Infernal Fall

Bryan Timothy Mitchell

Descendant Publishing

Printed in the United States of America

Cover Illustration and Design By: Damon Freeman

Edited By: Dawn Carter

First Printing, United States of America, October 2022

Library of Congress Control Number: 2022917328

ISBN 979-8-9869878-2-8 (Hardcover)

eBook ISBN 979-8-9869878-0-4

Descendant Publishing, LLC

PO Box 29

Byron Center, MI 49315

www.descendantpublishing.com

1 3 5 7 9 10 8 6 4 2

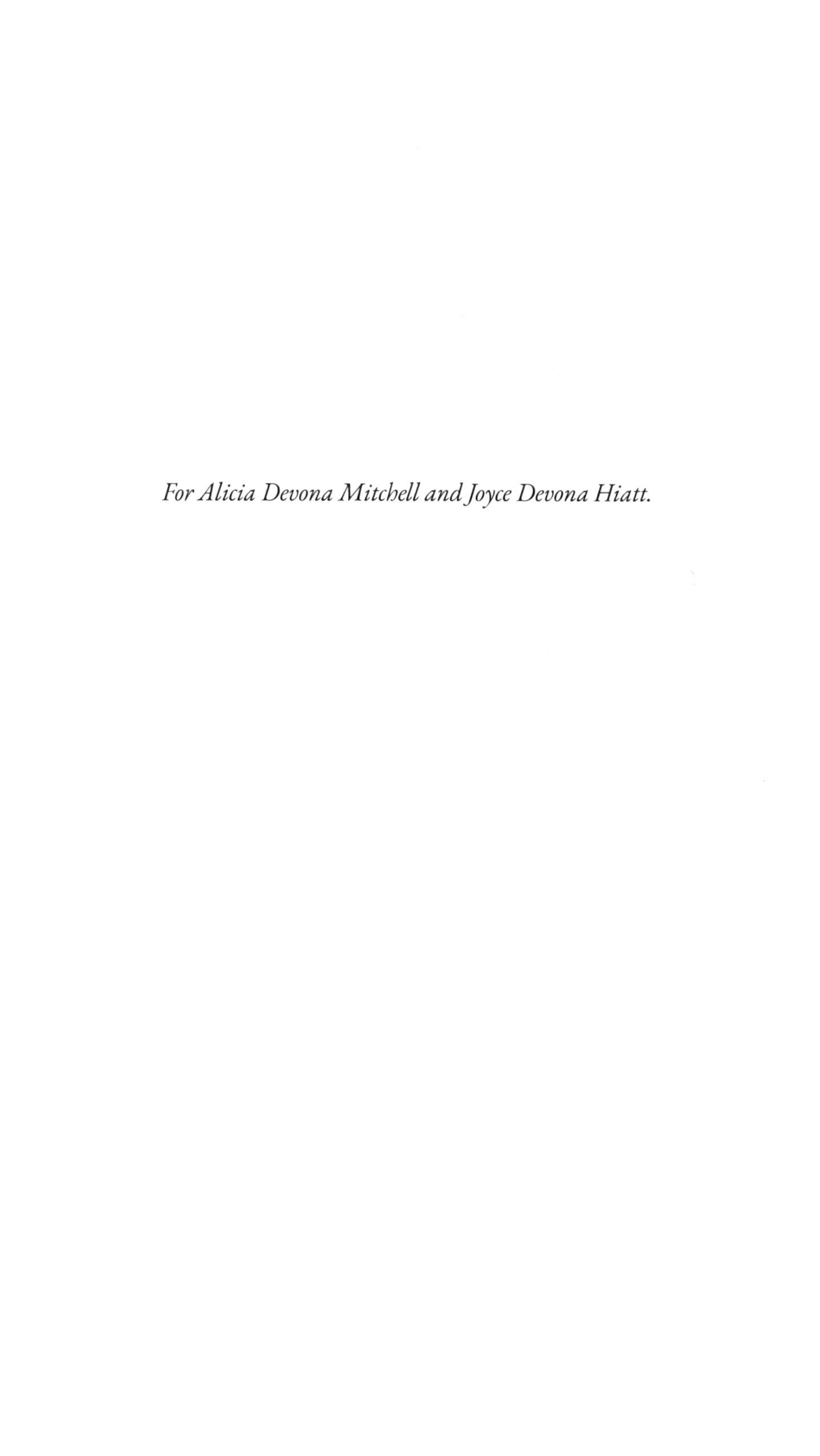

For Alicia Devona Mitchell and Joyce Devona Hiatt.

If you or someone you know is considering suicide, please seek help.

Suicide Hotline: 1.800.273.8255

Lust
Limbo
Greed
Gluttony
Wrath
Stygian lake
Heresy
Chamber 1
Tunnels of Boiling Blood
Chamber 2 Lake of Fire
Violence
Chamber 3
Sand dunes
Lake of Tears
Geryon
Fraud
Treachery
Satanus

Contents

1. The Tree and the Stone 1
2. The Purging Mountain 14
3. Spirit of the Undead 25
4. On to Grayton 38
5. The King's Secret 47
6. Enter the Storm 64
7. Eye of Lust 78
8. Cerberus Awaits a Meal 92
9. Ladies of Gluttony 105
10. A Fortunate Offer 117
11. The Goddess of Greed 131
12. Fuming Across Stygian Lake 144
13. The Heretics' Yard 157
14. Lord of Violence 169
15. Hot-blooded and Coldhearted 182
16. The Sad End of an Old Friend 193
17. Canteen of Tears 203

18. Into the Malebolge 215

19. The Malebranche 226

20. The Unchained Giant 237

21. Where Traitors Lie 247

22. The Hanging Disciple and Satan 260

23. The Scars 272

Thanks for Reading 286

Acknowledgements 287

About the Author 289

More from the Publisher 291

Chapter One

The Tree and the Stone

Something deep within Daniel Strong climbed into his throat and squeezed. Unwanted and unannounced shame rose from his heart and fogged his thoughts. He strained his neck to choke back tears. Glaring at the filthy lines in his palms, he formed fists to crush everything he was feeling.

Unaware of his internal battle, Kristine walked ahead of him, following the Bridge Trail to the summit of Grandfather Mountain. Why did he buy an engagement ring? How could he start a family after running away from home all those years ago? Would he do the same to her? *She'll probably say no anyway.* Horrible answers kept popping into his head until he remembered the last thing his father had said to him. *Just go then.* Those words roused his hatred and overcame his shame. The storm within relented, and the dark memories sank back into their place.

"There it is," Kristine said brightly. She stood several paces away along the rocky path lined with shining green leaves. Her red hair danced like fire in the cool morning breeze as she stared at the sky. She turned, and her smile waned. Shadows of trees camouflaged her face. "What's the matter?"

"Nothing." He stepped up next to her, craning his neck. "We're pretty close."

Almost directly overhead, The Mile High Swinging Bridge stretched over an eighty-foot chasm and moaned. Brisk winds passed through its steel supports and railings. Thick, long cables swayed to its eerie song. Dozens of people ambled along it while others paused to admire the horizon.

Vertigo swept through Daniel. He stumbled past Kristine to a boulder and braced himself. The warmth and firmness of the stone comforted him. It restored his sense of balance and helped him to focus—much like Kristine had months ago. If not for her, he would've dropped out of his first semester at Appalachian State University and reenlisted in the military.

"Hey." She came over and rubbed his back. "Seems like something's bothering you."

"Got a little dizzy, is all." Daniel raised his head.

The sun had darkened the freckles scattered along her flushed cheeks. With three years of college under her belt, Kristine was nearing graduation. That meant she'd soon leave. The thought of losing her twisted his stomach into knots.

He dug into his pocket and caressed the diamond ring nestled within. Before he could propose, he needed to come clean about last night. The truth may drive her away, but if he didn't tell her, someone else would.

"Let's take a break." Kristine took a seat on the boulder and tied her hair back. The wind sent a hush through the leaves.

He leaned against the stone beside her and looked at the bridge. A shadow darted across and sprinted along the outcroppings on the opposing ridge.

"What's going on with you today?" Kristine stretched her arms and back. "You seem off."

"I need to tell you something." Daniel jabbed his fist against the boulder.

She took his hand. "Tell me what?"

Even in this cool wind, she felt soft and warm. He ran his thumb over her knuckles. His heart pounded, begging him to keep silent. "I drank last night."

Kristine blinked. "Oh." Her expression hardened. She let go of his hand and folded her arms, looking away. She knew how ugly his temper could be when he drank. "Is that all?"

Daniel gazed down at his new boots, which looked more like shoes than what he wore in the military. "Remember what you said about me fighting?"

Kristine's body rose. Her eyes widened. "What did you do?"

"I punched a guy." Kristine pushed off the boulder and Daniel reached for her. "Wait."

She started back down the trail, stopped, and turned. Her face was flushed. "How bad was it this time?"

"I just—" Daniel swallowed. "I hit him once, and that was the end of it."

"You must have really showed him, huh?" She sounded tearful. They grew quiet as a couple and their dog hiked past them. She folded her arms and shook her head. "I'm sick of you fighting everybody, Daniel."

"It was minor. No one called the police. No one got kicked out." Daniel plodded over to her. "It was the first time in a long time. I didn't want to hit him, but he had it coming."

She remained still. Her eyes trailed the cliffs. "Seems like everybody has it coming."

"That's not true."

Tears rolled over her cheeks. She wiped her face. "Do I have it coming?"

"Of course not. I'd never hit you. I never hit a woman in my life!"

"But you're always getting in fights. It's like I'm dating Doctor Jekyll and Mister Hyde, and I never know which side of you is going to turn up." She huffed and looked over the red wildflowers stretching up the steep slope to her right. "I've tried to tell my friends that you're a great guy. That you're not the monster they think you are."

"You know I'm not a monster."

"Do I? Sometimes I wonder." Kristine's voice cracked. Anguished lines ran down her face. It hurt to know that *he* had caused those lines. "The look that comes over you when you get mad... They're all scared of you, and sometimes I am too."

"But I..." His throat locked up. He heaved a sigh. "I didn't want to fight. See? The guy was egging me on."

"So what, Daniel?" Kristine anchored her hands to her hips. "You should control yourself."

"You don't understand. An Army buddy of mine had just *died*." His entire body electrified at his own words. Fatigue swept through him. He massaged his forehead and ran his hand through his hair. "For some reason, that guy laughed when I told him, so I punched him. He apologized and said he misheard me. I could've stayed, but I paid my tab and left."

"Your friend died?" Kristine rested her hand over her heart.

Daniel nodded. Tears threatened to breach. He balled his fists to contain them. To his horror, he realized he was shaking.

Kristine took his hands. "It's OK."

Feeling too vulnerable for compassion, Daniel pulled away.

"What was his name?"

"Captain Jones." Saying the name conjured up his friend's face. Daniel picked up a fallen leaf and tore it into shreds. "Got the call from Fort Bragg last night. They said he committed suicide."

"Why didn't you call me?"

"I don't know. I should have, but—I wasn't thinking right."

Daniel reached into his pockets and grazed the ring. There would be no proposing today—not after this. Making it off the mountain with her by his side would suffice. "He was a good guy. Haven't spoken to him since leaving Bragg, though."

Terrible thoughts rippled through his mind. *Not much of a friend, but a good excuse to drink. You abandoned him like you did your parents. Ever notice how you ruin the best people?* The scar that ran along Daniel's neck prickled, and he dug his fingernails into it, satisfying the itch.

Kristine pulled his hand away. "Do you know why he did it?"

"No. I hung up before they told me. Honestly, I'd rather not know. It's easier to forget that way." Daniel slid his boot along the ground, clearing loose rocks from the path. "One thing I remember about him is that he'd listen to me drone on about my problems, but I never asked about his. Some friend I am, right?"

"It's not your fault," Kristine said.

Daniel nodded, but felt he had influenced his former commander in some way. Sunlight pierced through a cloud and darkened his shadow.

"Listen." Kristine spoke quietly. "If you love me, then talk to me about these things before going out and getting drunk. It's not healthy. Neither is fighting."

Daniel closed his eyes and asked, "Are you going to break up with me?"

She looked at the clouds inching overhead. "I don't want to, but the fighting and the drinking have to stop."

"I'm already back on the wagon," Daniel said. "No more excuses. I promise."

Kristine's smile couldn't hide the doubt in her eyes, but he could endure that. Over time, she'd see he was serious. He only had to stay out of trouble.

"Ready to hike up to the bridge now?" she asked.

"Let's get to it."

The gloom within Daniel dissipated the farther they went. The path hugged a cliff that curved to the right. Light beamed off the light-brown sand and green foliage. A steady breeze pressed into their faces. He thought he may propose after all. They rounded a sharp curve, and a tall, gangly man in a dark wool suit stood in their way. The man appeared to be in his seventies. He fixed his gray eyes on Daniel and removed his fedora with both hands, holding it at his waistline.

"Excuse us, sir," Daniel said.

He tried to pass the man, but the stranger planted his hand on Daniel's shoulder. He was much stronger than he looked. Daniel squinted at the man's crumpled face. "You sure you want to mess with me, old man?"

The stranger wrinkled his forehead. His lips tremored. "Do you know where you are headed, son?"

Daniel didn't like any man to call him son. Embers of anger stirred within him, but he took a deep breath and pointed to the bridge. "The trail leads to the bridge."

"Not out here." The old man jabbed a finger at Daniel's chest. "In there."

Daniel grabbed the lapels of the man's jacket and pushed the stranger against the rock wall beside them.

"Stop it!" Kristine grabbed Daniel's shoulder. "Let him go!"

Daniel pushed the man away. "Keep your hands to yourself, old man."

The man lowered his head and brushed dust from his hat. "There's a darkness locked inside you, and you fear the thing that can set you free."

Daniel glared at him. "You want to preach at me?"

Kristine gripped Daniel's shirt. "Choose life, like we talked about. Remember?"

Daniel took a deep breath and looked at her. Walking away would be so much easier. If he kept quarrelling with the man, he was sure to lose the only person he cared about. "I'm sorry."

He started down the path with her and felt the man's gaze against his back. It agitated him, but he kept walking until the stranger called after him.

"Just go then."

Daniel wrenched his arm from Kristine and turned. A prickling sensation fluttered over him. "What's your deal?" he asked, grimacing.

The stranger put his hat back on and walked away. "You should hurry home. It's getting late."

"Do you know me?" He started after the man.

Kristine grabbed his arm and turned him around. "Leave that man alone!"

"He said the same thing my dad said before I left home."

"It's just a coincidence. We don't know that man, and you had no business roughing him up." Kristine stared off to her right and blinked. She seemed confused. "That wasn't here before."

"What?" Daniel followed her gaze.

On a barren ledge, protruding from a shaded hillside, stood a stunted, dead tree, its hollowed branches splayed to the sky. A lightning-bolt-shaped crack splintered through it and expanded down the ledge, widening to the size of a cave.

"Did you notice this earlier?" She folded her arms as if chilled.

Daniel scratched his neck. "I wasn't looking that way."

"Seems like we should have noticed." She shivered as a cold wind passed over them. "Gives me the creeps."

"That tree gives you the creeps?"

"Don't laugh." Kristine's face paled. "I'm serious."

"It had to have been there. We just weren't looking because of the old man." From the cave underneath the tree, a light flashed. "Did you see that?"

"What?" Kristine said.

"I saw something in there."

"You're not funny." She nudged him. "Come on. Let's get to the bridge already."

"Wait a minute." Daniel studied the cave, expecting another flash. "I'm going to take a look."

"Are you kidding me?" Her voice trembled.

"Why not? It's just twenty yards off-trail."

"First you wanted to chase that man down—and now this?"

Daniel looked back down the trail. "Like you said, it was just a coincidence. But I saw something blinking in that cave. A light maybe. You didn't see it?"

Kristine shook her head. "It's pretty steep."

"We can climb that. This trail is steeper in some spots."

"But it's wet, and we'll get all dirty," Kristine said.

"Just wait here. I won't be long."

Daniel climbed the slope toward the ledge, knifing through the hillside. When he reached the crevice, he peered into the gap. The scent of cool earth burned in his nostrils and made his stomach groan. He heard Kristine climbing up behind him.

"This is not the way—you get back on my good side." Kristine breathed heavily.

"I'll make up for it." Daniel smiled.

Kristine screamed. A few feet away, a king snake slithered along some rocks and disappeared into the brush.

"Don't worry," Daniel said. "It's just trying to get away from us."

She scanned the ground. "Let's go back. This is ridiculous."

"Give me three minutes. After that, we'll head to the bridge."

Kristine's face soured, but she sighed and said, "Clock's running."

Daniel pulled out his smartphone and opened the flashlight app. With a twist, he stooped and stepped into the cave. A narrow passage took him six feet into the earth before the hard clay walls opened on either side. Overhead, a canopy of roots twisted into an impossible knot. Looking about, he realized he was in a circular chamber, about twenty-five feet in diameter and seven feet high. His boots slipped and sank in thick muck as he trudged to the center.

"Two-minute warning," Kristine said.

"Gotcha!"

Daniel used his phone to peer through the roots, and, lodged within them, a shiny black stone glimmered. *There you are.* It was almond-shaped, but three times the size. He reached and took it. It felt smooth against his fingers when he flipped it over. Someone had carved a perfect spiral on one side. Tracing the line, he counted it winding eight times before coming to a circle at the center. He wondered what a curator at the nearby museum might think of it.

He gripped the stone in his fist, and it warmed his hand, illuminating his fingers an orangish-red. The sudden light shocked him so much, he almost dropped it but managed a juggling one-handed catch. He took a hard look at the stone. *Maybe I imagined it.* He clenched the stone again, and his fingers glowed blood-red.

"Hey, Kristine. You won't believe this. I found something."

"What is it?" Her voice rang from the opening. "Time's up anyway, so bring it out."

"No. Come here. I swear, you need to see this. I promise no monsters, snakes, or anything like that. It's safe."

"Just bring it out here."

"Please. You need to see it in the dark. This stone makes my hand light up."

Kristine huffed. "Daniel, if this is some crazy joke—"

"It's not."

Daniel squeezed the rock as hard as he could. That orange-red glow traveled over his hand. From his fingertips to his knuckles, the redness darkened. The stone crackled like a bag of popcorn in his grip. He opened his hand. The spiraling indentation shimmered orange, yellow, and gold.

"Amazing," he whispered.

Kristine's body shielded ambient light reflecting from the entrance. "Smells awful in here."

"Do you see this?" He raised the stone. "See how it glows?"

"What is that?"

"I don't know. Someone carved a spiral in it. Not sure how it's glowing." He glanced at her. "Maybe ink or something. But look what happens when I squeeze it." Again, his hand lit up, darkening to red, then deepening to purple. When it crackled against his palm, he held on. The skin on his hand hissed and burned. His wrist cramped. He tried to let go, but couldn't.

"What's happening?!? Let go!" Kristine demanded.

"I can't." He dropped his phone and pried his fingers open. The stone, now on fire, plopped and vanished into the stinking mud. Tendrils of smoke rose from where it fell.

Blinking, Daniel dug into the mud for the fallen rock. "Did you see that?"

"Daniel, are you all right?" Kristine's voice shook.

"I'm fine. Can you pull out your phone and help me find it?"

When she did, light spilled over the mud. It was smoking and bubbling. He sniffed. "Is that sulfur?"

"Smells like it," Kristine croaked. "Daniel, you're sinking."

Daniel saw his feet buried. He tried to take a step, but the hot mud sucked his boots back down. The bubbling intensified, and, deeper within, the mountain stirred.

"Get out of there!" Kristine shouted.

Daniel couldn't move. The mud suddenly became hot and watery, and he sank to his waist. He breathed in rancid air. Dirt plopped from overhead, and everything shook violently. Unable to see, Daniel felt his way to a wall of crumbling earth and wrapped his arms around the thickest root he could find.

"Go," he rasped. "Get out!"

A deafening noise rattled his bones. The mud fell away as if a hatch underneath him had opened. The root unfurled. He held on tight. The hole beneath him seemed darker than anything he had ever seen. If he survived the fall, he'd likely be buried alive.

The madness soon subsided. The landslide and shaking ceased. Light spilled in from overhead. The noise drifted deeper into the earth. Daniel was relieved. He adjusted his grip on the slippery root.

"Kristine?"

"Oh my gosh, Daniel." Her voice reverberated from overhead.

Though they stung, he forced his eyes open. Through swirling dust, Kristine peered from the surface. She was only a few feet away. Golden beams of light cut through the darkness, reddening her silhouette.

"Don't worry. I can climb this," he said. "When I get close, take my hand."

Pulling himself up proved difficult. He lurched one hand over the other until he ran out of gas. But he managed to wrap a leg around the root and clamp it with his feet. He shook the tension from his arms, and the root unfurled even more.

Kristine clasped her head in her hands. "That root won't hold much longer."

"Yeah," he gasped. "At least you're safe."

"Is there anything else you can grab on to?"

Daniel looked around and cleared his itching throat. "No. But I can make it. Just need a moment."

With his arms slightly rested, Daniel tried to climb again, but it was too slippery. After very little progress, he stopped and looked down. Nothing but darkness. He had no idea how far he'd fall if he'd let go.

"Daniel, you've got to get moving."

"I can't." He used the root to scratch off sweat. "But I can hang on. Go for help."

"Daniel—"

"Go," Daniel said. "I promise I'm not going anywhere."

For a moment, Kristine hesitated. He wondered if she would say "I love you," but she darted from sight without another word.

Alone, Daniel sniffed in the harsh air. A high-pitched ringing sprang in his ears, and his temples throbbed in time to his pulse. He felt foolish and annoyed.

"Great way to spend your day off, knucklehead."

In the stillness, his heartbeat settled. The temperature seemed to drop. His muddy hands stiffened, but his arms felt ready for another try. Feeling strong and determined, he lunged higher onto the root.

It snapped.

In freefall, Daniel's stomach dropped. Light flashed when he hit his head. He tumbled deeper. The world darkened. Dirt pervaded the air. It caught in his throat. Death was certain. Terror blinding his reason, he clung to hope.

Chapter Two

The Purging Mountain

Daniel tumbled through pitch black and crashed onto sand. The world shook and roared as debris poured onto him. A glimpse of red light shimmering from a wide crevice gave him hope for escape, but the avalanche buried him before he could do anything about it. Kicking and clawing under mounting pressure, he lurched toward the gap.

Unable to breathe and with waning strength, he broke through the surface and sucked in a ragged breath. Within an arm's reach of the crack, he slapped his hands onto hot stone, sending jolts of pain up his arms. Gripping a thin seam, he pulled himself into a narrow tunnel as dirt filled the chamber behind him.

Daniel coughed and wheezed. Dirt coated his mouth and throat. His busted lips tasted of iron. With the mountain still shaking, he couldn't rest, so he shimmied toward the opening only ten feet away. Elbows and knees twinged with each impact. When he reached the edge, wisps of smoke twisted into a shattered red sky that flickered like fire over a dark and flat horizon.

"What?" Daniel had thought he would come out in a lower valley on Grandfather Mountain. This place seemed like a cavern but was too vast. It didn't make sense. Maybe hitting his head too many times during the fall had distorted his perception. Whatever the reason, he needed to get back to Kristine. Climbing back up wasn't an option. He had to find another way.

Though the mountain had calmed, Daniel's bones still quaked. He peeked over the brink. Sweat dribbled from his nose. A charred, smoldering valley lay fifty feet down a jagged cliff. Overhead, ink-black clouds rolled above a summit rippling with flames.

"What in the world?" He thumbed the irritation from his eyes. "I guess I better head down then."

He peered back down the cliff. It wouldn't be an easy climb. Without a harness, one slip could be deadly. He inched out until his toes found footholds. The rock burned his hands, but he held on.

CHARLES

An hour earlier, about a mile away from where Daniel fell, Charles sat outside his lodge on a dried-up porch, staring at the everlasting dark cloud billowing over the Purging Mountain Range and expanding through the northern sky. Overhead and southward, the pale-yellow burn of the day had diminished to orange. Soon, it would turn red, and then purple. Within hours, the frigid night would envelop Limbo.

He longed for the smoke that rose from the valley where he harvested dead souls. None were due in his district today, so he had nothing to do but wait upon his rickety stool, depressing the crown on his pocket watch. The metallic clicking and squealing of the spring pleased him. He clamped it shut and repeated the process.

Floating ash came to rest upon the lapel of his gray frock coat. Grimacing, he brushed it off and did the same for the bowler hat propped upon his knee. Seeing that his polished leather shoes remained untainted from the drifting cinders, he returned to clicking his watch.

A rotten stench drifted from the judge's quarters. Apparently, the Dishonorable Judge Baxter was paying a visit. Heavy footsteps clomped onto the wooden porch. The withering boards groaned, and the stink intensified. Baxter waddled forward as if in the third trimester of some sick pregnancy.

"Charles," the judge hissed. A worn black robe stretched over fluffy belly rolls and hung above his rotted gray feet. He patted his stringy, white, comb-over curls. "A soul needs fetchin'."

"That's not what you said earlier."

"Doesn't matter, filthy mutt." The judge's flabby jowls shook. "When I say fetch, you go."

Mutt? The same could be said for the judge, considering they had both been human once. Charles muttered to himself, "Hypocrite."

The judge gritted his teeth. "Do I need to remind you of who's in charge?"

Even in his position of authority, the judge had no real clout. The weakest inhabitants of Limbo called him Baxter the Brittle with no reprisals, but the sooner Charles gave in, the sooner he could enter the valley and breathe in its rich smoke. "You are in charge."

"You'll do well to remember that."

Charles opened his watch. Through the weathered glass, both hands neared the six o'clock position from opposite directions. Once they crossed, souls would spew from the mountain's mouth into the valley. "It's an odd hour to be harvesting."

"Doesn't matter. Just hurry before I report you."

Charles snapped his watch shut. "How many?"

The judge shuffled forward. The boards whined with each step. "I told you. *A* soul needs fetchin'."

"You mean one?" Charles glared. "Since when do we retrieve *one* at a time?"

"One more word," the judge's belly touched Charles's arm, "and I'll have you expelled like all the others before you."

"I find it more likely they abandoned their post to get away from you."

"Don't make me call the King of Grayton. I will not tolerate insubordination."

"Insubordination?" Charles pressed his mouth into contempt and placed his watch into his red vest. He had endured enough of the judge's empty threats. Slowly, he rose from his stool and stretched his back. Towering over the judge, he tightened his necktie and canted his hat onto his head.

The judge stepped back. "Go. Get to the mountain or—"

"If half of Limbo can call you Baxter the Brittle, I doubt there is much you can do to me." Charles leaned toward the judge and whispered, "I hear you scream every time your bones break. It happens so often, by the slightest of things."

Baxter's greasy lips shook. "Go, or kiss your harvesting days goodbye."

"Rushing me?" Charles walked toward the judge, who in turn backed away. "If I delay, will you have me banished, Mr. Brittle?"

"If you don't go now—" Judge Baxter stepped off the porch. "I'll send word to the king."

"Send your word." Charles paused at the edge of the porch. "Show him your incompetence. Or—stop this nonsense and ask me to do my work. Nicely."

"Nicely?" The judge blinked with confusion and then added, "Please, then."

Charles smirked. "Without the attitude."

The scowl on the judge's face twisted into a sarcastic smile. "Please go, and when you return, expect a reassignment!"

"Hmmm." Charles retrieved his watch, peeked at it, and then clamped it shut. "Good enough."

Charles stepped from the porch onto the gravel road. The judge's vile stench faded, but his insults traveled well until the sound of crushing pebbles drowned them out. The path cut through dried-out clay plains to the base of the Purging Mountains just below Charles's valley.

Charles rubbed his chin. He had always gathered at least a dozen or more souls at dawn every other day or so. Harvesting only one so late in the day was highly irregular. "Ah well. At least I won't have to deal with as much whining and begging. Oh, great. These two?"

Ahead, two wrinkled men in filthy white tunics lumbered along the path that came from Grayton and intersected with Charles's road. With so little entertainment in the old city, hundreds would journey here to attend the soul trials. The judge would read the charges, and everybody else would debate on which hell each soul should go to. Once sentenced, the defendants would receive a coin so that Charon would take them to their prescribed eternal hells. Unless they were dull enough to remain here in Limbo, of course.

One of the two old men called out to him. "Heartless Charles."

"What did you call me?"

Their smiles dropped. The other said, "Word is there's a hearing today. Are you off to harvest the souls?"

To show his disgust, Charles contorted his face when he walked past them. "Just one. Surely you have something better to do than attend one measly trial."

"One soul? Might be interesting."

"Thank you, Heartless—"

His companion elbowed him. "Shh, he doesn't like that."

"Heartless Charles..."

I ripped my heart out over ten years ago, and they still find it amusing. Charles reared, and they shrunk in fear. "Suffer the second death lately? Yesterday, maybe? Hours ago? Ready for it to come again? It will—at any moment. But hey, it happens to everybody, right? Oh, my mistake. Everybody but me."

"I doubt you're the only one," the denser of the two men said.

"You doubt me?" Charles asked, baring his teeth.

"No, sir." The wiser man took his companion by the arm and pulled him along. "He means no disrespect. We'll leave you alone. Sorry."

"You *are* sorry," Charles said. "Sorry as all the others who endlessly die in this place."

The two of them frowned and went their way. Charles came to the end of the road and onto a beaten path that led to his valley. The smoke oozing from the charred, cracked surface burned his nose and throat. He inhaled deeply and headed to a boulder where three metal chests sat beside it. After retrieving a single pair of shackles from the center chest, he climbed onto the large rock and sat.

About a hundred yards away, halfway up the cliff, he eyed the gash where dead souls would spew into his valley. His watch rang and shook in his pocket. Charles pulled it out and clicked it open. It stilled. Both hands pointed to the six o'clock position. Collection time had arrived. He returned his timepiece and stood.

Ensuring he looked his best, he brushed dust and ash from his suit. The road had tarnished his shoes, so he swatted the tips to bring out the shine. After buttoning his jacket, he entwined his fingers, straightened his shoulders, and waited.

A distant thundering noise swelled. Dust sprouted and smothered the fires in higher elevations. Charles removed his hat and scratched his head. The boulder shook and started to topple. He hopped off just before it crushed the three chests beside it.

The scar in the cliff collapsed and belched brown mist, but a small hole remained.

"Well, I'm not digging out whoever's stuck in there." Charles turned to leave, but stopped when he caught a whiff of the air. "What is that?"

He sniffed again. "Sweat? Can't be. Everything's dead down here."

A man crawled from the narrow hole in the cliff and paused at the ledge. Charles had to admit the old man was right. "This one *is* interesting. He's undead."

Daniel pulled himself onto a ledge and tried climbing down.

Charles half-smiled. "He's got some moxie about him, too. Very interesting."

Daniel lost his footing and fell into the valley.

"Don't go dying now, tough guy. Keep that heart beating. What's that?" Another strange presence made itself known. Charles narrowed his eyes toward the ridge and inhaled deeply. "Something is following you."

Fires had reemerged in the higher elevations, and, in them, at least a half-mile away, curling banners of black wrapped around a stout, pudgy body. "A shadow-man," Charles whispered.

Charles focused his voice on the man and spoke intently. "You weren't due, but you're stuck here now."

"Where are you?" The shadow-man looked about.

"Seeking the undead man? Hoping to take him back?" Charles clicked his tongue. "You know the rules."

"Who's there?"

"If you want to save him, you best come down—to me."

The shadow-man turned his thick face. Old and haggard, he scowled. Charles tipped his hat to the incensed, beady eyes.

"Hello."

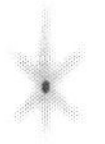

BEAU

Unhindered by the ground, a shadow-man named Beau passed through the earth's crust, hoping to save Daniel, but he was too late. The keystone lay beside the threshold to Hell. The man had already crossed over. After a century of watching souls pass on, Beau decided he had had enough. No longer would he assist in the misery of others, but leaving the keystone behind proved to be a mistake. It caused a man to enter Hell before his time. Beau couldn't let that stand. He took the stone and placed it in a pouch. After securing his horn, he attempted to enter, but a sea of voices commanded him to stop. He looked to his kindred shadows swirling in the darkness overhead.

A tall silhouette neared him. "How did you lose your keystone?"

"I didn't. I left it behind," Beau said. "A man found it and fell here."

"There is nothing you can do for him." The shadow glided above him in a large circle. "Leave him be. If you go in, you shall never return."

Beau set his eyes on the pulsing red tunnel. "I'd rather suffer Hell than spend another day sending souls there. I'll save him regardless of what comes of me."

"We are not saviors." The shadow twisted around itself as if agitated.

Beau closed his eyes and roused his courage. "Maybe that's why I can't stand what I am."

"We can't stop you from entering." The shadow stopped whirling and twisting. It unwound itself and came closer to Beau. "Do you know where to find him?"

"In the valley?"

Beau's fellow shadow nodded. "He will fall near the base of the most southern point of the Purging Mountains. Wait—"

Beau crossed through the veil, and the entrance to Hell closed behind him. Oppressive heat replaced the cool of the earth. Firelight shimmered and crackled ahead. It frightened him. On Earth, light compelled him to the shades. Such would not be the case in Hell, because he'd transformed into flesh and bone.

The air thickened and warmed as he continued through the tunnel. Fire roared, and wind howled. A strange sensation, a heaviness, pressed upon him and he dropped to the hot floor. The dark cloud enshrouding him tore into tatters. Under it, beefy hands and arms emerged. The floor of the cave burned his newly formed palms. He pulled them free and gaped at his blistering fingers.

"I'm flesh?" His voice cracked in his aching throat. "The keystone!"

He fumbled over his body until he found it nestled in the left breast pocket of his flannel shirt. There was something familiar about these clothes, but he didn't have time to think about it. Under his arm, the ram's horn hung from his shoulder by a leather strap. He had everything he needed to find the man and get out. He used the wall to rise and balance as he stumbled to an opening draped with fire and smoke.

Nearing the threshold, Beau grabbed his throat. Tears blinded him. His knees gave, and he fell forward. Placing the wide end of the ram's horn over his mouth and nose relieved his lightheadedness. Walking required control of the legs. Much harder to do than floating through darkness. He needed to figure it out along the way because if he didn't hurry, a demon would take the man to be judged.

After lurching to his feet, Beau lunged through the opening and onto the mountain's surface. Blades of fire ate at his flesh and clothes. Tatters of shadow fluttered from his body. He swatted at the bright flames, but they evaded his hands and set to his legs. The burning brought tremors, and his newfound flesh bubbled and melted. He pointed the large end of the horn at the blaze, and a powerful wind blasted from the cone. The fire retreated. Relieved, he dropped to the scorching-hot stone, struggling to breathe the hot carbonic air.

With shaking hands, he swigged brown sap from the horn's small end. His burns flaked to ash. Though his clothes remained charred, his skin rejuvenated. Buzzing with numbness, he regained his footing and staggered forward. The surface gripped his sandals upon every step.

"I need to—" Beau panted, "go down."

Smoke and fire limited his vision. The steep rocky slope glowed with heat. He couldn't tell how far he was from the valley or which direction was south. Heading downhill seemed like a good start. He lost his footing and fell into a gulch. Simmering coals and stones riddled the ground. He got up and used the horn to blow back nearby fires while carefully treading downhill.

A strange, echoing voice spoke. "A shadow-man."

Startled, Beau looked about.

The voice spoke again. "You weren't due, but you're stuck here now."

No one was around him, but the voice was near. "Where are you?"

"Seeking the undead man? Hoping to take him back? Tsk, tsk, tsk. You know the rules."

"Who's there?"

"If you want to save him, you best come down—to me."

A stabbing pain seized Beau's stomach. He hobbled downhill. Between flames and smoke, a demon stood in a low valley, tipping its hat. "Hello."

"The man doesn't belong here, demon."

"But he *is* here," the demon said. "Therefore, you are wrong."

"Where is he?"

"You sound as if I'm to blame." The demon's face soured. "But you're the one who caused this, aren't you? Never mind that. I want him alive, just as much as you. Best hurry. He's not faring well."

"Don't touch him."

The demon moved from Beau's sight. Beau was about a half-mile away from where the demon had been. If he hurried, he'd be there within minutes. Every second was precious. Trembling, Beau hastened his clumsy descent.

Chapter Three

Spirit of the Undead

DANIEL

Daniel's muddy boots slipped from a thin ledge. Unable to right himself, he fell and slammed into the valley below. Powdery ash engulfed him. He rolled onto all-fours, coughing. His back spasmed as he sat up. Gingerly, he bent forward and assessed the bruises and scrapes covering his arms. Thick abrasions traced the lines of his palms. Through the rips of his jeans, fresh cuts shone red along his legs.

Nothing looked or felt broken, but applying pressure around his knees and ankles brought sharp pain rather than relief. Daniel mopped sweat from his brow and grunted, "Not the best way—to get off a cliff."

Along the mountain's ridge, fire whipped and waved under a massive black curtain. He watched the blaze in awe until a cloud of smoke rising from the right stole his attention.

In the valley where he sat, a matrix of sunken, cindering paths zigzagged between countless dark mounds. Within the depressed trails, fiery cracks emitted wavering plumes of hot gas that blurred his immediate surroundings. Through a break in the smoke, he glimpsed where the purpling sky met a flat horizon.

This can't be Grandfather Mountain.

A sunlit morning thriving with life and light had drastically changed to a night of death and destruction. He bowed his head and huffed.

Beneath him, his vague silhouette danced upon the glassy black surface. He hated the fact he looked so much like his father that he stamped on his reflection. Embers stirred to flame and blew acidic kisses into his face. He swatted them away.

"Got to find Kristine." Carefully, he rose to his feet. His left leg could bear more weight than his right. With a hand pressed against the knotted muscles at the small of his back, he stooped forward. Bolts of agony shot from his feet to his spine. Still, he hobbled on—inches at a time. He figured if he followed the base of the mountain, he might find a path or a road leading back to civilization. If that didn't happen soon, he'd need to find a safe place to retire for the night.

Avoiding the mounds because they looked too much like unmarked graves, he limped along a sunken path oozing with tremendous heat. Red-glowing veins warned him to tread lightly or else stir the sullen cinders. His awkward stride improved as he grew familiar with the pain.

He stopped and scraped his eyes with his knuckles. "And to think I was going to give up drinking."

A ragged voice came from the right. "Hello."

Startled, Daniel faltered but kept his feet. Groaning, he braced his knee. A tall, sickly thin man in an old-fashioned outfit edged into the dim light shimmering from the mountain. Even from six feet away, the man smelled like a wastewater treatment plant.

Daniel tried to ignore the smell. "Man, am I happy to see you."

The stranger scowled and canted his hat forward, hiding his eyes. "Sure you are." His words slithered from his mouth slowly.

"I'm Daniel. Who are you?"

"Charles." His crooked grin revealed rotted, misaligned teeth.

"Sorry." Daniel gagged and shielded his nose. "I didn't expect to run into anyone out here. What is this place?"

Charles gazed uphill and wiggled the knot in his necktie. "We're at the foot of the mountain."

Daniel grimaced. "Yeah, but where are we? Linville?"

"Linville is north of the mountain," Charles said. "You're on the southern side."

"The southern side?" A wave of gray smoke brought tears to Daniel's eyes. He squeezed them shut and pinched the bridge of his nose. "Where are all the trees and hills?"

"Have you ever been on this side of the mountain before?"

Daniel shrugged. "I don't know, but this doesn't look like right."

Charles looked down at a golden pocket watch in his hand and clamped it shut. "Things will look more familiar when we reach Grayton."

"Grayton?"

"It's a nearby town about a thirty-minute walk from here."

Daniel rubbed the side of his head. "I never heard of it."

Charles's grin looked more like a sneer. "You aren't from here, are you?"

"No, but I'm a student at Appalachian State. It's not like I don't know the area. Linville, Boone, Blowing Rock ..."

Charles crossed his arms. "All you can name are three towns?"

Daniel's head ached. The anger rising from his gut didn't help either. It made him feel sick and dizzy. "Look, I almost died. If you want to get smart—"

"Take it easy." Charles extended an arm with his palm facing down. Darkness and smoke concealed most of him, though a sliver of firelight ran from his black hat down to his glossy shoes. "All those towns you mentioned are on the other side of the mountain. Let me get you to Grayton. There's a hospital there. You need one as banged up as you are."

"Do you have a phone on you?"

Charles tightened his necktie, which looked to be digging into his neck. "There's no reception down here."

Daniel caressed the scar on his neck and swallowed. He looked back up at the fire-covered mountain. "I need to call her," he whispered.

"Call who?" Charles asked.

"My girlfriend. She might be trapped up there."

"There'll be a phone at the hospital, I'm sure. But tell me something." Charles clicked his pocket watch open and frowned at it. "Do you feel like you are dying?"

"Like I'm dying?"

Charles closed his watch and rolled it in his fingers. His thin smile looked like it pained him. "Is it hard to breathe? Think you'll faint? Am I going to have to drag you to town?"

"You don't have to worry about me. I won't pass out. Not now." Daniel wasn't sure he trusted this man, but he wasn't about to turn away any help right now. No matter how off-putting this guy seemed, Daniel needed him. "How did it get so dark all of a sudden?"

"It grew dark gradually."

"But it was daylight!" Daniel's throat burned. He inhaled smoke and coughed. Once he settled down, he said, "I'm sorry it's just—everything's flipped upside down on me."

"Easy." Charles raised his hands and approached Daniel as if he were a wild horse. "Your lady friend is probably fine. There's no fire on the other side of the mountain."

"How do you know?"

"The fire is localized to the southern side of the mountain. If you came from the northern side, your friend is safe—most likely." Charles creeped closer. "All this will make better sense once we get you to the hospital."

Charles's face entered the light. His skin looked greenish and pale. He lifted his chin and exposed his eyes. They looked reptilian, with vertical slits that glowed. Daniel cringed.

"Why are you wearing contacts like that?"

"Contacts?" Charles backed away and tightened his necktie again.

"Are you trying to choke yourself?" Daniel winced and rubbed his neck.

"My tie keeps slipping is all." Charles adjusted his hat and took a deep breath. He pointed at the cliff while inching toward Daniel and asked, "Did you crawl from that small hole in the cliff?"

"Yeah." When Daniel turned toward the mountain, Charles's icy hand pinched the base of his neck. Numbness fluttered into Daniel's skull. Consciousness faded and Daniel collapsed.

CHARLES

When Charles had placed his hand upon Daniel, something alien and apart from the undead man had entered Charles's fingers, traveled up his arm, and seized his brain. An ancient face emerged upon the canvas of his inner eye and hummed a friendly, familiar song. Since his death, Charles had forgotten her and the song, but now, after decades of Hell, he remembered the only person he cared about in his past life—his grandmother.

Daniel lay in this valley of death, different from all the others who fell here before him. His pigmentation glistened. His chest rose and sank with life. The scent of salt and blood emanated from his warm skin. A heart thumped in his chest and his exhalations perfumed Hell's foul air. All these things were so remarkable to Charles. But the alien being residing within the man disturbed Charles. How did it bring back long-forgotten memories?

Daniel's thigh touched Charles's shoe. Charles nudged him off, and the man sprawled into a ditch. It whooshed and spat cinders. To keep his prize from catching fire, Charles pulled him to safety and rolled him onto his back. Slapping filth from his hands, he glared at the man.

"What was that?" Charles jerked his lapels down and loosened his tie. "Undead. Clinging to life like a child to his mum."

Charles rubbed his chin, gazing at Daniel. "You're infested with a spirit. Not one of ours. One of *theirs*. And I can think of only one that could do what it just did to me. Why are you still with this man, Holy Spirit? Because he's undead?"

Charles expected an answer but received nothing. "Typical silence," he muttered. "I guess nothing changes with you."

He took out his watch and clicked it open. The hands moved to the top of the hour in opposing directions. He clamped it shut and sensed the shadow-man approaching the cliff. "Come on! I got twenty minutes before Baxter reports me!"

The fires parted at a point along the ridge, and from it came the shadow-man, who was now a thick and meaty man in a dark flannel shirt and trousers. He held a ram's horn like a handgun, peering over the drop.

Charles stepped over Daniel's body and approached the cliff, waving his arms. "Get down here before he dies."

The shadow-man lost his footing and belly-flopped into the valley.

Charles palmed his face as the short, round man groaned and writhed. "Gotta watch your step around here."

The shadow-man brought the ram's horn to his lips. Charles expected him to blow into it, but he appeared to drink instead. He had piercing gray eyes, and a stringy beard resting over his barrel chest. Bushy hair hung below his shoulders.

"You changed when you crossed over," Charles said.

That got the shadow-man's attention. After fumbling to his feet, he staggered past Charles to Daniel. Though his skin and clothes looked soiled and disgusting, he smelled of earth and cool air.

"I'm not a shadow-man anymore, demon."

"Call me Charles. And you are..."

"I'm here for the man, not small talk." The shadow-man stopped by Daniel and tried to sit, but fell instead.

"Why are you moving so awkwardly?"

The shadow-man turned Daniel's head so that he could see his face. "What did you do to him?"

"What did *I* do?" Charles snorted. "You're the reason he's here, aren't you? Considering that I helped you find him, you should be more grateful. Yet you can't even tell me your name."

"The name is Beau," he growled. "What did you do to him?"

Charles intertwined his fingers behind his back and approached Beau slowly. "You don't get to ask me questions, but I'll overlook your insubordination to help you fix your mess."

"I don't answer to you!" Beau looked at Daniel. "And he doesn't belong here."

"This again?" Charles craned his neck. The sky was darkening. They needed to get to the city soon. "What comes here *stays here*. You know how this works."

"He's not dead."

Charles held up a finger. "Not dead—yet. It's only a matter of time until Hell kills him."

"He ain't dying." Beau pinched Daniel's cheeks and placed the small end of the ram's horn between Daniel's blistered lips.

Charles folded his arms. "I can't touch the man, but you can stick an animal part in his mouth?"

"Unlike you, I'm here to help him. This will keep him alive."

After a few seconds, Beau removed the horn and hung the strap back over his shoulder.

Charles gazed up at the Purging Mountains. "You plan to take him back to the north side?"

"Don't try to stop me. I may not have any authority here, but I don't need it to get past you." Beau lowered his head. "I'll get him out of here. I have to."

Decades of harvesting souls taught Charles a lot about those who fell here. All of them held expressions of deep fear but would react in different ways. Their actions spoke volumes about their characters. Beau seemed weary in his fear. Maybe the physical realm was too much for him after so much time as a shadow-man. This weariness told Charles that he could easily manipulate Beau to fall in line.

"You don't know what you're dealing with, Beau," Charles said. "You can't take him back the way you came."

"I'm not letting you take him to be judged."

"I have no intention of taking him to the court." Charles stepped on to the mound closest to Beau and held on to his lapels. He stuck out his chest to look more heroic. "I want the same thing you do."

Beau's face twisted. "There's no way you want the same thing as me."

"You want to get him out, right?" Charles stepped onto Beau's mound, towering over the shadow-man. "I can help you."

Beau lifted his head and blinked in confusion. "I don't need or want your help."

Charles checked his watch. "Within an hour, it'll be pitch black. The smoke will cease. The heat will be gone, and it'll become so cold that whoever's caught outside will freeze in place." Charles lifted his palms to the sky. "I'm already feeling a chill. Did you know that while Hell freezes over, the fires on the mountain endure?"

Beau rubbed his forehead, staring at Daniel. "Sounds like lies."

"Does it? What comes here stays here. Is that a lie?" Charles stepped closer to Beau. "Hope doesn't exist in this place—with one exception." Charles pointed at Daniel. "That's no lie, Beau. And you're about to cause the death of the one person to enter Hell with a heart still beating in his chest. You need me."

Beau's body language shrank in defeat. Charles sighed and clicked his pocket watch open. Ten minutes until Baxter reported him. "Suppose I let you take him back up this steep mountain. Not easy to navigate, as you just found out. You mishandle that horn or fall *once*, which is not impossible considering that clumsy gait of yours, and his life will be over despite your efforts."

Beau closed his eyes. His jaw quivered. "It wasn't his time."

"I'm not some arbiter you can plead your case to. People die every day through no fault of their own. You know that better than anyone. Time has no say in it."

Lines of doubt furrowed across Beau's forehead. "You're a demon and demons lie. I can't trust you. I'd be a fool to."

"Did I lie when I said what comes here stays here?"

Beau stared across the valley, shaking his head. "I won't listen to you."

"Demons speak true when it suits our purposes. No one leaves by way of the mountain. If it were possible, every demon in Hell would climb it right now."

BEAU

Beau brushed his fingers through Daniel's short brown hair. The medicine worked faster in Hell. The bleeding had stopped. Bruises had faded while swollen places had diminished. Daniel would soon wake. Beau tried to stand but fell back on his bottom.

"Good thing you weren't on the mountain," Charles said. "You're a wreck. Just look at you. You're putting too much on yourself. Burdens will ruin you here."

Pushing himself up, Beau peeked at Charles's leather shoes. They seemed to gleam in the firelight. Less smoke rose from the ground. The heat felt less pressing. *Maybe Charles wasn't lying.*

"Know why you struggle?" Charles opened his pocket watch and stared. "Not too long ago, you were a mere shadow. Immaterial. You're substantial now and taking in so much in such a short time. Feeling more than you ever have. That's why you can't see reason. You should humble yourself and accept my help."

"I'm not letting you take him to get judged. I'll fight if I have to."

"I told you I'm not taking him to the court." Charles returned his timepiece to his vest pocket. "But we need to get on our way. It's growing colder, and I'll soon be reported as a deserter."

"You think I'm a fool?"

"Maybe not a fool, but you are stubborn."

Beau looked at the mountain. The fire raged on. A ribbon of cool air brushed across his face. He realized he had no idea what to expect in Hell. Maybe the mountain was impassible. Heat rose into his face as he regretted listening to this demon. "Where do you plan to take him, then?"

Charles dropped his hands to his hips and stared off into the darkness. "First to the Town of Grayton. It isn't far. I'll get permission from the king to allow us to go deeper."

"Deeper?" Beau glared at Charles, who gave a slow single nod with a thoughtful frown. Beau couldn't believe what Charles was proposing. "You mean to take him to Satan?"

Charles stared up at the fiery mountain and folded his arms. "Still want to call me a liar?"

"Why?" Beau asked. "Why not just take him to the judge?"

"The judge will have him killed. Neither of us wants that."

Beau staggered toward Charles. "Satan will do worse than kill him."

"Satan could have him restored on Earth." Charles rubbed his hands together and squinted. "There'd be stipulations, of course."

"Then why doesn't Satan restore himself?"

Charles chuckled and looked down at his feet. "Ever notice the demons wandering about on Earth, or are you blind like everybody else?"

Beau looked away and closed his eyes. Images of dark entities whispering evil, unwanted thoughts to men, women, and children came to mind, tormenting them with lie after lie.

"You have." Charles smiled. "I can tell by the look on your face. Ever wonder how they get out?"

"No way I'll let you take him deeper. He'd lose his mind."

"There's no other way. Besides, you have that." Charles pointed to Beau's horn. "That'll keep him safe."

"It heals wounds, but does nothing for the mind."

"I see." Charles leaped to another mound and raised his index finger. "I know. We'll keep him focused on getting home. He mentioned a girl. The boy's in love. That will keep him from breaking."

"Love?" Beau glared at Charles. "Do you even know what that is?"

Charles shrugged. "He really wants to find her. I figure we could use that."

Beau looked at Daniel, then back at the cliff. The air was cooler, and the smoke had faded. Just like Charles had claimed. "Why do you even care?"

Charles creeped back over to Beau with a serious expression. "I'm sick of harvesting. You two are my way out of this."

"Your fate's been sealed," Beau said. "There's nothing I nor he can do to help you."

"Living people don't just fall into Hell." Charles sniffed at a plume of smoke that passed over them. "If I take him to Satan alive, it shows I am capable of more than harvesting crybabies every other day."

"Satan hates us. He's—"

"He's playing a long game against God—not man. Daniel's a new piece on the board. Satan could use him. We can bargain. That's how *we all* get what we want."

It was obvious now that Charles was telling the truth. Nothing that he said indicated that what he wanted was best for Daniel—only for himself. "We'll take our chances on the mountain."

"You'd fail," Charles whispered. "And I can't let this opportunity go to waste."

Beside him on the ground, Daniel stirred. Beau stooped and took Daniel's hands.

"Get off me," Daniel rolled away, scowling at Beau. When he saw Charles, he massaged his neck. "You. Stay back. Don't touch me."

Charles leaned to Beau. "If you won't listen to reason, maybe he will."

Chapter Four

On to Grayton

DANIEL

Daniel came to his feet, expecting pain, but it never flared. If not for the burning mountain, the ruined valley, and the two odd men in front of him, he would have considered he had dreamed everything, even hiking Grandfather Mountain with Kristine earlier that day. Unfortunately, the hot air stinging his eyes, the carbon wrestling his nostrils, and the fires dazzling his eyes confirmed that this was real.

He scowled at the two strangers. Tension built up around his joints. He flexed his arms to crush the irritation that dug into his bones.

Charles, who had pinched Daniel's neck with icy fingers, smiled and tipped his hat. "Rise and shine, tough guy."

"What did you do to me?" Daniel snarled.

Charles's crocodile eyes widened. He glanced at Beau, then back at Daniel with an incredulous expression. "You fainted. All I did was pull you out of the ditch, but Beau here gave you something while you were out."

"Don't trust this monster," Beau slurred. His movements were uncoordinated, as if he'd been drinking. He stood a foot shorter than Charles, but had a stronger and wider frame. His clothes were ragged and heavily soiled.

Daniel tasted something bitter and sweet on his tongue. “What did you give me?”

“It was medicine,” Beau stepped closer, “and it healed you.”

Daniel’s back no longer ached. The abrasions on his arms and the cuts on his legs were gone. He was confused. This had to be a dream. Or maybe he'd been drugged. “What kind of medicine?”

Beau presented a ram’s horn. “A special mead from my horn.”

“It’s empty, by the way,” Charles added.

Daniel figured it was alcohol, which would explain the numbness he felt running beneath the surface of his skin. It didn’t matter. Nothing mattered except finding Kristine. “Do you have a phone on you?”

“No.” Beau staggered to him, squinting. His pale gray eyes seemed to light up the night. His puffed cheeks trembled as if he were on the verge of tears. “You need to understand something, Daniel. You’re in Hell.”

Daniel wasn’t sure if this was an elaborate joke or some form of odd luck. He nearly died and out of nowhere, two very strange individuals show up. “You’re kidding, right?”

“It’s true.” Beau cringed and wiped his eyes. “And it’s my fault.”

Beside Beau, Charles swayed from side to side. He shrugged when he looked up at Daniel. “I don’t know what he’s talking about.”

Daniel took a deep breath to settle his nerves. “I’m not dead, so this can’t be Hell.”

Beau craned his neck and touched the center of his forehead. “You’re alive, but—”

Daniel had had enough of Beau. He turned to Charles. “How far is that town again?”

“A thirty-minute walk from here.” Charles clicked his watch open and huffed. “We best get moving.” He strutted off, and Daniel followed him, lightly treading the ditches that bore deep-red veins.

"Wait," Beau called from behind. "He's taking you deeper into Hell."

Charles called over his shoulder, "Of course I am. We can't go higher for obvious reasons."

"Don't trust him, Daniel." Beau struggled to keep up, staggering behind them. "We need to climb the mountain. He's trying to trick you."

"When we get to town, things will make more sense," Charles said. "If not, you can come back and climb that mountain all you want."

"Can't you see what he's doing?" Beau gripped Daniel's shirt sleeve and turned him around.

Daniel shoved Beau's hand away. "Stop with that nonsense."

Beau scoffed. "Look around you. Can't you see what this is?"

Daniel took a breath to quell the anger rising within him. The horizon had blended with the sky. He didn't want to stand around. He wanted to get moving. "Heading to town makes sense. Climbing into a forest fire doesn't. So, that's it."

"You don't understand." Beau pointed at Charles. "He's a demon."

Daniel squinted at Charles, then back at Beau. "If that's the case, then what are you?"

"I'm not sure." Beau looked at his sooty hands and curled them. "I was a shadow."

"Wow!" Charles chuckled. "Sounds like someone's been drinking a little too much magical mead."

Beau bared his teeth. "He wants to take you to Satan."

Charles folded his arms. "What a thing to say. Maybe you want to take him to Satan. I'm pretty sure the ruler of Hell would be on top of a burning mountain."

"Stop!" Daniel shouted. "All I care about is finding Kristine, so let's get moving."

"I apologize." Charles placed a hand over his chest and bowed. "Follow me."

Daniel trailed after Charles. He tried to ignore Beau, but the chubby little man came alongside him. Tears ran down his filthy cheeks and disappeared into his beard. He stumbled over his feet, but managed not to fall.

"Don't go," he slurred.

The air began to chill. Daniel rubbed his arms. "You're drunk, Beau. You can barely walk or talk."

"No. No." Beau shook his head and tripped over another mound. "I was a shadow for too long, is all. This is the first time I've used my legs in ages."

"Whatever," Daniel said. "You don't have to come with us."

"I'm going wherever you go."

"Then I don't want to hear another word about Hell."

They came to a path riddled with holes and loose rocks that cut through a dark plain. There were no trees. Nor were there any signs of a nearby town. Charles turned left, and the decline slowly steepened.

Beau slipped and stumbled, trying to keep up. He panted, "I won't say another word about Hell if you promise me one thing."

"What's that?" Daniel asked.

"That you won't listen to *his* excuses when we can't find a phone or Kristine."

"Fair enough."

Ahead of them, Charles shouted, "You're falling behind!"

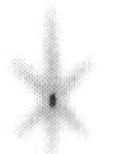

CHARLES

Daniel and Beau ambled like the two old oafs heading to the courtyard for a soul trial that would never occur. Baxter would've reported Charles by now, but they were far enough along the trail to Grayton that any reactionary force would miss them. Deserters avoided cities and stayed in the wastelands of Limbo. No one would look for them along this route since it led straight to Grayton.

Once they got into town, Charles would need to meet with the king and explain the situation. Surely, His Majesty would see reason and allow him to take the undead man to Satan. If not, the king would strip Charles of his demonic status and send him to the Acheron with a coin for Charon. Charles doubted he'd get pulled out of the seventh ditch of the Malebolge a second time.

Behind him, Daniel hollered, "Hold up a second, Charles."

"Great." Charles stopped and turned. He folded his arms, shaking his head. "What is it?"

A staticky sensation prickled over his hands and face as Beau and Daniel neared him. Charles backed away. He was certain this electric feeling came from the Holy Spirt. If only he could stamp it out. Maybe prolonged exposure to Hell would weaken it.

"You need to slow down," Daniel said. "It's dark. There are potholes and loose rocks everywhere. It's hard to keep up."

Charles shrugged. "The sooner we get there, the sooner we find your friend. It's not much farther, so come on."

Charles turned to go, but Daniel took hold of his sleeve. Daniel's blue eyes stood out in the darkness. It had been ages since he'd seen the color. It reminded him of the sky he stared into the first time he had died.

"Why are you dressed like that?" Daniel asked.

Charles didn't like getting questioned. When the souls he harvested asked him anything, he usually answered by breaking their fingers. That hushed them up, but he couldn't deal with Daniel that way.

"You have a problem with how I'm dressed?" Charles asked.

Daniel gestured to the surrounding darkness. "You're all dressed up in the middle of nowhere." His face seemed to glow. His eyes beamed with confidence and determination—unlike Beau.

Charles removed his hat and placed it over his chest. "I visited my grandmother's grave..." He squeezed the brim of his hat and winced. Her withered face returned, so did the song she often sang. "I meant my—father's. He gave this suit to me, so I wear it when I visit his grave — not far from where you fell."

Daniel quirked his lip and nodded. "Sorry for your loss."

"Don't be." Charles returned his hat. "She passed ages ago."

"Is it *he* or *she*?" Beau said. "See, I told you. You can't trust him."

Charles looked down the trail toward Grayton to hide his grimacing face. "My mistake. I meant she—I mean *he,* of course."

Daniel sighed and caressed the scar on his neck. "How much farther?"

Charles shrugged and swatted a few rocks off the trail with his foot. "If you keep up, we'll be there in no time."

"Just slow down some," Daniel said. "We don't know this path like you do."

Charles shrugged and resumed the walk, with Daniel and Beau trudging behind him. Their muffled steps jabbed into the eerie silence. The red plains on either side of the trail disappeared into the blackness, and the air continued to cool. Ahead, a massive cloud lingered over dark silhouettes that rose from the flat horizon. He took out his watch and started clicking.

BEAU

The mountain's firelight faded the farther they marched along this abysmal road. Charles kept his head slightly turned so he could eavesdrop on whatever was said. He opened and closed his watch steadily. Beau's thoughts drifted as he listened to it click and snap. He staggered less as he grew more familiar with walking. Still, the downward trek and treacherous path made it difficult for him to control his gait. His shaky breath and stuttering steps remained offbeat compared to Daniel's, who walked in time to the watch's cadence.

Lost in thought, Daniel stared at the ground. His body swayed side to side with every step. He and Charles were about the same height, but Daniel was broader and more muscular. He looked healthy for a man who had just fallen into Hell, which gave Beau an idea.

Beau cleared his throat and said, "You're getting along pretty well."

Daniel narrowed his eyes. "I'm lucky to be alive. I'll give you that."

"You're alive because of the medicine that comes from this." Beau raised the horn.

"Magical mead," Daniel quirked his lips, "that comes from a ram's horn. Did you find that at the Family Dollar?"

"I know you don't believe me." Beau slipped over loose rocks. Daniel helped him right his balance. "You were bad off back there, but look at you now."

Daniel glanced at his palms. "I was lucky nothing was broken. I was cut up a bit, but not too much. And hiking isn't too difficult when you're heading downhill and pumped full of adrenaline."

Beau twisted his beard between his forefingers. The slight tug and thickened string of hair felt familiar to him. "You fell through a mountain, crashed against rocks, scraped against rugged surfaces, and got torn up along the way—and you think you're running on adrenaline?"

"It's more believable than your story," Daniel said with a hint of laughter.

Beau reached into his pocket and retrieved the keystone. "Recognize this?" He held it out with the golden spiral facing up.

Daniel's face drained. He slowed to a stop. "Where did you find that?"

"The truth is that I'm drawn to it." Beau gripped it, and his chubby fingers lit a soft, orange glow that traveled over his fist. The heat emitting from his hand wrapped around him like a warm blanket. It could have sent Daniel to Heaven, but it had chosen Hell instead. Why? Maybe if Daniel held it again, he would return to Earth. "Here, you take it." Beau opened his hand and offered the stone. The warmth and the glow faded.

"No. It burned me, but what makes it light up?"

"I'm not sure." Beau flipped it like a coin and caught it. "It's called a keystone, and it takes whoever squeezes it to Heaven or Hell. Part of my job as a shadow was to place it in the hand of the dying. They'd give it a squeeze and if it was their time, they'd take off one way or another."

"How could you carry anything if you're a shadow?"

Beau twisted his beard. "It was part of the shadow realm. Only shadows can interact there. It is part of your world, but you can't see it. For some reason, when I left the keystone behind, you were able to find it and take it. If I had any idea that could happen, I would've kept it."

"You're the one who left it under that tree?"

"I—"

"What you got there, Beau?" Charles walked toward them.

"It's none of your business." Beau returned the keystone to his pocket.

Charles's lips curled with contempt. "If you say so." He looked over his shoulder. "Grayton is just down this hill."

"Finally!" Daniel trotted to Charles, and Beau trailed after him, looking about in the dark, wary of unseen dangers.

As he neared Daniel and Charles, a lonely city crushed by torrential rains emerged three hundred yards down a low-grade slope. A huge, low-hanging cloud loomed over the town. Steam jetted upward from its empty roads. Yellow streetlamps flickered in front of two-story buildings, stretching along the outskirts.

"What's that smell?" Daniel covered his nose.

"We're near a landfill." Charles pointed ahead. "The hospital's only a few blocks that way. Come on."

Charles trudged downhill with Daniel right behind him. Beau sucked in a ragged breath. Though he couldn't convince Daniel to turn back, this miserable town would certainly reveal that this world was Hell and that Charles couldn't be trusted.

Chapter Five

The King's Secret

DANIEL

A putrid odor filled Daniel's nostrils, and unrelenting heavy rains hammered the steaming, ruined streets of Grayton. Charles hurried over potholes and crumbling asphalt, which exposed the brick beneath the road. They came upon a sidewalk riddled with newspapers, rotten food, and broken glass. Behind them, Beau stumbled along with his chin down and shoulders hunched.

The engagement ring pierced Daniel's thigh. He pulled it out, worrying that the gold band might have bent or one of the smaller diamonds had come loose. Thankfully, it was fine. Maybe, like this ring, he and Kristine could weather through their rough patch and come out more resilient together.

He couldn't wait to see her smiling face when she found out he had survived the fall. She had told him when they were signing up for classes last semester, *You can do anything you want.* Joking, he had asked, *Anything?* She had laughed. *Well, almost anything.* Escaping death would be one thing he could do, apparently.

Charles turned into a narrow alleyway. Hot rainwater poured from the rooftops onto dozens of vagrants, who sat with their backs to the wall on either side. Daniel gazed into their sunken faces. They stared at the stream coursing through the alley's center. Seeing none of them blink or lift their eyes to meet his unnerved him.

When they reached the other side of the alley, Charles stepped out onto a larger road that was as empty and ruined as the first and pointed left. "The hospital's this way."

"What about these people in the alley?" Daniel said.

Charles shrugged. "What about them?"

"What do you mean by that?" Daniel asked. He couldn't believe Charles's lack of empathy. "They're stuck out here in this downpour, and no one is helping them."

After clearing his throat, Charles slid his fingers along the brim of his hat. "You see, the wildfire displaced a lot of people—too many. Very unfortunate. Most terrible thing, I must say. I'm sure the authorities are trying their best—their absolute best to help."

"Their best? There are dozens of them. And look at all these buildings—there's plenty of shelter."

Charles pressed his lips together and adjusted his necktie. "Maybe they're unaware of these poor, poor fellows. After I show you where the hospital is, when I run over to the police station to check on your friend, I'll let them know about these people too."

From the alley, Beau's voice blasted like a cannon. "You know where you are?" At the end of the alley, Beau interrogated an elderly man who shielded his sobbing face with both arms. "What is this place? Say something, will you?"

"What are you doing?" Daniel marched to Beau. "Leave him alone."

"Not until he answers my question."

Daniel grabbed Beau's sodden shirt and pulled him away. "I won't let you bother these people."

"Look at their faces," Beau said. "Their skin is gray. They don't even blink. They're dead."

Daniel looked at the poor man sitting at the end of the alley. He had his face buried in his shaking hands. The woman next to him looked away, covering her mouth. Their bruised skin was wrinkly and swollen, likely because of prolonged exposure to the rain. They were not well off, but not dead either. "Do any of you want to go to the hospital with us?" Daniel asked.

When none of them answered, Beau said, "Can't you see how messed up this place is?"

Daniel looked at the others sitting in the alley. They stared through him with glazed eyes. He's seen this before and knew all too well that these alley-dwellers had grown numb to their dreary reality. "Let's get to the hospital, OK? Charles will tell the police about these people."

"Is that what he told you?" Beau looked both confused and disgusted. "Daniel, I know you don't believe me, but open your eyes. See this place for what it is."

"Don't patronize me." Daniel took a deep breath and swallowed his anger. Something was off with this place. The rain was hot. The town was in ruins. The sickly faces of these people and their haunted expressions gave him pause. Charles's eyes and ghoulish skin soured his stomach. "If we can't find a phone or Kristine in the next three or four hours, we'll go up the mountain. OK?"

Beau nodded.

A block down, on the opposite side of the road, Daniel spotted seven people standing in a single file by a bus stop sign. Why they would stand here in all this rain was beyond him, but he jogged past Charles and crossed the street.

"Excuse me." Daniel panted as he neared them. "Can I borrow a phone? Please, it's important. I'll be quick. I promise."

They glanced at each other. Some shrugged. Others shook their heads. They grumbled amongst themselves until a lady in a tight skirt pursed her lips and said, "There aren't any phones here, sweetie. But if you're lost, I can help you."

"Hey, I'm lost," another man snickered. The others erupted with laughter.

"No one has a cellphone?" Daniel couldn't believe this. What were the chances that out of seven people waiting at a bus stop, none of them would have a phone?

Beau hurried past Daniel, panting. "One of you needs to tell him what this place is."

A large man dropped his folded arms and scowled. "You think you can march around here and bark orders at us, fat man?"

"Settle down." Charles walked over and raised his watch as if it were a badge. "Don't mind him. He's not all right upstairs, if you know what I mean."

The group became awkwardly silent. They fidgeted and looked at each other, frowning.

"Don't you get it?" Charles's reptilian eyes widened. He bared his rotted teeth into a smile. "He's not all right *upstairs*. It's a *joke*, people."

The group burst into false laughter. Their mouths stretched, and their jaws jerked left and right.

Beau's eyes shimmered with tears. "All of you know what this place is. Just say it."

Charles answered him. "The town of Grayton, of course."

"There you have it," one traveler said. "The miserable town of Grayton."

Charles started to pat Daniel's shoulder, but stopped. "The hospital is just down the street. It's not much farther."

"Come on." Daniel tugged on Beau's sleeve and followed Charles deeper into the city. The odd laughter continued until the tallest one roared and started punching the bus sign. When he stopped, he shouted at the sky. "I'm through waiting on that stinking bus with these squawking loudmouths. The grass may be greener over there, but it's filled with a bunch of do-gooders who think they're better than everybody." He stomped off, splashing through every puddle in his path.

Beau placed a heavy hand on Daniel's shoulder. "Don't you find it funny how they reacted to Charles?"

Daniel swallowed. Never had he seen grown men and women act so strangely, but that didn't mean they were in Hell. "They probably thought he was a police officer. Did you see how he held up his watch like it was a police badge? People get nervous around law enforcement. He kind of saved you there. That was a big and angry man."

"It was more than that." Beau stepped into a pothole and stumbled. "They were afraid of him."

"Charles isn't scary, just weird."

Charles peeked over his shoulder and gave Daniel a wink. "Believe it or not, an angel drives the bus. Picks up passengers for Heaven. Most don't make the trip because it's such a horrible place. But don't take my word for it, I'm a demon. Can't trust me. Right, Beau?"

Beau grimaced at the buildings along the right side of the street. They looked abandoned and looted. Shattered glass, trashed displays, and junk riddled their floors. Baseball bats and lead pipes were strewn about the street. Manhole covers were missing and there wasn't a single car parked anywhere.

"What happened here?" Daniel asked.

Charles sniffed the air and squinted. “There was a protest. It was mostly peaceful, but things got out of hand.”

Daniel pointed to a smashed window. “Shouldn’t the police be out here protecting these businesses?”

“Well,” Charles said, “the rain hasn’t let up in a while. Everyone’s sick of it. It’s why there aren’t any rioters and protesters out here now, but never mind that. There’s the hospital.” Charles pointed to a dark structure with several dimly lit rectangular windows. “I’ll head over to the police station from here, but will catch up with you afterward. I’ll tell them about the people in the alley and see about your friend.”

Daniel was relieved to see the hospital. “Thanks Charles. Ask the police to look for Kristine Groves. She’s a student at Appalachian State and lives on campus. If they need more details, have them come talk to me. I’ll cooperate.”

“Sure.” Charles started off.

“Wait.” Daniel trotted to him and offered a handshake. “Thanks again for your help.”

Charles recoiled. “I don’t shake hands. But I’ll come to the hospital and find you. Maybe I’ll have some news.”

“Good news, I hope,” Daniel said.

Charles backed away, looking at Daniel’s chest. He seemed frightened. “See you soon.” He darted off to an adjacent street.

Daniel and Beau hurried along the sidewalk and across the hospital’s empty parking lot. EMERGENCY flickered in bright red letters over the entrance. The automatic glass doors squealed open, and they entered. The waiting room flickered under buzzing fluorescent lights. Dozens of small, cushioned chairs sat along the walls and back-to-back throughout the center. Old beauty magazines lay mangled on side tables. The black-and-white–tiled floor echoed as they approached the nurse at the front desk.

"Ma'am, may I use—"

"Check-in is at the kiosk." The nurse scowled at her computer screen. Her fingertips punched hard against the keyboard.

"I don't think I need to see a doctor. I just need a phone."

The nurse stopped typing and glared at Daniel. "If you're not here for a medical emergency, you need to leave."

"O-K." Daniel walked over to the kiosk. A sheet of paper that read: CHECK-IN HERE was taped to the wall over it.

Five people waited in this massive room.

"Should be more crowded from the riot. Don't you think?" Beau said.

"You are extremely persistent, Beau." Daniel typed in his name and pressed enter. "Are you signing in too?"

"No." Beau plodded to a seat facing the exit and sat. "We'll leave when you're ready."

Daniel went back to the front desk. The lady slapped her hands on her desk and gave him a stern look.

"I checked in," Daniel said. "May I use a phone, ma'am?"

The nurse rolled her eyes. "Phones are for office use only. Take a seat and we'll call you when we're ready."

"Forget that," Daniel muttered. He spotted a man feigning sleep. The man doubled over and even peeked. "Sir, are you awake?"

The man turned away and started snoring. Daniel walked over and jostled his shoulder.

The stranger slapped Daniel's hand away and screamed, "Don't touch me!"

"Sorry. But do you have a phone I can borrow?"

The man sobbed and repeated, "Don't touch me. No touching."

Daniel backed away. The disturbed person folded over and pretended to fall back asleep. Daniel looked around the room. Everyone squeezed their eyes shut—except Beau, who pointed at the door.

Daniel shook his head and walked toward another fake sleeper.

"Sir," the nurse said tersely, "if you harass anyone else, I'll have hospital security escort you out. Do you understand?"

Daniel rolled his eyes. "You can't be serious. I only asked for a phone."

"I asked you a question, mister. And I require an answer. *Do you understand*?"

"Yeah, yeah, I understand." Daniel waved her off. "I'll take a seat."

Walking to Beau, he saw they'd tracked muddy footprints across the floor. A small puddle was under Beau's feet and chair.

"I didn't realize you were wearing sandals this whole time."

"Yeah? They're brand new."

Daniel groaned as he inched into a chair beside Beau. "We are filthy." Relief rose in his aching legs and back. Cold and wet, his clothes clung to his skin. He shivered. "Let me see that horn, Beau?"

He handed it over.

"Heavier than it looks." Daniel peered through its center. The inside was brown and wet from the rain. "There's nothing in here. Except the strap running through it."

"Try taking a sip."

"Looks nasty." Daniel handed it back. "Besides, it's not a drinking horn. It's a blow horn."

"I've blown it a few times," Beau said. His eyes widened. "I should've done that."

"Done what?" Daniel asked.

"Sounding the horn scares off demons. One blast and they'll—" A smile spread across Beau's dirty face. "They'll run off."

"Are you going to blow the horn at Charles?" Daniel chuckled. "See if he runs off?"

"If he does, will you believe this is Hell?"

"No. But don't let me spoil your fun."

"You wouldn't find that odd? Most people don't run off when they hear a simple sounding from a horn."

"Beau, a sudden loud noise can startle anybody," Daniel said. "Startles me sometimes."

He picked up a magazine that lay on the seat of the chair beside him. Someone had defaced it with black markers. The name of the magazine and stories were blotted. The close-up of a woman's face was altered to have a beard and look like a skull. He tossed it back in the chair.

"Notice how you can't use a phone?"

"Yeah, kind of noticed that." Daniel rolled his neck and shoulders. "But I'm not ready to hike up into a forest fire just yet."

"What if you find out I'm right? That this is Hell."

Daniel slouched into his chair, closed his eyes, and grinned. "Then I guess I'd have a bus to catch."

CHARLES

Charles ran three blocks to City Hall, where the provincial king's office was one floor down from the police department. Charles climbed the cement steps and opened the double doors. Swirling dust gleamed underneath nine halogen lights symmetrically aligned and spaced on the ceiling in three rows of three. The police officer stationed behind a bullet-proof window chuckled when he saw him.

"Heartless Charles. Surrendering yourself to the king?" Having no teeth, the officer spoke with a lisp. His beady eyes narrowed to slits. His greasy, swollen face glistened like melted wax. "You'll be more than heartless by the time His Majesty finishes with you."

Charles stopped a foot shy of the window. He folded his arms and huffed from his nose. "I don't have time to deal with you. Call 'im."

The officer came off his chair in a pathetic attempt to intimidate. Grimacing, he snatched the phone from its base and pushed a button with a thick, stubby finger. He put the receiver to his ear and scowled at Charles. His face softened when someone answered. "Charles is here. Do you... OK. I'll send... Thank you. You do excellent work too... Yes. Thank you. I'll catch up with you after work, pal. You're the best too." He hung up and slumped back into his chair.

"Pitiful," Charles said, shaking his head.

The toothless officer frowned. "You may have made a name for yourself when you pulled your heart out years back. I always wondered how you kept it from growing back, but it doesn't matter. The king loathes deserters."

Charles scowled. "Judge Baxter called every harvester who's ever served under him a deserter. What does that tell you?"

"You abandoned your post, failed to deliver the soul for trial, and left the mountain." The officer sneered. "You're toast, *Heartless* Charles."

Charles leaned close to the glass and whispered through the horizontal slot. "Do you want to know how I kept it from growing back?"

The officer's demeanor lightened. He blinked with interest. "How?"

"First, rip out your own heart." Charles straightened his back and folded his arms.

"Yeah." The officer edged closer in his chair, licking his lips.

"Go on," Charles said. "Do it."

"But I'm on duty."

"Then you're wasting my time," Charles took out his watch and rolled it in his fingers, "and the king's time."

The guard slapped the window. "You'd better be glad there's a thick sheet of glass between us. Otherwise, I'd wring your scrawny little neck."

"I wring my own neck well enough, thank you." Charles tightened his necktie. "Now unlock the door."

"You're in for a world of hurt, punk." The guard pressed a button, and the heavy door to Charles's left popped open.

Charles adjusted his hat. "Am I not already in a world of hurt?"

Charles's footsteps echoed as he entered a stairwell reeking of bleach. After two flights of stairs, he came to the narrow hallway that led to the king's office. Steel walls on either side reflected like clouded mirrors. Circular light-fixtures, occupied by shadowy bug carcasses, hung from moldy ceiling tiles and shined hot light upon the beige linoleum floor. At the opposite end, two guards in black uniforms stood before a red door where white smoke emanated from the cracks.

The larger of the two guards had puffy eyes and a gray-headed buzz-cut. He waved a bulky hand. "Come forward, Charles."

The temperature rose several degrees as Charles walked to the two large men. "Looks like His Majesty enjoys smoke too. I think we'll get along splendidly."

"That's far enough. Turn and place your hands on the wall."

"You want to search me?" Charles complied, but the idea of them touching his suit disgusted him. "You think I'm stupid enough to attack the king?"

"It's protocol." Mr. Buzz-cut came up behind Charles and checked his bowler hat. "We don't much like touching you either."

"Hurry up then. I have things to do."

The guard came to Charles's vest and gripped the watch.

"Hands off the watch," Charles hissed.

The guard let it go and frisked Charles's pants. "How 'bout I break your stupid watch?" He finished and said, "He's clear. Tell the king."

Charles adjusted his coat and tie while the other guard opened the door. Smoke wafted into the hall. "Charles is clear for entering, Your Highness."

"Send him in." The king's voice sounded ragged.

Charles breathed in harsh smoke and sighed upon entering the king's chamber. "Ahh, this is nice."

Despite the haze, Charles could see clearly. The king sat on a throne that had two bull horns protruding from either end of the top-rail. In front of him was a golden desk placed near the center of the room. Two marble fireplaces roared on the far side of the office. Red and orange light glimmered against the purple ceramic floor and walls. Overhead, decaying drop-ceiling tiles dripped with moisture. The king worked alone, which explained why the guards checked Charles at the door.

When the king didn't acknowledge his presence, Charles said, "I see you enjoy your privacy, Your Majesty."

The king grunted while scribbling onto a piece of parchment with a pen shaped like a curling snake.

"Fine taste indeed, Your Majesty." Charles inhaled deeply. "Burnt pine. Harsh, sweet—"

"Just take a seat, Charles."

"Thank you, Your Majesty." He went to the dark-green chair in front of the king's desk. When he sat, its horrible leather upholstery grabbed at his clothes and made impertinent noises.

The king wore tiny spectacles, and his blistered skin hung loosely from his skull like moth-eaten garments. He dropped his pen into an ink jar, ripped his brown gloves off, and slapped them onto his desk. Leaning back in his chair, he said, "You disappoint me. You swelled the attendance of our soul cache, making it the most popular in all of Limbo, then out of nowhere you desert your post!"

"I'm not a deserter. I was—"

The king came off his throne. "If you're here and not on the mountain, you're a deserter!" The king's head quivered. He blinked, scratched his chest, and sank back into his seat.

"I apologize, Your Majesty. I assure you. There's good reason."

"There's no good reason. Once I take your watch and have your eyes gouged, you'll realize that." The king massaged his forehead. "I thought you were destined for greatness. I venerated you to all of Limbo and my superiors. Once word of your desertion gets out, I'll be the laughingstock of Hell." The king pounded a fist on the desk and groaned. He cupped his hand behind the desk and nursed it in his lap.

"Your Majesty. No one will laugh." Charles crossed his legs and clutched his left elbow. "You will become the envy of kings. I have an undead man and a shadow spirit. If you allow me—"

"You have nothing." The king rose from his seat again. "They belong to me. Even you belong to me." His nostrils flared and his breath sent smoke into swirls over the grand desk. He brought his hand up as if preparing to slam it, but thought otherwise. He sat back down instead. "Nothing here is yours. Your ridiculous clothes. Your watch. Even your eyes are mine."

Charles came to the edge of his noisy chair and whispered, "Your Grace, I must tell you the man has the Holy Spirit inside him. The shadow is dead set on escaping. If they stay here, they'll be a burden. I'm certain you'd be better off having me take them deeper."

The king squinted with confusion. "The Holy Spirit—here?"

"It's possible. The man *is* alive and still has hope."

"I suppose." The king caressed a large blister on his cheek and leaned back in his throne. "But how are you so certain of it?"

"I didn't realize it at first, but when I forced the man asleep, it attacked me." Thinking about it made Charles feel uneasy. He fidgeted in his chair. "Wreaked havoc in my head. Injected images of my former life. It isn't worth your trouble, I assure you, Your Majesty."

"The Holy Spirit spreads like a disease, you know." The king pinched and pulled at a slab of skin hanging from his jaw. "Perhaps it has infected you."

The gentle, smiling face of his sweet grandmother, her frail hands, and melodic humming lingered in Charles's mind like gunpowder over a battlefield. He swallowed and cleared his throat. "It didn't spread to me, but the man *is* infected."

The king scowled. "If that is the case, I'll have him killed within the hour."

"Sir, that's wasteful."

"I won't have that Holy Spirit running amuck in Limbo. Everyone in Grayton will be lined up for that God-awful bus."

Charles sat up straight and tightened his tie. "Then let me take him and the shadow deeper into Hell. We'll be off your hands."

The king sighed with boredom. He drummed his fingers on his desk. "Humor me then. Where do you intend to take him?"

"Him *and* the shadow."

"Of course, both of them."

"I'll take them to the Ninth Hell," Charles slowly stretched out his arms to either side, splaying his fingers, "where I'll offer them to Satan as gifts from you."

The king huffed. "We don't send gifts. We send souls to their proper place. Furthermore, Satan hates man. You'll fester his anger and he'll blame me."

Charles sat back in his seat and brought his hands together. The king's response demonstrated the problem with the demons of the First Hell. They lingered in the frail power they held rather than work to achieve more. "Allow me to take them anyway. Here, they're a useless burden."

"Enough. Hand me your pocketwa-wa..." The king gripped his neck and tried to clear his throat. His eyes widened. Gagging, his withered face grew red. Yellow and white pus burst from his blisters. Steam plumed from his nostrils. The king bent behind his desk, heaving.

Charles grimaced to hide his delight. "This isn't a good look for you, Your Majesty. I see why you prefer your privacy. I suppose no one knows you suffer the second death."

The king's unpleasant noises ceased. His furious eyes emerged from behind his desk. He attempted to speak, but disappeared and heaved more. The most powerful man in the province struggled for breath and groaned pitifully as he came upright again. Behind strained, arthritic hands, the king's face contorted until he spouted sizzling water upon the desk. When finished, His Majesty leaned against an arm of his throne, gripping his belly.

Charles took one of the king's gloves and tried it on. "You know, my day has been filled with coincidences, Your Highness—whatever you call yourself. First, harvesting a single soul—late in the day, mind you. Very strange. Turned out the soul survived the fall. He remains alive, but how? Oh, that's right. A shadow spirit, of all things, along with his life-giving elixir, rained like manna from the mountain. Like I said, so many coincidences." Charles brought his elbows upon the king's desk and perched his chin on his gloved hand. "And now this."

Still weak, the king brought a kerchief to his mouth. "It's nothing."

"Such tiny hands." Charles removed the glove and tossed it to the floor. He sat back in his seat, crossed his legs, and steepled his fingers. "Everyone assumes you're a pure demon. If someone, besides me, found out who you were and that you suffer the second death—why, they might test your authority, wouldn't they? And very well might remove you from this position you've held for so long."

The king scowled while massaging his throat.

Charles dropped his aching smile. "You can keep your secret if I can take the man and the shadow to Satan—with my watch and my eyes intact, of course. Otherwise, I'll sing your death song all the way to Charon's skiff."

The king tried to sit up but couldn't. "I'll have your tongue cut out."

Charles leaned to the side rubbing his thumb across the tips of his fingers. "You can't do it alone. You're too weak to overcome me. Besides, all I need to do is say your name loud enough for the guards to hear. We both know how fast word gets around."

"You don't have the gall to test me."

"I hope you're not a betting man." Charles cleared his throat and exclaimed, "Ladies and gentlemen. Anyone with ears who can hear, indulge in the news I bring. His Royal Highness, the King of Grayton, is none other than the man, the myth, the legendary—"

"Quiet!" The king's hands and blistered face trembled. He bent over his desk and looked down at his golden reflection. "I will let you go, but I cannot send you straight to the Ninth Hell."

"What do you mean? Hundreds have been sent straight there since I've been here."

"Charon won't carry the undead, and I can't force that monster to do anything. I'll send you, along with the man and shadow, to the Second Hell through alternative means. From there, you're on your own."

"Lust is a perpetual storm." Charles pulled out his pocket watch and rolled it between his fingers. "How do we get out of that?"

"You're so smart, you figure it out." The king opened a drawer and pulled out a piece of parchment. When he took out the snake-shaped pen, it stretched and curled around his hand twice before he scribbled his instructions.

"If you utter another word in my Hell, your eyes and tongue are mine. Do you understand?"

Charles appreciated a promising threat and gave a closed-mouth grin while tipping his hat.

The king rolled up the parchment and slung it across the desk. "Give it to my guards. One will escort you to the man and shadow. Gather them and leave."

Charles came to his feet. He twirled the parchment in his fingers and pointed it at the king as if it were a pistol and winked. The king glared nastily. Charles sauntered to the door and took the knob. Before leaving the room, he inhaled the smoke and sighed loudly.

Chapter Six

Enter the Storm

BEAU

In the emergency room, Beau wrung his hands. Grime fell from his fingers like snow. He wracked his brain over what he had said. *Demons ran away from the sounding of the horn.* It stirred a frail memory of a time before he was a shadow. He was a man chasing after someone in the woods.

"My past is coming back to me," he muttered. "But why?"

Daniel wriggled in the chair beside him. When he had plucked the keystone from the earth, Beau felt a stinging pain in his chest. From miles away, he had a clear vision of a hellhole opening up to swallow Daniel. When it did, Beau didn't hesitate.

"I *chased* after him." He believed he had done the right thing, but that provided little comfort.

He sighed and stared out the foggy automatic doors of the exit. Charles had planted a seed of doubt in Beau. There was some truth in what the demon said. The mountain would never suffice. If they lost the horn, they'd suffer, but that wasn't all. Daniel needed to change his ways, or he'd end up here even if they escaped.

Caressing the thin, red scar on his neck, Daniel sat at the edge of his seat, staring at the muddied black-and-white–checkered floor beneath his feet. Every moment counted. Sitting there with nothing to say wouldn't help Daniel at all.

"How did you get that scar?"

"I got it in Iraq." Daniel sat up and wrapped his arms over his stomach.

"What happened?"

Daniel sighed and scratched the back of his head. "I don't want to talk about it."

"Someone tried to kill you?"

Daniel didn't respond. He squirmed in his chair. The muscles in his jaw flexed. His face reddened. He closed his eyes and exhaled.

"We may as well pass the time while we're waiting," Beau said.

"If you *must* know," Daniel said, glaring at him, "a ten-year-old kid jumped on my back with a steak knife."

"Did you, you know, kill him?"

"Sometimes I wish I did." Daniel sneered. "I know what you're up to. You're trying to figure out why I'd be in Hell."

Beau shrugged. "Well, why would you?"

"I don't believe in any of it." Daniel's brow furrowed. "I used to. I went to church but stopped a long time ago."

"That's it? You don't believe in God?" Beau asked.

"Oh no. That's just the short answer. You see, I'm a sinner." Daniel shifted in his seat and glared at Beau. "And I don't care. If that means I'll burn in Hell someday, then so be it."

Beau didn't understand why Daniel was so bitter and angry. He shifted his approach, hoping to get on Daniel's good side. "Your friend, Kristine. You care about her, don't you?"

The mention of her brought a genuine smile to Daniel's face. His eyes teared up, and he looked back at the floor. "I want to marry her, but I got issues."

"What kind of issues?"

Daniel curled his lip in contempt. He looked to the emergency room door, to the nurse, and back to the floor.

"You don't want to talk about it?" Beau asked.

Daniel let out an exasperated sigh. "Not sure why you care to know every single thing about me, but I'll tell you what. I love Kristine. I've never felt this way for anyone else."

"What's the problem, then?"

Daniel twisted the arms of his chair, causing them to groan. They remained bent when he let go. "If I tell you something that's been on my mind, would you stop with all these questions?"

Beau kept his eyes on the warped chair longer than he intended. He nodded. "Sure."

Daniel stared past Beau to a far corner of the emergency room. "I got into it with my dad years ago." He looked back to the floor, his knees bouncing nervously.

"Why?"

"He was overbearing." Daniel looked at Beau and stiffened. "He was a poster-boy for Alcoholics Anonymous and he had all these standards that he wanted me, his *only* child, to live up to, so when I came home drunk *one time* after eighteen years of toeing the line, he kept coming at me and I lost it." Daniel sucked in a breath. "I tried to leave. He got in my way," his brow wrinkled, "and I pushed him over the coffee table."

Beau placed a hand on Daniel's shoulder, but he nudged it off.

"Mom ran over to him. They were crying there on the floor." Daniel closed his eyes, shaking his head. "I was about to say I was sorry. That he was right, and I didn't have any business going back out at three in the morning. But he looked me in the eye and said, 'Just go then.'" Daniel's knees started bouncing again. "So, I did."

Beau lowered his head and rotated the horn in his hands. “I see.”

“I’d had enough.” Daniel glared at the far corner of the room. His face soured. “I mess up one time, and he does that.”

“You regret it?”

Daniel’s mouth opened, but he struggled for words. His head swiveled like a plane out of control. “He *told* me to go. Told me to get out. Go drive drunk, son. Do whatever you’re gonna do. Just go away.” Daniel sighed. He palmed his face and shook his head. “If I was a stranger, he would’ve cared. But yeah, I regret it. I’ve wanted to call them for years but haven’t. It’s too late now. Wouldn’t make a difference, anyway.”

“Are you kidding? Of course it would. Don’t let that moment dictate your life.”

Daniel righted his posture and gave Beau a stern look. “It doesn’t. I’m better off without them. Shamed and judged for every little thing I screw up. I’m through with that.”

“I can tell that it bothers you,” Beau said, “and even if it didn’t, maybe your parents need you. Maybe your father wants to make things right. Ever think about that?”

Daniel’s face was red. His glistening eyes shot up at Beau. “I’m over it.”

Daniel’s tone was harsh, but his hard expression melted away. He seemed to be frightened to reach out to his parents. Maybe he’d be willing to face this fear once he realized the truth about where he was.

Daniel glared over his shoulder at the nurse. “Why hasn’t anybody been called back yet?”

“One more outburst from you, and I’ll call security,” the nurse said.

“Isn’t she the sweetest?” Daniel chuckled. “You know, not that long ago, I would’ve lost my cool with that lady by now.”

“Why haven’t you?”

"Kristine." Daniel nodded with a smile. "Being around her... Her way about things.... On our first date, she told me something that flipped a switch in my head."

"Yeah?" Beau propped his elbow on the arm of his chair and leaned toward Daniel.

"I was mad about something, and she took my hands and said, 'Choose life.' I didn't know what she was talking about, but she told me that regardless of the situation, I get to choose how I want to be. She said I can decide to let things live or die, but if I want peace, I should choose life."

"Sounds like good advice to me," Beau said.

Daniel looked back to the entrance and huffed. "I'm worried about Kristine. I really can't live without her."

Beau intertwined his fingers and eyed Daniel carefully. When they made eye contact, he said, "You can live without your parents—but not her?"

Daniel looked away, quirking his lip. "That's right."

"Has she ever asked about your parents?"

"Enough with all these questions."

The doors to the emergency room squealed open. Charles and a large police officer in a dark uniform marched toward the nurse. Her jaw dropped, and she stiffened in place. The officer handed her a document. Charles gestured for Beau and Daniel to join them.

"Did you find her?" Daniel asked, springing to his feet and heading to the nurse's station. Beau trailed after him.

Charles nodded with a thin smile.

"We'll take you to her in a moment," the officer said while eyeing the nurse. "Open the doors already."

The doors clicked open, and the officer led them through a cold, barren hall. Green floor tiles glistened. Light fixtures hummed overhead. Cinderblock walls were coated off-white. Their clamoring steps echoed past empty offices and closed laboratories.

Mindful of the officer and Charles's speedy gait, Beau lingered behind. "Where are we going?"

No one answered. They came to a freezing lobby with red carpeting and matching velvet furniture. Lingering dust irritated Beau's nostrils. Through large, fogged windows, the downpour blurred the streets of Grayton. A television on the wall displayed silent static.

"This way." The officer pulled keys from his belt loop. They reached the main entrance and came to a corridor of elevators. He walked up to a keypad, inserted a small key, and entered a code.

An automated voice buzzed from the speaker beneath it. "Select a level."

He pressed 0010.

Daniel asked, "She's on the tenth floor?"

"That's right." The officer raised his eyebrows at Charles.

When the doors opened, Charles and Daniel stepped in. The officer turned and stared at Beau with daring eyes. Beau's chest pounded as he inched into the elevator. Utter dread clamped his mouth shut. Words seemed distant. Thoughts turned to mush.

Once Beau was in the elevator, the officer returned his keys to his belt loop. As the doors closed, the officer flitted his hand over his head and said, "So long, Heartless Charles."

"Heartless Charles?" Daniel squinted.

Charles folded his arms, unfolded them, and shifted his feet.

The elevator lurched.

Beau gazed at the mirrored walls and frowned at his rugged reflection. His ghostly gray eyes compelled him to look elsewhere. He spied on Charles, wondering what this was all about.

Behind him, Daniel groomed his hair using the walls, no doubt expecting to see Kristine. He huffed and said, "Shouldn't we have stopped by now?"

Charles checked the shine on his shoes and brushed wet ash from his pants. He tightened his tie and removed his hat. A heavy, red line was etched across his forehead two inches below his short, blond hair. Charles glanced at Daniel and flinched.

Beau cocked his head while pinching his beard. It dawned on him. "You're *human*," he said to Charles. "Aren't you?"

Daniel suppressed a laugh. "That's quite a change, Beau. Good for you."

"Excuse me?" Charles smiled nervously, rotating his bowler hat in his hands. His inhuman eyes stood out due to the overhead lights.

"What happened to your eyes?" Beau's voice shook.

"They're just contacts," Daniel said.

"Contacts," Charles echoed, while replacing his hat. His face grew stony. He blinked and looked away.

"No." Beau squinted. He seemed confused. "They did something to you. Did they try to turn you into a demon?"

Daniel placed a hand on the crown of his head. "Goodness, I thought we were past that. What's up with this elevator?"

The elevator jostled to a stop. Beau, Daniel, and Charles grasped the steel railing. The overhead lights brightened, grew hot, and exploded. Darkness and the stench of burnt electrical wires filled the compartment.

Beau grabbed Daniel's arm.

Charles whispered, "Brace yourselves."

A swirling, whistling noise wavered in intensity. The elevator rose and fell slightly, making Beau feel queasy. Overhead, a metallic clanging grew louder, as if something sped toward them. When it struck, the elevator car shot downward.

They bounced all around the interior and into each other. The elevator car soared through the unknown. A massive impact sent it tumbling. Shattered mirrors rattled within it until a final, jarring crash brought them to a halt.

A ferocious wind whipped against the exterior. Maniacal screams oscillated to the wind's rhythm.

Disoriented and aching, Beau managed to keep Daniel in his clutches. "Are you OK?" Daniel didn't respond. Beau shook him. "Daniel."

"Use the medicine," Charles grunted.

Beau reached for it, but the strap had broken. "I lost it."

"It can't be far. Find it."

Fumbling into his shirt pocket, Beau gripped the keystone and held it overhead. Charles shrank away from the warm, golden light. Shards of glass riddled the floor. The horn lay nearby; its leather strap had broken, but he fixed it by tying a square knot. Beau brought the small end of the horn to Daniel's mouth.

"Whatever you do, don't lose that," Charles said. "We have a long way to go."

Thuds jostled the walls. Hands scraped against the exterior, and voices pleaded for help until winds swept them away. Their cries dissipated in the whirl.

"What do you mean?"

"We're in Lust." Charles took out his watch and clicked it open. "It's the Second Hell. We need to get to the Ninth."

"No, we don't," Beau growled. "Daniel will be through with you after this."

"There's no other choice."

Beau glared at Charles. "You can't make us go anywhere with you."

Charles looked about the floor, found his hat, and placed it on his head. "There's no way back. We can either stay in Lust, or head to Satan. That's it."

"You lie."

"Not about this." Charles picked up a triangular mirror shard and assessed the cuts on his face. "Sure, I misled Daniel to make him think he wasn't in Hell, but it was necessary. There's no way up that mountain. I am certain of that."

"There's got to be another way." Beau slung the strap of his horn back over his shoulder. "We can't take him to Satan."

"If you want him to live, you must come with me. Otherwise, this is it, for all of us."

Life blossomed in Daniel's still body. Shards of mirror pushed out from his skin. Scars scabbed and withered away. Bruises faded and swellings fell. Daniel's chest rose and sank lightly again.

"When he wakes up, we'll need to move and keep moving." Charles eyed the two closed doors overhead and tried to pry them apart.

"Don't open those!" Beau shouted. "People are banging around out there. Try the trapdoor."

DANIEL

When the elevator car dropped, a thrilling sensation rose from Daniel's gut. His head swam with euphoria and trauma. Each time his body slammed against a wall, flashes erupted from the corners of his vision until he lost consciousness.

Within an internal void emerged spatial awareness. Darkness extended in all directions. Pale gray lines fluttered from where he focused. Then a shape—a circle—increased in size as if coming to him. He passed through its center. More followed, but faster. Centered at the far end of his awareness pulsed a black sphere. A red and green haze spun into a spiral around it. A thought germinated and grew into a memory. Her eyes and hair. *Kristine. The fire.* He screamed, and though his vocal cords vibrated, no sound came out.

He felt alone and hopeless until a stoic buzzing voice blared in his head. *I'm coming.*

Who's there? His words traveled toward the spiraling colors in the form of long, stringy waves.

A trickle of light zipped back to him, and in his head, the voice spoke again. *Azrael.*

"He's awake." Beau shuffled closer.

An oppressive heat stole Daniel's breath. A whistling and howling noise swelled in his ears. Golden light beaming from Beau's glowing fist hurt his eyes. The door to the elevator bent in from overhead. The walls were black and dented. A buzzing noise fluttered in his ears. It reminded him of something. He rolled to his side and pushed himself up. Shards of mirror lay scattered. Beau brushed the debris from Daniel's sweaty back.

"How did it get so hot?" Daniel wiped his face. Flies zipped across his vision; they were everywhere, landing and taking flight. He waved a hand to shoo them away. "What's with all the flies?"

Beau was stooped over him, breathing heavily. "We fell into another realm of Hell. A violent windstorm filled with flies."

"Will you drop the talk about Hell?" Daniel murmured.

Beau pointed at the emergency trapdoor. "See for yourself."

Charles sat at the far side with his legs folded up to his chest. He stared at his open pocket watch, undisturbed by the flies.

"What is this, Charles?"

Charles clamped his watch closed and rested his arms on his knees. "The elevator crashed."

Something struck the exterior of the elevator car. The wall bowed and someone pounded against the outside, screaming, "Help me!"

The panicked cry and the grave look on Beau's face sent a wave of fear through Daniel. He shimmied to the trapdoor and rested his hand on the latch.

"Wait." Beau pointed the large end of his horn at the door. The winds eased, and the noise quieted. The walls of the elevator popped back out. "Go ahead."

The trapdoor shrieked open when Daniel pushed it. The stench of rotting fish and more flies gushed in. Daniel shielded his mouth and nose. "Ugh, what in the world?"

"Take a look." Beau continued to point the wide end of the horn at the opening.

Daniel swatted flies away and peered outside. Bodies writhed in a barren desert. Swarms of flies dashed about aimlessly. Along the horizon, reddish-black clouds rolled counterclockwise through a bright tan sky.

Daniel's head felt heavy. He held it with both hands. "It was night. We were in a hospital. Rain was pouring."

"We're in a different place now." Beau kept the horn pointed at the opening.

Charles shifted with agitation. "We need to get moving."

"We'll get swept up by the storm," Beau said.

"Not if you keep your horn out." Charles gestured to the opening. "See?"

Beau glared at Charles. "If I drop it, everything becomes tornado-land again."

Charles scoffed. "Not too long ago, you were ready to scale a burning mountain with it. This is a desert. Far easier to navigate."

Daniel couldn't believe what he was hearing. They both sounded insane, but he understood it was too hot to walk around in a desert during the day. It was best that they stayed put. "We should wait 'til nightfall."

"Help." A man in filthy rags reached through the trapdoor. The smell of decay swept through the enclosure. Flies crawled over his boney face as he tried wriggling through the opening. "Help me." The man's burnt, withered skin was cracked and crumpled like an old brown paper bag. Reaching for Daniel, the man's puny arm trembled. His bald head held a few long hairs that hung like broken wisps of cotton.

Daniel grabbed the stranger's hand and dragged him in. The frail, naked body of the stranger had little weight. His spine and ribs pressed against the blistered, red skin of his back. No muscle. Just skin and bones.

"How is he alive?" Daniel backed against the far wall, staring.

Charles crawled to the trapdoor and clanged it shut. "Why did you let him in?"

The unsightly man smelled like a dead animal. Though it sickened Daniel, he needed answers. "If anyone can tell me where we are, it's him."

"Good idea." Beau lowered the ram's horn. Furious winds resumed, causing the walls of the elevator to bend again. The buzzing flies reminded Daniel of something, but he wasn't sure what.

"He's in no shape to talk." Charles screwed up his face with exasperation. "Throw him back outside."

"Beau, if you can heal people with your horn," Daniel said, "now is the time to show me."

Beau nodded and touched the man's burned shoulder.

The man recoiled. "It hurts!"

"Have a drink?" Beau asked. He raised the horn as if it were a pint.

The old man's withered lips mouthed, "Please."

Beau crept closer to the man. "What's your name?"

"Joseph." He took the horn and held it over his head. Once his mouth opened, a string of brown sap oozed from the horn's small end.

Daniel thought it was some sort of magic trick. "How are you doing that?"

Beau ignored him. "That's enough." He took the horn from Joseph.

Charles let his head drop back against the wall behind him. "We don't need him to tell us where we are. I can just tell you."

"You put us on an elevator that crashed into a desert swarming with flies." Daniel cringed at the audacity of his own words. "I'm not listening to another word you say."

Charles held up a finger. "Actually, it was the security guard who put us in the elevator. Not me."

"It's because of you and you know it," Beau snarled.

"Doesn't matter." Charles bared his teeth. "We need to get moving."

"I'm not leaving until I get answers." Daniel turned to Joseph. "You want more to drink?"

Joseph flinched and nodded.

"Then answer my questions!" Daniel shouted. "Understand?"

"Ask me anything."

Chapter Seven

Eye of Lust

DANIEL

Joseph peered at the fragments littering the floor and picked up a mirror shard. He studied his burned and shriveled face and whimpered. The piece of mirror slid from his grasp and he sobbed. "Dear God, what's become of me? I'll tell you everything, but swear you'll give me more to drink."

Despite the torrential downpours in Grayton, dark soil still plagued Beau's leathery skin and clothes. His fist glowed red, and bright golden beams shone from under his folded fingers. He gazed down at Joseph. "Answer our questions and we will."

The blisters and lacerations that covered Joseph's sunburnt body seemed to have diminished. "What do you want to know?"

"What is this place?" Daniel asked.

"Lust." Joseph arranged broken pieces of mirrors underneath him. "It's the Second Hell."

Daniel shuddered. Beau couldn't have talked Joseph into spinning his absurd story, not with Daniel and Charles right in front of them. Daniel considered all the impossible things he had experienced firsthand. A thin string of mead oozing from Beau's empty horn. A mountain burning under a fiery, cracked sky. An elevator crashing through the floor of a hospital and into a desert teeming with flies and whirling bodies.

Overwhelmed by all this, he looked at Joseph and asked an irrational question. "Are you dead?"

"I died in 1974," Joseph said, frowning at the floor.

Daniel pressed his fingers against his temples and closed his eyes. He was here, and this was real—not a dream.

"How did you end up here?" Beau asked.

"I was sentenced as a fornicator." Joseph itched his crooked nose. "Apparently, I made too much love—as if that's such a crime. I shouldn't be here." Joseph bent over and cried. "I don't deserve this."

"Lovely." Charles sneered. He sat back against the wall, flipping his watch between his fingers. "This is just flat out lovely."

"What happened after you were sentenced?" Beau asked.

"The judge gave me a coin with images of Asmodeus and Lilith on it." Joseph scratched his nose again. "They brought me onto a dock where some monster in a boat came and took me."

"That would've been Charon," Charles said, staring at his golden reflection on his closed pocket watch.

"Yes. Charon brought me here." Tears burned red streaks down Joseph's cheeks. "Please, give me more to drink. I'm telling you everything."

"This man reeks." Charles straightened his hat. "It's hot. Flies are everywhere, yet we sit here marinating in this filth when we should be moving."

"If you're in such a hurry, why don't you leave?" Daniel said, clenching his fists.

"He's not giving us anything useful," Charles said. "It doesn't matter how he got here. He's here. So, what?"

"Have some more." Beau brought the horn over Joseph's head. Once Joseph parted his lips, the amber thread resumed from the small end.

The shriveled folds of Joseph's face expanded. His skinny, flabby arms inflated like balloons. When Beau pulled the horn away, Joseph no longer looked shriveled and on the brink of death. He seemed younger—maybe in his fifties. This was impossible. Daniel's eyes must have deceived him into thinking Joseph was older and frailer than he was.

Joseph swallowed and gasped. "Thank you." His voice sounded fuller. "You have to save me from this place."

"How bad is it out there?" Daniel asked.

"Every day, the storm carries us wherever. Sand blasts from all directions. It's hot. Hard to breathe. It never stops." Joseph gasped and wiped his eyes. "Never stops."

"That is actually useful." Charles tightened his tie. "Tell 'em about the night."

"It gets cold. Horribly cold." Joseph shook his head. "It stings all over, but heals your wounds. Then it starts all over the next day."

Charles raised his eyebrows. "They call it eternal suffering, Joseph."

Joseph gripped his stomach and groaned. Burns marked where his tears ran dry. He grimaced, and teeth sprouted from his gums.

Daniel couldn't believe it. He looked at Beau. "You were telling the truth."

Beau frowned and nodded.

Daniel turned to Charles and sank back against the wall. "Those aren't contacts. They are your eyes." He gasped. "Are you really a demon?"

"Sure," Charles looked at the trapdoor, "and you're in Hell. Can we go now?"

Daniel felt sick to his stomach. Beau crawled to him and placed the wide end of the horn over Daniel's mouth and nose. He could smell honey, which cleared the growing fog in his head. After a few breaths, his body relaxed.

"Don't worry. We'll get you out." Beau turned back to Joseph. "Do you know a way out of here?"

"There's a pit at the eye of the storm. Lilith and Asmodeus direct the storm from there, but I don't know how you'll get past them."

"You've proven me wrong, gentlemen." Charles rubbed his hands together. "This has been quite useful, after all. We'll head to the center of the storm and jump into the pit. It'll likely take us to the Third Hell."

"I'm not going anywhere with you," Daniel said.

Despite the deep cuts under his cheeks and above his eyes, Charles didn't bleed. He glared at Daniel. "You have no choice, tough guy."

Daniel tossed the horn aside and lunged at Charles. The demon dodged him and snapped his watch shut. Flies swarmed Daniel's ears, mouth, and nose. Daniel swatted at his face and rolled on the floor, littered with shards of mirror.

A deep tone blared in the small room. Everything stilled. The flies dropped dead, and Charles crouched in a corner, shielding his ears. Beau had the horn.

He helped Daniel sit and placed the horn in his hands. "Breathe through this. You need to brace your mind, body, and spirit, or you'll lose yourself in this place."

Daniel nodded. A storm ravaged within his head. Nothing made sense. Hell wasn't supposed to be real, yet here he was. He wiped his tears away. "I didn't know. I should have listened."

Charles uncovered his ears and picked up a dead fly. "You should've killed these annoying little pests earlier."

"You do anything like that to Daniel again, and I'll blow this thing until your head pops off," Beau snarled.

"What could I possibly do to him?" Charles asked, smiling. "He's fallen through a mountain. Crashed into this desert. Rolled around in this broken glass, and doesn't have a scratch on him."

Daniel opened the tears in his shirt and pants and found no scratches or bruises. After everything he had been through, he was completely unscathed. He pressed his fingers to his eyes. "This can't be happening."

"The mead healed you," Beau said. "Just breathe through the horn."

Charles laughed. "Yeah, get a grip."

Daniel swung at Charles, who slunk back and brandished his pocket watch like it was a deadly weapon. "Wanna see if I can resurrect the flies, tough guy?"

"You're the reason I'm here!" Daniel's voice shook. His throat burned. He strained his arms and neck.

Charles nodded to Beau. "Thank him for getting you here. Not me."

"I tried to get him up the mountain," Beau said. "Your lies got him here."

Charles stretched his neck and tightened his tie. "I already told you there's no way up the mountain. We have to go to the deepest pit of Hell to escape."

"What year is it?" Joseph's whimpering voice brought a hush among them. Outside, the wind whistled in low, oscillating tones. Sounds of groaning traveled with it.

Daniel sighed. He scratched his tingling scar. "It's not 1974 anymore. I wasn't even born then."

Joseph gasped. His eyes glistened like shot glasses filled with scotch. "Maybe you can escape to the outer edges of the storm where Charon comes and goes."

Charles craned his neck and huffed. "Charon won't take the undead. The pit is the only way."

"We should at least try," Beau said.

Charles folded his arms. "If you don't have coins, you're not getting on his skiff, dead or alive."

"Can I go with you?" Joseph asked.

"No," Beau and Charles said together. They looked at each other, amazed they agreed on something.

"Why not?" Joseph bawled. "I told you everything."

"You belong here," Charles said.

Joseph cried. "No one *belongs* in this place."

"Let's go." Daniel wiped his face with his damp shirt. "And let him come too. I don't see any problem with it."

Charles muttered incoherently and pointed at Beau. "This is your fault, so you fix it."

"Daniel, this man is dead," Beau said. "You're not. He can't leave like you can."

"If you and Charles can leave, why can't he?" Daniel demanded.

"He's sentenced here," Charles hissed.

"All he did was sleep with a few women out of wedlock," Daniel said. "It's not like he's some kind of monster."

"I'm not a monster," Joseph pleaded. "I promise."

"He hasn't told you everything." Charles bared his rotted teeth at Joseph. "Tell them what you did. Don't lie, 'cause I'll know."

Joseph turned to Daniel. His face wrinkled as if the medicine was wearing off. "I met a girl who was visiting family close to where I live. She was in her teens. I can't remember her name, but she was a virgin. I treated her right, and she fell in love with me. Gave herself to me before going home." Joseph's face soured. "A few months later, she came back *pregnant*. I suggested we get rid of it, you know, but she wouldn't hear it.

She wanted marriage, and I can't live like that. Love should be free, not tied down to one person."

"Maybe you didn't have to marry her," Daniel said, "but did you try to work something out?"

"It wouldn't have worked out." Joseph scoffed. "I hardly knew her. She wanted to tie me down. Neither of us would've been happy. I set her free, man. That's what love is all about."

Charles leaned to Joseph and whispered, "You wooed the girl. The one you *hardly* knew. Took her innocence and told her to kill your child. Is that real love, Romeo?"

Joseph looked at the floor. He placed his hand on the mirror shards he had gathered under him and pushed them away. "She could have saved us both some time and said no. She knew what kind of man I was."

"Why don't you own up to your mistakes, you coward?" Charles's face contorted with disgust. "Your kind is the most pathetic in all of Hell. You whirled through life chained to sexual desires. A slave to pleasure."

"Enough," Daniel said.

Charles wasn't finished. "Your needs turned you into an ignorant stepping-stone for anyone willing to aspire."

"Enough!" Daniel shouted.

Charles scowled at Daniel. "You're down here for a reason, too. Are you a coward like him?"

Daniel curled his hands into fists.

"Wanna hit me?" Charles asked. "Go ahead, tough guy. Let's see what you got."

Daniel hurled a fist hard against Charles's jaw. The demon fell against the wall and dropped to the floor, holding his face. Beau came between them.

Charles sat up, sneering. “Very instinctive.” His eyes reduced to thin slits. “Seems like you do this often. Resorting to violence.”

Daniel could barely contain his fury. “After what you did to me, you’re lucky I don’t break every bone in your body. ’Cause I promise you, I can.” Intense hatred flowed through him. He felt strong and predatory.

Charles picked up his hat and brushed it off. “Do whatever you feel is necessary, tough guy.”

“Stop riling him up,” Beau said.

“Maybe he should evaluate how he responds to simple slights.” Charles plopped his hat on his head. “We’ve heard enough from Casanova. Let’s go.”

“I’m not going anywhere with you,” Daniel said.

“It’s not like you can get rid of me.” Charles pressed his tongue to the left side of his lip. “I’m coming, like it or not.”

I’m coming. Remembering the dream, Daniel sank back to the floor. Bright tones rang in his ears. Beau brought the horn to Daniel’s face. He pushed it away. “Not now.”

“What’s wrong?” Beau asked.

“I had this dream.” Daniel stared at the shattered bits of mirror on the floor. “Someone or something called Azrael said it’s coming for me.”

Beau ran his hand down his chin and gripped his beard. His fearful eyes looked at Charles, who squinted with bewilderment. Neither of them seemed willing to speak. Daniel believed things had just turned drastically worse.

“What’s the problem?” Daniel asked.

Charles huffed. “Do you know who Azrael is?”

“No. Sounds like a name from the Bible though.”

“He’s the Angel of Death.” Beau’s lips trembled.

“Why would he be after me?” Daniel asked. “I’m already in Hell.”

"You're alive." Charles breathed on his pocket watch and brushed it with his coat sleeve. "He's coming to finish you off. If he gets to you, you'll be stuck here. It's a good thing I've taken you deeper."

"Like I'll ever trust a word from your mouth again," Daniel said.

"I'm afraid he's right," Beau said gravely. The light in his hand wavered. His hand shook nervously.

"It's just a dream," Daniel said.

"Down here, there's no such thing as *just dreams*." Charles sniffed the air and came to his haunches. "Something's coming."

The winds silenced and stilled. The walls of the elevator car groaned with relief. Two hard thuds from the outside shook the ground. Daniel's heart pounded. His mind raced with images of Death in a long dark cloak swinging a long scythe at his neck. He sent both hands through his short hair and held on to either side of his head, wincing.

"Is it Azrael?" Beau whispered.

"No." Joseph cowered on the floor. "It's Asmodeus and Lilith."

CHARLES

The light flickering in Beau's hand hurt Charles's eyes and made his skin crawl. The presence of the Holy Spirit was worse, but Charles discovered that if he angered Daniel, its presence diminished considerably, although it seemed to reemerge faster than Charles liked. Now there was the issue with Azrael. Having a heavenly adversary coming after Daniel was concerning, but Charles understood the fine art of manipulation. Make that which is good evil in the eyes of the man.

But first, he needed to handle the rulers of Lust. Just outside the elevator car, a masculine voice shouted, "Come out, you imposters!"

Joseph became a tearful mess. Daniel looked at Beau, who stared back, dumbfounded.

"Coming, Master!" Charles turned to Beau and whispered, "Can't keep them waiting. Hide the horn and the stone. If they see it, they'll take it, and there'll be nothing we can do about it."

"What do we do?" Beau asked, while stuffing the horn into the waistline of his pants.

"I'll go first." Charles looked at Daniel. "You next. I think they'll be too interested in you to worry about whatever Beau's carrying. Whatever you do—don't offend them. Let me do all the talking."

The trapdoor squealed as Charles pushed his way through. The hot surface burned his hands. Overhead, a light-brown sky radiated tremendous heat that pulled tendrils of steam from Charles's wet coat. *Wish there was smoke here.* Charles came to his feet and observed the perpetual storm raging a half-mile out along the horizon. Bodies whirled like flocks of birds. Behind him, the elevator car sat at the deep end of a trench where it had skidded to a stop.

He heard a deep voice behind him. "Do you not know your place, Harvester?"

Charles turned, kneeled, and bowed his head. He glimpsed Asmodeus's bald head and gray eyes. He and Lilith were both pale blue and twice his size. "Please, forgive me. Your world—it's fascinating."

The trapdoor squealed again. The desert heat fell several degrees, and the presence of the Holy Spirit prickled at Charles's skin. Daniel fell with a grunt. The ground sizzled, and he recoiled, groaning.

Lilith strutted to him. She was lean and feminine, while Asmodeus was brawny and stoic. "This one is alive," she said. Her silky voice sounded delighted. On his knees, Daniel held his burned hands out and seemed to be holding his breath. Lilith swayed her way to him and brushed her fingers through her long, black hair. "I've seen better-looking men, but you're quite nice. Stand, so I may see your face, little one."

Daniel came to his feet. His posture was rigid, and he cowered away from her. The heat rising from his body looked like light. Lilith smacked her lips and leaned toward him. "Closer."

He took a hesitant step forward. Lilith caressed his cheek with her sharp nails and took his chin, forcing him to stand up straight. He shuddered.

The trapdoor squealed again. Beau crawled out carefully. Charles squeezed his eyes shut, worrying that the horn may fall out onto the sand.

"A shadow?" Lilith said with disgust.

"Move beside the harvester," Asmodeus commanded Beau.

Beau crept beside Charles and bowed beside him. "You know what you're doing?" he muttered.

"Don't speak," Charles whispered.

Asmodeus pursed his lips. His cheeks puffed and a great wind escalated in strength until it sent the elevator car rolling and whirling away and into the storm, with Joseph still inside.

"You could be mine," Lilith said to Daniel. Her body shifted seductively. She lowered her hand to Daniel's chest and pinched something under his shirt. "A crystal?"

Daniel nodded. "My fiancée gave it to me."

Lilith leaned closer. Her lips were inches from his ear. "Crystals break easily, love." Daniel tried to pull away, but Lilith gripped his shirt. "Don't be frightened." She lifted his rigid chin so that their eyes met. "Never fear me." She sucked air through her teeth. "I'm the greatest friend you could ever have."

"No." Daniel stumbled back and fell.

Lilith turned. Her pure black eyes looked to Asmodeus. "I like him."

"He's undead." Asmodeus folded his thick arms over his bare chest. "None of them belong here."

Charles came to his feet. "Master, I am taking them to Satan."

"Quiet." Asmodeus held up his hand. "Come here, Harvester."

Charles obeyed, but knew he was in trouble. Asmodeus showed no emotion when he gripped the shoulder of Charles's coat and tore the seam. "Don't speak unless spoken to." He pushed Charles back to the ground.

Lilith turned back to Daniel. "You must be parched, my love. Here. Have this." She presented a black apple. "Take it. It'll help." Her voice was soothing and seemed to enchant Daniel. He reached for the rotted fruit. Its flimsy, bruised skin gave and oozed brown sludge when he took it.

"That's it," she whispered. "Eat."

"Don't eat that!" Beau yelled. Daniel flinched, and the apple fell from his hand. It splattered and sizzled on the ground. Rotted insides teemed with maggots and worms writhing in the heat.

Daniel drew away from Lilith. Covering his mouth, he fought the urge to be sick.

Asmodeus stepped forward until Lilith said, "No need to intervene, dear. The shadow-man wants to steal my sweet Daniel away from me. Sorry, but he's mine now." She blew a kiss at Beau, and his face distorted into a foggy mist. He fell to the side and became motionless.

Daniel shouted, "Beau!"

Lilith took her eyes off Beau and looked at Daniel. Beau's head returned to normal. He blinked and raised his eyebrows to keep his eyes opened. Asmodeus stomped past Lilith, took Daniel by the shirt, and lifted him from the ground, bringing him nose-to-nose.

Grimacing, Daniel gripped Asmodeus's hands and tried to pull away. "Something stronger than either of you is coming for me."

Asmodeus's gray eyes turned blood red. "You know nothing of power, boy."

Charles came to his feet. Asmodeus may punish him again, but Daniel needed help. "Azrael is coming for him."

Asmodeus turned his head to Charles. His mouth hung open. His eyes turned yellow. "How do you know?"

Charles knew Asmodeus was afraid. Confidence flooded through him, and he stepped forward, knowing he could weaponize the Holy Spirit and Azrael against the ancient demon. "Can't you sense it?" He asked. "It's faint, but it's there."

"Speak plainly, Harvester," Asmodeus said brusquely.

"The Holy Spirit is in him," Charles said. "He blacked out and heard Azrael speaking. Your old foe is coming for that man."

Asmodeus peered into Daniel's eyes and studied him. His eyes became green. "It's true." He dropped Daniel to the ground and stepped back. "They must go."

"Are you sure?" Lilith squatted beside Daniel, lifting his chin with a sharp nail. An impressed smile rose from her discerning gaze. "I have other fruits. If you eat, Azrael will never find you. You'd be safe from his sting."

"No." Daniel crawled away from her, grimacing. The scorching sands hissed against his hands.

Asmodeus raised his arms parallel to the ground and stretched them outwardly. He seemed to take an inward breath as he raised his face to the sky.

"Goodbye, sweet Daniel," Lilith said, winking.

Sands swirled skyward, and the surface rumbled. Wind blasted one way and then another. It grew stronger and stronger until a gale blasted from Asmodeus's lips and sent Beau, Daniel and Charles skidding across the ground. Another powerful gust came from Lilith, and it propelled them into the air.

Soaring higher into the sky invigorated Charles. Never had he felt such overwhelming sensations. He pressed his hand upon his hat to keep from losing it. Sand blasted from every direction. Swarms of flies and screaming souls twirled about. The madness was over in less than a minute. There were no flies, sand, or whirling bodies. Just him, Beau, and Daniel falling away from the storm and all the noise.

Charles peered down at a dark, massive pit. "On to Gluttony."

Chapter Eight

Cerberus Awaits a Meal

BEAU

Lilith's kiss had scrambled Beau's senses. The world tore into shreds and his brain rippled like fire. A hot pain had rolled over him and suddenly, he was somewhere else.

He woke in a golden field littered with dandelions and daisies. Crystal sunshine spilled from the sky onto his skin. A brisk wind whipped across his warm face. The sights and smells were earthy and familiar. Although it was quiet and lovely, something chilled him. Something sinister hid behind this serenity. He came to his feet and looked in all directions. Thirty feet away, a long dirt road stretched along the valley and continued over a slight incline. The forests that edged either side of the field caused his stomach to turn. Underneath the green canopies of oak and beech trees, a small voice, distant and childlike, echoed from the depths of the eerie wood. *Can't catch me.* Fear sprung from his heart. He had to hurry.

A sharp throb pulsed against the inside walls of his skull. Sand thrashed against his face. A piercing scream swirled in his ears. The weightless sensation of flying sent bouts of euphoria through his body and stole his breath. Were they stuck in Lust forever? Shame overwhelmed him. He did more harm than good by trying to save Daniel.

The sand disappeared. The noise diminished. The winds ceased. He drifted through the air, away from the thick brown storm peppered with flies and pale, flailing bodies.

To his left, Charles held onto his hat, smiling gleefully. "We're at the eye!"

Daniel brushed against Beau, twirling unconsciously. Beau grabbed and pulled him close. They plummeted into the pit below and icy air refreshed Beau's hot skin. The walls went from brown, to gray, to black the deeper they fell. They plunged headlong through ice and into water. The impact jarred Beau, and he lost Daniel.

Beau resurfaced, struggling for air. The odor was noxious. He inhaled freezing water and coughed. Fumbling into his trousers, he retrieved the horn, but it slipped from his fingers and drifted away. While fighting to stay afloat, he took the keystone from his shirt pocket and squeezed. Its golden light warmed him and supplied a surge of energy.

A few feet away, the horn submerged. Beau swam under, and through the murk, he saw the horn descending and grabbed it. He returned to the surface and brought it to his mouth. One inward breath cleared his lungs and warded off the foul stench lingering in this dark chamber.

"Over here." Charles's voice echoed from behind.

Beau twisted around. About 20 feet away, Charles had dragged Daniel and dropped him onto an icy blue surface. A heavy brown mist enshrouded them. Ice glazed the stone wall behind them. Beau swam over. The frosted slab stung his bare hands as he pulled himself from the water.

Daniel lay shivering and shuddered when the light from Beau's fist reached his pale, wet skin. With a broken nose and two swollen eyes, he was barely recognizable. Charles slunk away, wincing at the light. Beau passed him and knelt beside Daniel, offering him the horn.

"I don't want it."

"You need this," Beau said tearfully.

"I can't go—any deeper." Daniel's voice trembled. A thin plume of steam jetted from his stiffened lips. "I'm waiting for the angel."

"You mean the Angel of *Death*," Charles said, examining the tear in his jacket.

Beau gripped Daniel's shoulder. "Kristine told you to choose life. Are you giving up on her?"

"I don't want to." Daniel groaned as he shifted his back. "It just—hurts too much."

"Remember what Joseph said about the cold nights in Lust?" Charles asked. "How it stings and heals? That's what you're experiencing. The pain will ease once you warm up."

Overhead, the hole shaped the distant tan sky of Lust into a large full moon. Condensation dripped from overhanging stones. Beau tugged on his beard. The keystone had warmed him in the water. He scooted closer to Daniel, hoping it would warm him faster. "You'll be on your feet soon. We can still get out of here."

"We can't beat Death," Daniel said through gritted teeth.

Charles removed his coat and tossed it aside. "If you die here, you stay here. You want to freeze in this wretched hole for eternity, or at least try to get back home?"

"Do you really intend to take me to Satan?" Daniel sat up. He seemed more limber. The light had dried his skin. Color had returned to his cheeks. His nose had righted itself and the swelling on his face had gone. A few cuts and bruises still remained.

Using the glassy surface of the rock wall as a mirror, Charles tightened his necktie and canted his hat. He turned his head to examine the scars that had thinned on his cheeks. "It's the only way."

Looking at the ground, Daniel shook his head. "It can't be."

"I'm afraid he's right." Beau stared at the light emitting from his hand.

"What about the mountain?" Daniel pleaded. "The bus stop in Grayton? Or was that a lie, too?"

"Doesn't matter." Charles smoothed the wrinkles from his vest and checked that his watch was still in his pocket. "We can't get back there. Even if we somehow climbed this pit back into Lust, we can't climb the sky and reenter the hospital. Besides, Azrael will come from that direction."

Daniel scratched his neck. He looked skyward and then to the water littered with thick shards of ice. "What about that boatman?"

"We covered this already," Charles said impatiently. "Charon won't let us on his boat."

"Then we'll take it from him," Daniel demanded.

Charles snorted. "You need to understand there are things here that are far greater and more powerful than the three of us combined."

"But it's not just us, though, right?" Daniel tilted his head and pointed at Charles. "You said the Holy Spirit's in me."

Charles waved off the statement and turned back to his reflection. "I just told them that to throw them off. Lucky for us, it worked."

"That was a bluff?" Beau asked.

"Of course it was." Charles righted his posture and gripped the lapels of his jacket.

"No way." Daniel said. "They looked in my eyes. Somehow, they saw it."

"They aren't all that smart," Charles said. "Think about it. They're in Lust. They don't think with their brains."

Somewhere deeper in the darkness, a low grumbling noise occurred. Daniel stumbled to his feet. "What was that?"

"*Shh.*" Charles peered into the darkness. Save for the sounds of dripping and sloshing water, it was dead silent. Charles creeped into pitch black. "There's a tunnel over here. It must lead to Gluttony."

Daniel turned to Beau and whispered, "Do you really think we should go with him?"

The thought of taking Daniel deeper into Hell seemed counterintuitive, but he knew that escaping Hell would take a lot more than finding the nearest exit. With Azrael coming after Daniel and no knowledge of what was to come or where they should go, Beau felt as if they had no other choice in the matter.

He nodded. "For now, at least until we find a better way."

Daniel glanced at the glossy rock wall and looked away. "I'm sorry I didn't listen earlier."

"I understand. Go ahead, take a drink from the horn. You need it."

Daniel turned the horn in his hand. "I don't know. After seeing what it did to that guy, Joseph."

"It healed him. He just needed a lot more of it."

Daniel took a hesitant sip and shuddered. "Oh man. That's bitter."

Beau clapped him on the back. "Seems appropriate, considering the circumstances."

Daniel drank heartily and shuddered. "I don't want to give up. I've got good reasons to live. It's just that I'm not afraid of Azrael."

"You should be," Beau said.

Charles emerged from the darkness. "Did you guys hear me? This cave leads to the Third Hell."

"How many are there?" Daniel sipped from the horn.

"Nine," Charles said. "This one is called Gluttony."

Daniel grimaced and looked through the horn. "We're going through all of 'em?"

"We have to get to the bottom." Charles looked back at the darkness that led to Gluttony. "All we need to worry about now is this one, so listen. There's something ahead that's far more dangerous than Asmodeus and Lilith."

"What is it?" Beau asked.

"A ferocious beast with an insatiable appetite," Charles said.

Daniel chuckled. "Well, I'll drink to that." He took a long swig.

"How do you know what's ahead?" Beau asked.

"The demon I worked with in Limbo told me about all the hells. He was a bore, but I listened."

"You trust him?" Beau asked.

"As I told you earlier, demons speak the truth when it suits our purposes. Besides, he was dead on about Lust." Charles looked up toward Lust and scratched his neck. "Although he didn't mention the flies. If he's right about Gluttony, we're heading into a filthy bog. And there, lurking in that mess, is a giant wolf infested with snakes. That rumble we heard..."

"Let me guess," Daniel's speech had slurred. "That's the wolf."

Charles nodded. "It's called Cerberus, and it can scarf us down in a few bites. It's at the other end of this tunnel—waiting."

Daniel scratched his head. "It picked up our scent that fast?"

"It smells *you*," Charles said. "Your flesh and blood are rich with life. Unlike the nasty, decrepit souls lying around in its disgusting bog."

"Lucky me, I guess." Daniel wiped his mouth. He squinted at the ice floating in the water, appearing more sluggish. "A giant, snake-infested dog—who wants to eat me."

Beau twisted his beard between his fingers. "The horn killed the flies. Maybe it'll kill Cerberus."

"I doubt it." Charles began to pace with his hands behind his back. "It's much larger than a fly. It's legendary. No sounding from a horn will best it."

"It may scare it off," Beau suggested.

"Don't count on that," Charles said.

Daniel chuckled. "Why not play some *fetch* and give her a biscuit?"

"Fetch." Beau picked up Charles's jacket. It was heavy with water. "You're done with this, Charles?"

Charles frowned. "Asmodeus ruined it."

Beau wrung the excess water from the coat and laid it beside Daniel. "I'll need the horn for this."

Daniel handed it over. "What're you thinking?"

"We'll soak the jacket with mead and give it to Cerberus." Beau sucked air through the small end of the horn and then turned it up over the coat. Brown sap leaked on to it. "If that doesn't satiate it, nothing will."

Charles rubbed his chin. "It may want Daniel more."

"All Cerberus needs is just a little taste," Beau said. "The mead heals everything—including hunger. This will work."

Charles took out his watch and rolled it in his fingers. "If it doesn't, then our little journey will end much sooner than intended."

Daniel neared the tunnel leading to Gluttony. "If we get past the dog, how do we get to the next hell?"

"Gluttony is an endless canyon that wraps around in a giant circle." Charles opened and closed his pocket watch, squinting in thought. "But it's only a few miles wide. From here, we'll cross to the other side and climb a cliff to the Fourth Hell. But I must say that Gluttony is a real wasteland. I mean that literally. The stench there will be very foul."

"Thanks for the heads-up, but I'm more worried about getting eaten alive right now." Daniel patted his pants pocket while looking up at Lust. "Why not just wait for Azrael?"

"This again?" Charles's eyes bulged.

"He's an *angel*." Daniel shrugged. "I am the one who heard him, and he sounds like he's coming to help me—not kill me."

"Not all angels sit on clouds playing harps," Charles said. "Guess who God sent to kill the firstborn in Egypt?"

"I'm telling you," Daniel marched to Charles, who backed against the rock wall, "he doesn't want to kill me."

"We face better odds against Cerberus and the rest of Hell than Azrael," Beau said. "If he gets to you..." Unable to finish the sentence, he shook his head.

Daniel huffed and walked along the wall, touching his chin. "Wouldn't he just kill me if I make it out?"

"Not if Satan works out a deal with God," Charles said, folding his arms.

Daniel stopped and turned. "What? They're enemies."

Charles lifted a finger like a teacher giving a lesson. "In the Book of Job, Satan spoke with God in *Heaven*."

Daniel squatted down by Beau and stared at the coat. "I could just pray."

"Prayers aren't heard here," Charles said.

"Go figure." Daniel stood up and paced. "Hurry up, Beau. Let's get this over with."

DANIEL

Daniel's heartbeat thudded in his head. Beau's magic medicine had warmed and numbed him, but his hands remained stiff from the cold. The scent of honey stuck in his nose. Much better than the stench he endured before drinking. He still struggled to believe any of this. Monsters and demons? Falling out of skies and through mountains? To him, Hell had been nothing more than a fear tactic used to fill pews and collection plates. Knowing now that Hell was real, his doubt in God turned to animosity. Why would an all-mighty, all-loving creator require everyone to worship Him or else suffer eternal damnation? Maybe he would be better off in Hell than under the supreme rule of an all-powerful dictator.

His parents were the only reason he went to church. Running away from home had lopped off the last thread tethering him to what he considered a fantasy. God eroded from his thoughts, but fragments of Him drifted through Daniel's mind like tumbleweed. In those fragments, he heard his father calling out to him.

Just go then.

"It's ready." Beau handed Daniel the horn and tied Charles's jacket into a knot, cinching it with the sleeves. He tucked it under his arm and staggered to Charles. The light from his hand bounced around the walls, making Daniel's head spin.

Charles shielded his eyes. "Keep your distance with that light."

Beau tossed the jacket to him. "You don't like the light?"

"If your plan doesn't work," Charles furrowed his brow, "we'll need to run. Obviously, Daniel can't get caught, and I know the way. Understand what I'm saying?"

"This will work," Beau said. "Trust me."

Charles grimaced. "Trust doesn't exist here." He backed away into the narrow passage.

They filed into a muggy tunnel. The temperature warmed considerably, and the brown mist thickened around them. The slimy walls and floor looked like the throat of a tremendous beast. Light shining from Beau's fist produced shadows that toyed with Daniel's imagination. Dark slivers along the ground seemed like snakes. Along the walls, they looked like spiders or dark tentacles luring them to nightmare-land. When his face prickled, he thought of cobwebs. Cool drafts grazing the back of his neck felt like icy breaths from unseen stalkers—Azrael with the scythe. *Whoosh.*

Daniel pressed the horn over his mouth and nose. The smell of honey made his belly grumble. Something growled in the darkness ahead.

"We're close," Charles whispered.

Daniel pressed the crystal pendant against his chest. The horn made his breathing louder. A steaming mist pressed against his face. A cloud of dust emerged from the black and distorted everything that could be seen. Darkness pulsed at the outskirts of Beau's wavering light. He closed his eyes and thought of Kristine.

Daniel ran his fingers along the wall, longing to go back the way he'd come, but he marched forward, disregarding his rising sense of doom. Something grabbed his upper arm, and he jumped.

"Calm down," Beau said softly.

"Put away the light," Charles whispered, shielding his face. "We need Cerberus focused on the jacket."

Beau nodded and gave Daniel's arm another squeeze. "Keep the horn. Blow it if I say so."

Shadows rolled along Beau's face as he pocketed the keystone. A rancid stench wafted from the other end of the tunnel. Daniel gagged but kept moving. In utter darkness, his heart quickened. Intermittent flashes of light startled him. Distant rain and occasional drips of water echoed.

Charles whispered, "It's watching us."

Watery, red eyes from a dark silhouette shimmered to life. A large glistening nose sniffed the air. Fog rose from its mouth and pooled over its massive head. A long snake the size of a light pole slid between Cerberus's shoulders and down its neck. Another hissed from the rear of the beast, licking the air with a thin, forked tongue.

"We need to move closer," Charles whispered.

They edged toward the end of the tunnel. Cerberus froze. The snakes slithered excitedly on and around the giant wolf. Another flash of gray light disturbed the darkness. The mangy fur of Cerberus was muddied and matted. Thick white foam caked its large fangs, ran down its jaw, and slopped to the cavern floor. Its blood-red eyes were wide with madness.

"The canyon is to the left," Charles muttered.

Cerberus was massive. Its head was as tall as Charles and about five feet wide. A long growl rumbled from its throat. Both snakes hissed and bared fangs.

"You like the smell?" Charles tried to sound alluring, but his voice sounded ragged and high-pitched. "Come. Take it. It's yours." Charles shifted closer to the threshold of the tunnel, holding out his wadded-up jacket. Cerberus started to move, but hesitated. The snake around its neck hissed, while the other curled behind Cerberus's hind legs.

Cerberus pinned its ears and growled at the snakes until they settled, then warily, it inched closer to Charles, narrowing its large, red eyes.

Sharp teeth glistened in another flash of light. It licked its chops but seemed reluctant to take the offering.

Charles shifted closer and stretched his arms farther. Cerberus froze and snarled. The scruff of its neck stood like spikes. A warm stench steamed from its mouth. The snake around its neck coiled, and Cerberus snapped at it. The snake retreated. Only a foot from Charles, Cerberus sniffed the jacket.

It reached with its teeth to take the offering, but Charles pulled away. Cerberus barked and snapped. Saliva sprayed. It whimpered and reared. A snake had bitten its hind leg and remained clamped. Cerberus chomped into the snake's body and shook it violently. The other snake lunged at Charles, but Cerberus pounced on it.

"Hey!" Charles yelled.

With a large paw pressed upon the writhing snake, Cerberus growled at him. Charles slung the jacket to the right. Cerberus ran after it, dragging one snake with it. It snatched the jacket and dashed deeper into the cavern.

Charles sprinted left.

Beau pulled Daniel by the arm. "Come on."

As they ran for the exit, the remaining snake snapped at Charles and missed. It writhed with excitement. Beau tripped over its head and Daniel slammed against its body and fell back. The snake reared and coiled at Daniel. Its long tongue tickled his belly.

When it lunged, Daniel rolled, and it missed him. Beau jumped onto the snake's head and dug into its eyes. "Blow the horn!"

"I lost it." Daniel looked about frantically. Though his eyes had adjusted to the darkness, all he could see were rocks and mud littering a swampy floor.

A sound blared. Daniel covered his ears. The snake dropped and ceased fighting.

"Here." Charles tossed the horn to Daniel and ran for the exit. "Hurry up."

Chapter Nine

Ladies of Gluttony

CHARLES

Charles sprinted from the cave and into the cold, slanting rain. His shoes splatted through sloppy mud. He lunged over sprawled bodies. Pale-gray lightning rippled left to right, illuminating the low-lying clouds of Gluttony. Panting, he stopped and looked across the canyon. Sheets of dark rain obscured the distance. Muck covered the bottom hems of his pants, but he didn't care, because he was succeeding.

Behind him, at the threshold of the cave, an argument played out between Daniel and Beau. Daniel grimaced as he spoke. Charles couldn't hear their conversation, but he knew Daniel wasn't happy. "Stay angry, Daniel. It'll serve you well in this world."

Those suffering in Gluttony groaned and writhed in the sludge. Charles folded his arms and looked into their dreadful faces. "Not as deplorable as those in Lust. At least you crave something substantial. Still, you're a vile mess."

Another round of lightning revealed the mud-caked face of an elderly lady. Charles's grin shriveled. Her vacant eyes stared beyond him. She stretched an arm like a beggar to a passerby and slapped her hand into the soupy swamp and pulled. A horrendous gurgling noise occurred, and she slid back into the shallow mud puddle she must've dug over time.

This woman favored his grandmother. His throat locked. Another memory blossomed in his head. Her voice returned to him. At bedtime, she'd sing to him while caressing his hair. Afterward, she'd ask, *Shall I sing another hymn for my sweet boy?*

"No, thank you," Charles whispered to the ugly woman. He swallowed and turned his attention back to the far side of the canyon.

His vision blurred. Something warm and wet streamed from his eyes. He touched his cheeks. *Tears?* A breath quivered through his clenched teeth. He hadn't cried since he was a child. Though he hated to admit it, the Holy Spirit hiding within Daniel had infected him.

"Move it!" Charles's throat burned when he called to the stragglers. With sour, hanging faces, they trekked into the icy rain, tucking their heads and hunching over. Beau took care to step around the pitiful souls lying in the mire while Daniel tripped over one of them.

Charles whispered, "Hear me, Holy Spirit. Daniel's anger weakens you, and your influence diminishes with every step he takes. Antagonize me further and I'll end you."

DANIEL

Daniel's heart pounded. Somewhere in the darkness behind him, a giant wolf gnawed on Charles's coat. Though he knew Cerberus could come back, he needed to talk to Beau alone. He grasped the back of Beau's shirt and pulled him to a stop just short of the cave's exit. Lightning flashed and distant thunder grumbled. Rain splattered into the swamp ahead of them.

Beau placed his hands on his knees. Huffing, he pointed into the cave. "That snake might wake up. Cerberus—could come back."

"Let's break off from Charles." Daniel inhaled the stink of the Third Hell and gagged. He put the horn over his mouth, and the light scent of honey dulled the stench. "We can't trust him."

"I know, but..." Beau shook his head in resignation, "he knows the way."

"Are you kidding me?" Daniel's arms tightened. A surge of violent energy rolled through him. He took a deep breath through the horn and exhaled. "He's taking me to Satan."

"That's all we can do right now," Beau said. "If Azrael catches up, he'll kill you."

Lightning flashed, and Charles's glowing eyes looked back at him from the muddy gray bog of Gluttony. A dark smile stretched on his pale face. Daniel shivered. "Satan may do something worse than kill me. Did you think about that?"

"I know how it sounds." Beau dropped his hands to his hips and stared at the ground. "But if Azrael kills you, you're stuck here."

"How do you know that?"

"Because your soul isn't right with God," Beau said plainly. His hardened face softened. "It's why you fell in the first place."

The words jabbed hard into Daniel. Hearing this made it difficult to breathe or stand. It hurt more than he expected because it was true. Feeling exposed and ashamed didn't sit well with him. He turned to his anger, which felt more empowering and familiar. "Of course, I'm not right with God. Look around, Beau. Should I be right with this? If He thinks everyone who doesn't *worship* Him belongs here, then I don't think I want to be *right* with Him."

Beau's mouth twisted into a scowl. "You think *this* is what God wants?"

Daniel sighed and looked back out into the rainy swamp. "If God doesn't want this, then why does it exist?"

"Move it!" Charles screamed.

"We stick with Charles for now," Beau whispered. "If we find another way, we'll take it." He hunched forward and entered the swamp.

For a moment, Daniel considered turning back into the cave without Beau or Charles, but the thought of being here alone filled him with dread. He closed his eyes, tucked his chin down, and stepped into the mire. His arms sprouted gooseflesh. The rain had a gritty texture and smelled horrible, even with the horn pressed over his mouth and nose. He tripped over a rock and almost fell. Turning back, he found the rock was actually the head of a man half-buried in gooey mud. He stumbled back into Beau.

Beau steadied him. "Mind where you step."

Lightning revealed dozens more writhing in the brown sludge. Their movements were weak and slow. "They're everywhere," Daniel muttered.

"Don't look at 'em. Focus on getting across the canyon."

"These are people." Daniel's eyes filled with tears. "Stuck here for eternity by a loving God you say I need to get right with?"

Beau took Daniel by the shoulders. He opened his mouth to speak, but closed his eyes and exhaled. "I know you're angry, but these people had a choice, and this is what they chose."

Daniel looked past Beau at Charles, who stared at a poor lady writhing near his feet. The sight stirred the fire within him. "I hate Charles. If anything can get me right with God, it's that."

Beau trudged on. "He's stuck here, you know. No Heaven. No chance for redemption. There's no hope for anything—but power."

"Is he really a demon?"

"He's a man." Beau took out the keystone and squeezed. "I think he's tricked himself into thinking he's a demon. It probably makes him feel less miserable and more in control."

The light enshrouding them had the warmth of a fire on a frosty night, and it dampened the foul odor. Daniel stared over the gauntlet of bodies and thought of the people in the alley and those in the sandstorm. Whatever was ahead—would be worse. "Are you sure there's no other way?"

Now within earshot, Charles slapped his pocket watch shut and returned it to his vest pocket. "Why do I need to keep telling you the only way out is through? Stop complaining or lie down with the rest of these brain-dead losers."

"Losers?" Daniel growled. "You're no different from them."

"I'm nothing like these pathetic pigs." Charles sneered at the supine, muddy bodies. "None of these lowlifes can ever dream to aspire to what I am."

Daniel marched toward Charles, who in turn backed away. "Like them, you're stuck here, and you *are* human. No matter what you say."

Charles's face twitched. "I evolved. Earned everything I've achieved. They chose me to become one of them over countless others, and I proved my worth. Ripped out my heart. Defeated the second death. And I'm just getting started. These imbeciles are finished. This is it for them!"

"Where would you be without me or Beau?" Daniel asked.

"Know where you'd be without Beau's little slip-up?" Charles shot back testily. "With the little girl earning your way here. And get this, tough guy. If Azrael gets to you, you'll be nothing more than another dead soul in Hell; beneath me, bowing and begging for mercy that will never be granted."

Daniel grabbed Charles by the lapels and pulled him close. "I'll be just like you." He looked at a nearby lady writhing on the ground. "Just like her. And everyone else here."

He pushed Charles away and started across the canyon.

BEAU

Charles glanced at Beau and righted his tie and hat. "Find this amusing?"

"Why are you pushing his buttons?" Beau asked. "He already wants to give up. Is that what you want?"

"What I want is for you to keep that light out of my face." Charles frowned at the souls writhing nearby. "Go. Catch up with him."

Beau came closer. Charles winced in the light. "You pulled him ashore back in that pit."

"So what?" Charles shielded his eyes. "It meant nothing."

"It means he's right. You're pretty humane for a man trying to be a demon."

"I'll do what I must to achieve our ends," Charles hissed. He looked over his shoulder at Daniel, who continued slogging his way across the canyon. "We shouldn't let him wander too far."

Beau trudged past Charles after Daniel. Rain continued to pour in droves. Slippery mud bubbled and fizzed. He pushed himself through the stinging rain. Another flash of lightning revealed a high ridge breaking through the dark mist. Groaning and writhing, countless souls wallowed in the slush. Their dumbfounded faces bearing sleepy expressions stretched as they reached, clawed, and pulled.

When he caught up, Beau took Daniel by the arm and pulled him to a stop. "Don't go off alone like that."

Daniel glared at him. Brown streaks of rain had dirtied his face. Beau thought Daniel was about to throw a punch, but he walked off instead. "It was all I could do to keep myself from hitting him. It's an improvement in how I normally deal with things, I'd say. Besides, isn't this what you want? To keep pushing through Hell—maybe pick up a few nightmares to share with my friends back home?"

"Let's not talk about nightmares." Beau peered at the bodies along the ground. "This one is enough."

Daniel glanced over his shoulder at Charles. "Glad he's keeping his distance."

"The light bothers him." Beau held up his glowing fist.

They spoke little while they walked across the swamp through the hazy mist that slowly revealed more suffering. The monotonous groaning had become nothing more than background noise along with the pattering rain. Flashes of lightning rippled overhead sporadically. Beau and Daniel's attention remained with those lying in the mire. Beau thought it was sad how they passed and stepped over one failed life after another.

Daniel must have been thinking the same thing. "Why are these people here?"

"I'll tell you." Charles had caught up and marched past them, keeping at the threshold of darkness just beyond the keystone's light. "They are consumed by worthless endeavors. Excessive drinking and eating. Some of them took too much stock in worldly fashions. There's more to it, but overall, it's their selfishness."

"Eating and drinking too much?" Daniel asked. "What's wrong with that? They aren't hurting anybody."

"If they owned the world, they wouldn't offer you a blade of grass," Charles said. "They'd watch children starve while eating a four-course meal served by well-dressed servants without batting an eye. I have to hand it to them, though—at least they're honest about who they are."

"Do you think your father may be here?" Beau felt uncomfortable bringing this up, but Daniel was in a dark place and the years he'd spent avoiding his family seemed to be a major reason he had fallen here.

Daniel's face was pensive. "He's not dead."

"Are you sure about that?" Beau asked.

"What makes you think his father would be here?" Charles asked.

"He was an alcoholic," Daniel said solemnly. "He gave it up when I was born. Didn't matter though. The whole town still thinks he's a drunk. Who knows? He may have picked it back up when I left."

"Well, if he stopped, then he's not consumed by it." Charles opened and closed his pocket watch. "He wouldn't be here, but I know a man who should be. The pastor at the church I attended before my first death. He was a slobbering drunk. Every time we locked eyes, he turned in shame. Imagine what good he did, preaching the gospel."

"The punishment doesn't fit the crime," Daniel said. "They ate and drank too much. So what?"

"They don't see it as a punishment." Charles creeped closer, grimacing in the light. "When Charon brings them here, he tells them they'll find what they desire most at the end of the canyon. With that, they leap from the boat and bound out through this muck. In time, they grow tired and start crawling. Eventually, they get stuck and bury themselves."

"You told us this canyon went in a circle," Daniel said.

"That's right." Charles twirled a finger. "A never-ending, disgusting loop."

"Can they ever leave?" Daniel asked.

"They wouldn't want to. They love this slop too much." Charles shrugged. "They indulged in slop all their lives, so in the end, they *do* get what they want."

"Is that why you're here?" Daniel asked.

"No." Charles's smile displayed dark, rotted teeth. "My sins are far more noble."

Beau scoffed.

"My hell is deeper than this," Charles said. "Harsher too, but I'm beyond that now."

"You really think that given the choice, no one would leave this?" Daniel stepped around a larger mud puddle, where several souls clawed at the sides.

"Whatever they think is at the end of the canyon is too valuable to them," Charles said.

"Let's wake one up and see." Daniel raised the horn.

Beau peered back behind them. The mist had swallowed the other side of the canyon. "Cerberus could still come back."

"If Charles is right, it wouldn't take long," Daniel said. "They'll either take off down the canyon or come along with us. We could use some extra help. They may know a better way out of here."

Charles glared at Daniel. “These people know nothing. It would be a waste of time.”

Daniel looked about the swamp and stepped over to a younger-looking woman caked in mud. She was sprawled in a shallow puddle, gazing ahead with one arm stretched before her.

Beau rubbed the back of his neck. “Maybe we should leave her alone.”

“But we could save her, Beau.” Daniel squatted by the woman, flipped her over, and cradled her in his arm.

Charles folded his arms. “Waste. Of. Time.”

Daniel placed the small end of the horn between her lips. She blinked and bolted upright. When she tried to pry the horn from Daniel, he wrenched it from her grasp.

She screamed and tried to run.

Daniel caught her by the wrist. “Wait. We want to help you.”

“Let go of me,” she growled, yanking herself free from Daniel. Clumps of filthy mush plopped from her arms. “Where is the end? How much farther is it?”

“This is so stupid.” Charles hid his face while massaging his forehead.

“What’s your name?” Daniel asked.

“Holly Fairchild. It’s freezing.” Trembling, she picked up handfuls of mud and rubbed it on her arms and legs.

“This path you’ve been following...” Daniel pointed down the canyon. “There’s no end to it, Holly. It just goes in a circle.”

“Liar.” Rain had washed mud from her long hair. “You’re just trying to trick me so you can have it all to yourself.”

“No.” Daniel shook his head. “I just want to help you. Do you have any idea where you are?”

“Not where I’m supposed to be,” Holly cried. “I’ve been alone. Freezing for ages with nothing but mud to keep me warm.”

"Alone?" Daniel looked at the others digging themselves into holes. "Just come with us. Maybe if you get out of this mess, you'll see more clearly."

"Never!" Holly slapped Daniel hard across the face.

"This wasn't a waste of time, after all," Charles said with a big grin.

Daniel's eyes glazed with fervent anger. His expression went cold and dark. He seemed to grow two inches in height. Beau cringed, expecting the worst.

"Your choice, Holly." Daniel walked away, carrying the horn with him. "Go wherever you think you need to go."

"How much farther?" Holly screamed.

Charles came up beside her and pointed down the canyon. "You know, it could be just around the corner."

Holly gazed at Charles for a moment and then she darted off, slipping and tripping over others as she went.

Charles checked the knot on his tie and came up beside Beau. "Maybe next time, we won't entertain fruitless ideas. It's foolish to wake the dead to see if they'll change their minds."

"Daniel isn't like you or me." Beau walked on. "He has hope—even in this wretched place."

"Azrael's coming to kill him," Charles said. "We can't help anybody here. We can't change who they are."

Beau didn't trust Charles, but he believed him in this regard. He hastened his steps to catch up to Daniel. The thunder grumbled, and flashes of lightning revealed they had less than a mile to go. The cliff ahead darkened the swamp with its shadow.

When he caught up, he placed a hand on Daniel's shoulder. Like he had before, Daniel nudged it off. Though Beau saw a lot of good in Daniel, the young man was stubborn and prideful. It was probably what kept him from reconciling with his parents. In a sense, Joseph and Holly suffered because of their pride too. Joseph believed he was innocent and wouldn't hear otherwise. Holly only cared about getting what she wanted, with no regard for anyone else. Beau believed Daniel could overcome his pride and reconcile with his parents.

Beau looked at Daniel, who glared ahead. "Holly made her choice. You have a choice, too."

"I don't have a choice," he grumbled. "All I can do is head for Satan, remember?"

"I mean when you get you back home," Beau said. "You can fix things with your parents. Marry Kristine. Figure things out."

Daniel shook his head and became sullen.

Chapter Ten

A Fortunate Offer

CHARLES

Holly, that filthy glutton, had slapped Daniel silly. It was glorious, but when Daniel walked away, the Holy Spirit swelled around him. It had strengthened when it should've weakened. Charles maintained his distance; it had affected him enough. He remembered more about his past than he cared to. The drunk reverend. His grandmother and her lullabies.

Less than a half-mile from the cliffs, mud hardened to a shiny brown clay. Rain subsided to a lingering mist. Though the stench and cold remained foul and brisk, fewer souls lay ahead. Lightning dazzled Charles's eyes. The swampy ground trembled at the sound of thunder. Daniel and Beau marched behind him with their heads low. Charles preferred the quiet, but over time, the silence lured his mind back to those long-lost memories. He could almost hear his grandmother beckoning to him.

Her wrinkled smile had always shined. When he was a small child, he had sought her withered hands and loving, blue eyes for cuddling and safekeeping. Soft-spoken and gentle, she had no enemies. Never quarreled or spoke ill of anyone—even when tested by the loose-lipped gossips at church. She had always deflected such nonsense. Each night, she'd brush her fingers through his hair while singing songs to lull him to sleep.

I sang these same songs to your mother when she was your age.

Nana, will she ever come back?

Sorry, dear. Your mommy passed on to Heaven when you were born. She'll be the first one to greet you when your time comes.

Why'd she leave? Didn't she love me?

Oh, she loved you and didn't want to go. But giving birth took a hard toll. She doesn't hurt anymore. She's smiling down from Heaven on her greatest miracle. That's you, Chip.

He glared over his shoulder at Daniel and shouted, "Stop calling me Chip!" He hardly believed the words he spat from his lips.

"Chip?" Daniel looked bemused. "I thought they called you Heartless Charles."

Beau peered at Charles as if seeking a blemish. "Neither of us said anything."

Charles broke his glare. Fog plumed and spiraled from his nose. Never had he felt such shame—even when he spent time in the Seventh Ditch of the Malebolge. He took out his pocket watch and clicked it open. "I prefer Charles, if you don't mind."

"Why did they call you Heartless Charles?" Beau asked.

"They're jealous." Charles clamped his watch shut and turned to the cliffs. He realized his breathing was quick and shallow. He closed his eyes and tried gaining control of his emotions. "I ripped out my heart and replaced it with a lump of coal. No one else in Limbo could bring themselves to do it, so they call me that to hold some kind of ownership over me. Nobody owns me."

"Why would you rip out your own heart?" Daniel asked.

"I'll tell you along the way." Charles resumed the walk.

Daniel and Beau trailed behind him. Charles didn't want them too close, so he spoke over his shoulder while keeping a brisk pace.

"Everyone in Hell suffers the second death," Charles said. "It's called the second death but reoccurs throughout eternity. It's more painful than the first and could come at any time. Maybe in minutes, even seconds, after it stops. Oftentimes, it comes hours or days later. One may go weeks before it strikes again, but it comes, nonetheless."

"Does Satan suffer the second death too?" Daniel asked.

"The fallen angels were never human," Charles said. "I figure they suffer differently."

"How do you die over and over?" Beau asked.

"You already know about the cold." Charles pushed his hat lower onto his head. "It heals everything, including death. When I replaced my heart with a lump of coal and sewed myself up, the night came and went. It only healed the scar on my chest. I haven't suffered the second death since. I'm the only one who's beaten it."

Daniel's mouth hung open. "You're walking around without a heart?"

This amused Charles. "I'm dead, tough guy. The only reason we breathe and bleed in Hell is to suffer."

"How did ripping out your heart stop you from dying again?" Beau asked.

"On my first death, I died from a gunshot wound. My heart burst in my chest. The second death mimics the first. With my heart gone, it can't explode again." Charles shrugged. "The cold still thinks it's inside me."

"Does it hurt walking around without your heart?" Daniel asked.

Charles rubbed his chest. "It hurts regardless. But enough about me. Look for a crack in the rock face that stretches up to the summit." He nodded toward the cliff. "There's lots of them, so it shouldn't be too difficult to find one. Each of them has a ladder that can take us on to the Fourth Hell."

DANIEL

Despite the cold and being drenched, Daniel's skin burned. With each step, his blistered feet inflamed. He ached all over, and his stomach groaned in unison with the thundering sky. He scanned the cliffs for long cracks and pressed his palm to his gut. The way out seemed distant and downright impossible, but so did everything else. If he set his mind to it, he could make it.

"Mind over matter," he muttered.

"What was that?" Beau asked.

"Mind over matter." Daniel nudged Beau's shoulder. "I don't mind, and you don't matter."

Beau frowned. "Why say that?"

"My drill sergeant used to say it." Daniel smiled at Beau. "Oddly enough—it helps."

"I see." Beau dropped his head. With his arms hung and shoulders slouched, he looked like a kid walking home after losing a fight.

"What's with you?" Daniel asked.

Beau tugged on his beard while squinting ahead. "Did you notice how Joseph and Holly were?"

Daniel stepped around a body that curled into a fetal position. "I don't think I could forget if I tried."

"Notice how they didn't think they did anything wrong," Beau said. "They were both selfish and blamed everybody else for their issues. Their ignorance made them blind. There's no way they'd repent, because everybody else is the problem. Not them."

Daniel kept his eyes on the cliffs but felt Beau staring at him with anticipation. "Will you stop nagging me about changing? I got enough to deal with already."

"You need to repent."

Daniel felt the usual storm gathering within, but he had already exhausted most of his rage. He was tired of fighting but was in no mood for any more lectures about changing his ways. His father told him to leave, so he did. In a sense, Daniel had acted in obedience. Still, the image of his parents crying on the floor caused him to feel ashamed.

"I'm not talking about this now, Beau."

"You have to," Beau said. "Don't let your pride—"

"My *pride*?" Daniel came to a stop. "Really?"

Beau gazed at the muddy ground. Rain had washed muck from his round face, giving him a ghoulish look in the quivering light emanating from his hand. Daniel no longer saw him as a drunken recluse and had grown to respect him since learning the truth.

Daniel huffed and walked on toward the cliffs. "I know there are things I need to work on, but stop pushing me. I need time."

He felt Beau's eyes boring into his back. Charles had drifted farther ahead but glanced back with those off-putting eyes.

"I'll back off," Beau said, "but you're running out of time."

"What do you know about time? You were eternal."

"I don't think I was always a shadow." Beau caught up with Daniel. "I keep getting visions. I was in a place that felt like—home. Sunlight touched my skin, and it felt natural."

"You think it was a memory?"

Beau squinted. "It was, but something horrible happened to someone I loved." Beau's brow furrowed and his eyes glazed. "I wish I could remember more."

"Have you tried thinking back to the first time you used the keystone?"

Beau frowned and shook his head. "All I can think of now is the last one." He wiped his eyes. "A little girl was struck by a car and left for dead in a ditch. I had sent on many children before her, but for some reason, her face is stuck in my head. I don't know why."

"It's a shame." Daniel smacked his lips. "I sure hate it for her parents."

Beau stopped. His eyes widened.

"What is it?"

Beau's stony face relaxed, and he resumed walking. "I may have been a father."

"Stop straggling!" Charles shouted. He turned and continued toward the cliff, clicking his watch open and shut.

Daniel whispered, "What's going on with Charles? He's acting more erratic toward me than he was before."

"It's because *you* are alive," Beau said. "Unlike him, you breathe and bleed to live—not suffer. You remind him of what that was like."

Daniel half-smiled and took a breath through the horn. Above them, the canopy of clouds sputtered with lightning flashes. The few bodies lying on the hardened surface were still as statues, unlike those who dug their own graves back in the sludgy puddles.

"I see an opening." Charles pointed ahead and trotted toward it. "Come on."

"One less hell." Daniel patted Beau's back and hurried after Charles. He wasn't eager to find out what was in the next hell, but would be happy to leave Gluttony behind. All the souls strewn about in this wasteland heightened his resentment toward God. They shouldn't have to spend an eternity in this filth for a few decades of overindulging. Holly chose to stay, but only because she believed in a lie. If she or any of the others knew the truth, they wouldn't want to be here.

Charles slowed to a stop beside a three-foot-wide crevice and leaned against the cliff. He rolled his pocket watch around his fingers. Daniel came up next to him and peered into the crack. Stones littered the ground. The walls were carved out as if a monster, maybe Cerberus, had clawed them out. Despite the abrasions, the walls didn't appear to be suitable for climbing, and the low gray clouds shrouded the height of the cliff.

"You said there'd be a ladder in here?" Daniel asked.

"There is, somewhere." Charles looked at his watch and flipped it shut. "Go take a look. You'll see."

Daniel stared into Charles's reptilian eyes.

"What is it now, tough guy?"

"Why were you shot in the back?" Daniel asked.

Charles huffed. "I was trying to escape a ten-year prison sentence. A guard, obviously, didn't approve of my departure."

"Why were you locked up in the first place?"

"I was a thief. Stole fine art, jewelry, and clothes from gluttons." Charles gestured to the canyon. "They locked me up with murderers and rapists over a few trinkets. Then I got a bullet in the back for trying to get out of that place. It's ridiculous."

Daniel lowered his head. "Do you regret anything you did?"

Charles took off his hat and brushed it off. "I told you, they were gluttons. If anything, I was helping those fools learn humility."

Daniel looked back at Beau, who walked rather than ran. "Beau thinks everyone down here is unrepentant and prideful. He believes it may be why I'm here. I'm too proud to work things out with my parents. Too proud to admit that I was wrong. Too proud to care. Maybe he's right."

Charles blinked at him with stunned silence as Daniel went into the fissure. After miles of trudging through the swamp, his feet flared with tenderness on the stone floor. The stale, warm air caused him to sweat, which tingled his scar. A pleasant burning sensation spread around it when he scratched. He took a seat on a rock and stretched his back. After brushing sludge from his arms and clothes, he scraped excess mud from his boots with a flat rock.

To his right, the ladder that Charles had mentioned reached into the overhead fog. He gripped one of the sharp stone slabs jutting from the wall. Cold and damp, and without railings, he'd need to pinch with his thumb and forefingers to climb, however high it went. Difficult but doable.

Footsteps approached. It was Charles. Behind him, Beau slouched without the light beaming from his hand.

"Before we go, I should warn you," Charles said. "There is a war going on in Greed."

"A war?" Daniel rubbed the back of his head. "What for?"

"There are two types of sinners there, and they loathe each other." Charles leaned on the rock wall opposite the ladder, clicked his watch open, and flipped it shut several times.

"They're all greedy. How different can they be?" Beau asked. He took a seat on a small boulder and stretched his legs out.

"The hoarders keep and never give. The squanderers waste whatever they receive. Trust me, they hate each other." Charles stared into the fog. "Kind of hilarious, really."

"It won't be very funny if we get caught up in that mess," Daniel said.

"We'll get through it," Charles said. "I've gotten you this far, haven't I?"

"Not on your own, you haven't. We worked a plan to get by Cerberus." Daniel rubbed his head. "If we're heading into a war zone, we need to know what to expect."

"They fight over rocks." Charles laughed. "Stupid rocks! It's the one thing they value, and their weapon of choice. Hoarders fashion them into spears, hammers, knives, and swords. When they aren't using them, they store them in underground silos. Cue the squanderers, who raid these silos endlessly. Should they get a stone or even a knife, they just sling it at the hoarders. That's pretty much how it goes there."

Daniel ran his hand through his hair. "What about the terrain?"

"After the climb, we'll be heading downhill until we reach the main battlefield. We'll have to cross it to get on to the next hell."

"Can we wait for nightfall and cross then?" Daniel asked.

Charles looked incredulous. "No. Azrael is coming. Besides, they'll be so focused on each other, we'll probably slip through unnoticed."

"If they're interested in rocks, we should hide our belongings." Daniel removed his necklace with the crystal pendant and stuffed it in his pocket. "Keep that keystone put away, Beau. If they see that, they'll be gunning for us. Will they care about the horn?"

Charles shrugged. "It's just a bone to them."

"Just in case." Daniel took a quick swig from it and tossed it to Beau. "Put it away until we get through this."

Beau took a sip and then tucked the horn under his waistband.

Daniel patted his pants pockets and felt the outline of the ring in one and the crystal in the other. "I'm all set. You'll need to keep your watch out of sight, too."

"I'll put it in my vest pocket before we head up."

"And the chain," Daniel said. "If I can see it, so can they. Hide it."

"They won't care about my watch." Charles squeezed it in his hand. "They're fixated on rocks."

"You were a thief once," Daniel said. "If you saw someone walking around with jewelry hanging out, wouldn't you take it?"

"Thieves are in the seventh ditch of the Malebolge. Not Greed."

"For goodness' sake," Daniel's face flushed, "hide it."

Charles shoved the watch into his pocket, detached the chain from a buttonhole of his vest and tucked it away. "Satisfied?"

"It will do." Daniel grunted while coming to his feet. He stretched his arms and legs. "Anyway, see you up top."

He locked his mind on the task of climbing. The smell of sediment displaced the stench that clung to his clothes. The cool mist of Gluttony gave way to chalky, white fog the higher he went. He stiffened and slowed, but refused to stop. The sharp edges of the slabs cut his palms, which stung each time he slapped them on the next step. He gasped for breath. His heartbeat echoed in his ears, and his fingers numbed and slipped with blood. His legs ached, but he was too high to turn back. Drained of energy, he kept pushing and wondered if he would ever reach the summit until, finally, a ledge emerged.

Using cracks and edges, he pulled himself onto a four-foot-wide ledge and rolled to his back, coughing and gasping. Sweat burned his eyes. He relieved them with his shirt. On his left, the cliff continued. He twisted to his stomach and peered down the cliff.

"I reached a ledge!" he shouted.

"OK!" Beau called back breathlessly. "We're coming."

Daniel swallowed, and his throat creaked like a rusty door hinge. A dizzy spell swept through him. He pushed himself up and rested his back against the rock wall. To his left and right, powdery scars riddled the ledge's granite surface.

A warm gust brushed his face. The smell of wet stone soothed him. Unfolding his fists, he peeked at the blood congealing in the creases of his palms. He rolled them up into the hem of his T-shirt and squeezed.

The throbbing of his hands slowed. Closing his eyes, he leaned back. The strain on his neck eased.

His lips vibrated, and both ears rang in unison. After several deep breaths, he fell asleep.

BEAU

Beau's arms and legs jittered with fatigue. He clung to a flat piece of stone jutting from the cliff, unable to climb any higher. His face burned and his vision blurred. Thoughts of falling crept into his head. Still, he held on and adjusted his fingers when they slipped.

"Move it, Beau," Charles snarled from under him.

"I can't. Need to... catch... my breath."

"If you fall, you're taking me with you, and this whole thing is over, so get over whatever it is and go."

Beau's upper body wrenched away from the cliff. Gritting his teeth, he heaved his body closer to the strange ladder and adjusted his hands. He pressed his head against a razor-sharp edge and winced. "I can't."

"Keep thinking like that and you'll fall," Charles said. "And we're done. Daniel dies. Hand me the horn and your little pebble and just jump off."

Beau flared inside. "You. Aren't. Helping."

"You're wrong, Beau. Not all of us are unrepentant. There're many repentant cowards down here, too. They gave up trying to do the right thing and succumbed to what they know. They are who they are. And just like them, you're giving up and giving in."

Beau closed his eyes and remembered the little girl who died in the ditch alone. He pictured her alive and smiling. *Hurry Daddy.* Beau pursed his lips and filled his cheeks with air. Straining his arms, he pulled himself to the next stone. *Hurry!* Using his chin and knees to keep from slipping, he pulled to the next. Grunting and groaning, he continued. His arms and legs tightened and burned, but he found a rhythm and kept moving. Every step up brought misery, but eventually, he made it to the ledge and crawled next to Daniel, panting and wheezing.

Charles came up next and stood over them. To no avail, he tried brushing the muck caked on his clothes. "Seems you found a little grit in you."

"Mind over matter," Beau gasped.

"Whatever it takes to get you going." Charles glared at Daniel. "Wake him up. We need to go."

Beau sat up. "Let's give him a minute."

"You forget where we are and who's coming after him?"

"But he might hear from Azrael," Beau said. "He did the last time he fell unconscious. We'll get an idea of where Azrael is. Maybe he's not planning to kill Daniel."

Charles peered out into the fog. He picked up a rock and slung it. Seconds later, it struck the opposing wall. "Azrael is trying to trick him into giving up. Any information we get from him is useless."

Charles reached for his watch but found it concealed in a buttoned pocket. He shook his head and scoffed. "This can't continue to happen. No more resting after this. When I get back, we go." He started for the path that led to the right.

"Where are you going?"

"To find a way up. Be ready to go when I get back."

"Did someone from your past call you Chip?" Beau asked.

Charles froze in place. He turned his head slightly.

"You're remembering your past, aren't you?" Beau said.

Charles turned and stared at Daniel sleeping against the wall. There was longing and sadness in his expression. He closed his mouth and seemed like he was ready to cry. "It's no good to dwell on it. It's a weakness. We're here and that's all that matters."

"I'm starting to remember my daughter," Beau said, "but I don't think it's a weakness."

"It's no use to you here," Charles said.

"It got me up that cliff."

Charles tightened his necktie and swallowed. He looked away. "Remember what I said before—about the Holy Spirit?"

"It's in him, isn't it?"

Charles pressed his lips into a thin line and nodded. "I've never dealt with anything like it since coming here. Not for nearly a hundred years."

"If it bothers you so much, why do this?"

"Destiny doesn't call every day, but when it does, I answer." White fog swallowed Charles as he walked off. "Just like you."

"We're *not* alike."

Beau pulled out the ram's horn and took a sip. A rush of energy trailed down his spine and spread through his body. Soreness evaporated, and his limbs no longer shuddered with fatigue. He pressed his fingers into his eyes and exhaled. Beside him, Daniel twitched and snored. Beau murmured, "Mind over matter."

He heard a feminine voice in his head. *Beau.*

"Charles?"

I am not Charles.

Beau came to his feet. He tucked the horn back into his waistband and looked around. "Who's there?"

I'm a friend. Call me Fortuna.

"What do you want?"

You possess something that belongs to me. Return it and I may help you.

"You'll help me get Daniel out of here?"

If he chooses.

"How can I trust you?"

To some, I am evil, but to others, I'm the most pleasant of angels. For you and your companions, I am essential. Without me, you will never escape. Come in good faith, and I will help you.

Beau squatted down and rubbed his head. "Should we leave Charles?"

Without Charles, you fail.

"Where do we find you?"

When you reach the summit, you'll find a valley. Follow it. Mammon will beckon to you, but give him nothing. He is chained and cannot reach you. You'll pass through the greedy mob and find smoke rising on the far horizon. It derives from Stygian Lake. There, I will come to you.

Chapter Eleven

The Goddess of Greed

BEAU

Daniel woke gasping and sweating. He jumped to his feet and stumbled into the rock wall. Beau grabbed him by the shirt, but he wrenched away and fell to his knees.

"Settle down," Beau said. "We're on a cliff. Remember?"

Daniel wiped his face. After several breaths, he said, "He's getting closer."

"You saw Azrael?" Beau stood up and dusted off his pants.

"I saw through his eyes." Daniel stared out into the fog. "He was next to Kristine on Grandfather Mountain. She was crying. A small crowd was with her on the trail. Some were praying." He squinted at the ground. "He wanted me to see that."

"Was that all you saw?"

Daniel looked up at Beau and came to his feet. "After that, he leaped up the hillside and into the hole I fell through in a single bound. He's faster than us. Much faster."

"Then we should get moving," Charles said, emerging from the fog. "I found a way to the summit."

Charles and Daniel started to leave.

"Wait," Beau said. "There's something I need to tell you. Good news, actually."

"Good news?" Charles sneered. He started off. "Tell us on the way."

Beau almost had to jog to keep up with them. "A spirit named Fortuna told me she'd help us. She said we need to ignore Mammon and meet her at Stygian Lake."

"Really?" Charles looked overhead. "Fortuna gives and takes, so what does she want in exchange?"

"She said I have something that belongs to her." Beau huffed. The pace was too quick for him. "But I don't know what she means. Everything I have is mine."

Charles brought his hand to his vest pocket. "It must be the horn."

"We can't give that up." Daniel kicked a rock off the cliff. "It's helped us more than anything. What could she possibly do for us, anyway?"

"She can grant us good fortune," Charles said. "That may be your ticket out of here."

"What's Mammon?" Beau asked.

"He's a fallen angel," Charles said. "I'm told he likes to stay in Greed. Holds sway over everyone sentenced there. He's some kind of wolfman. When he's a man, he goes by Mammon. When he transforms into a wolf, he's Plutus."

"So, we just ignore this wolfman and go to Stygian Lake?" Daniel rubbed the side of his head. "I don't know. Sounds too simple."

"She's the author of fortune." Charles seemed giddy. He smiled and rubbed his hands together. "She could make it that simple."

"Wait a second." Beau stopped and pointed at Charles. "She whispered like you did on the mountain."

Charles turned. "What are you getting at?"

"You pretended to be her," Beau said. "That's why you walked off."

Charles put his hands on his hips and shook his head. "Do I sound like a woman to you, Beau?"

"Er—no."

"Why would I sabotage what we're trying to do?" Charles asked. "This whole thing was my idea."

"We'll find out at the lake." Daniel stared out into the fog. "We need to move."

DANIEL

Charles led them to a fork and took a rightward path up a steep grade. The dry air had hardened Daniel's clothes. His pants chafed his inner thighs as he lunged uphill. His feet and hands stung and throbbed. Heat and irritation burned his throat. Abdominal muscles cramped, and a dizzying headache persisted. None of it dissuaded him, but he wished he had taken a sip of Beau's medicine before they had set off.

He doubted Charles had fabricated Beau's encounter with Fortuna. His mind was more drawn to the entity that had jumped into Hell to find him. He wondered why Azrael would let him see Kristine's tearful face before jumping in. Was he trying to tell him something—taunt him, maybe? Though he believed Azrael meant him no harm, the fear of death overpowered his gut. And seeing Kristine had renewed his determination to get home.

The summit was solid rock. Walking inland, they came upon a sharp descent, where they followed a winding path downhill. The fog became clouds. The path led to a pale valley that cut between two rocky escarpments. When they reached the narrow valley, they climbed over scree and followed it at a slight descent. After an uneventful mile, clanging metal prickled Daniel's ears.

A small party of scrawny men dressed in rags toiled along the trail ahead. Hunched over, they tapped at the ground, widening the path with pickaxes. Two of these men filled burlap sacks with debris by hand. With tired, trembling movements, they all seemed on the verge of collapse.

"Who are these guys?" Daniel asked.

"Hoarders," Charles said.

"You told us everyone would be fighting," Daniel said.

"These guys are too old and frail to fight." Charles tightened his necktie. "They spend their days in perpetual labor—gathering whatever they can for Mammon and the other hoarders."

"Should we be worried?" Beau touched his breast pocket.

"Look at them," Charles gestured to the workers. "They'd keel over before causing us any trouble."

As they passed by, the hoarders kept to their work. They smelled of musk and stale cigarettes. Their dried, wrinkled faces, deprived of sustenance and care, sagged with deep folds that ran from either side of their noses and extended past their pointed chins. One of the two men filling sacks slung a filled sack over his shoulder. The momentum of the bag sent the man stumbling.

Daniel caught him before he fell over. "Want me to carry that for you, sir?"

"Find your own," the old man growled. The grimace on his powdered face made him look like a pointy-eared goblin. "I worked for what I have, you lazy bum."

"You were about to fall over," Daniel said. "Thought you could use some help."

"Sure, you want to help." The man's swollen eyes became thin slits. He bared his teeth, revealing rotted gums that glistened in contrast to his dried-out, withered lips. "Ya think I was born yesterday?"

Daniel rubbed his chin. Certainly, a man in Greed would be selfish, but Daniel wondered if this man's main issue was his pride. "Mind if I ask you a few questions?"

"Can't you just move along and leave me alone?"

"Goodness, Daniel," Charles said. "The man doesn't want to be bothered."

Daniel glared at Charles. "Like you care." He turned back to the man. "This is Greed, right?"

"Boy, you're a fool if you don't know where you are," the old man said.

Daniel spotted a golf ball-sized rock and picked it up. "I'll give you this if you'll tell me why you're here."

The old man craned his neck like a turtle stretching its head from its shell. He grunted and his face scrunched up as he eyed the rock in Daniel's hand. "Fine. I died with money in my pocket. Quite the crime, wouldn't you say? The world is a wreck. Full of uncertainty. But the Good Lord doesn't want you to keep what's rightfully yours. *No.* He insists you give your belongings away to weak-minded imbeciles and watch them trash it."

"You mean the squanderers?" Daniel asked.

"There're only two types of people." The old man held up two fingers for emphasis. "Those who have the sense to save, and those who treat everything like trash."

"You think you're here because you were rich?" Beau asked.

The old man brought his bag higher onto his shoulder. "That's right. Because I had sense enough to not waste my keep."

"Did you ever give to someone in need?" Daniel asked.

"Do I look like a fool, boy?" The old man scowled. "I don't fall for panhandling fakes or charities. I'm no sucker. No one needs my money. What they really need is a swift kick in the pants."

"Considering where you are," Beau said. "Do you regret you didn't give more?"

"My only regret is bumping into you three."

"Is Mammon down this way?" Charles asked.

"I'm bringing this bag of marble to him." The old man motioned ahead with his chin. "He'll be outside his cave on the left embankment. Keeping one eye on his treasure and the other on the thieves." He glowered at Daniel. "I've told you enough, so hand over that rock."

Daniel gave it to him, and the old man tucked it in his mouth like a wad of tobacco. The path began to incline, and a loud ruckus could be heard. Dust and smoke lingered over the horizon. They crested the hill and started down the other side, which was much steeper. The valley widened between two escarpments that extended into the sky on either side. A raucous crowd brawled in a field that lay at the mouth of the valley.

At the foot of the hill, four men hid behind a boulder while several others hurled stones at them. The bag carrier trudged uphill to the left, using a small staircase that was carved into the hillside.

Daniel, Beau, and Charles stopped and analyzed the chaotic situation. There was no break in the crowd anywhere. It looked as if they would have to fight their way through everyone to get to Stygian Lake.

"I don't know about this," Daniel said. "Any ideas?"

"Looks like we'll have to push through it." Beau looked at Charles. "What do you think?"

"We stay close. Move fast and don't engage unless we have to."

A long snarling growl hushed the crowd. On the hill to their left, a large, dark-green wolf with pinned ears emerged from a cave onto a thin ledge that jutted out from the cliff. It looked directly at Daniel and barked. "Rah Sah Tan Rah Sah Tan Con que ror Con que ror!"

The battle ceased. All eyes were upon the wolf. It rose onto its hind legs. Its canine head fell back like a cowl. Large hairy arms flung its fur coat behind massive shoulders, where it draped down his back like a cape. Green skin, clad in golden armor, Mammon glared at them with his hands held out, as if expecting gifts.

"Give," Mammon commanded with a deep, guttural voice.

The bag carrier struggled to traverse a small path that led to Mammon. He took short shuffling steps while holding out a hand to the rising slope to keep his balance.

Daniel looked at Beau. "Fortuna said to ignore him?"

Beau nodded.

"To pass, you must bear gifts," Mammon hissed, lowering his arms. His green eyes glowed with fervent desire. He gestured to the crowd below. "Do so, or I'll sic my people on you."

"We have to ignore him," Beau said.

"What should we do then?" Daniel asked. "Head back? Find another way?"

Mammon hunched on all fours and howled. Half the crowd turned to Charles, Beau, and Daniel. A few stones soared their way. All of them fell short, but one sailed to the left and struck the bag carrier. He fell onto the path holding the sack, and shards of powdery stones cascaded down the hillside. The crowd dashed after the loose pebbles.

The voice of Mammon returned. "Bring me the three infiltrators, and I'll give you gold."

A large group of hoarders wielding stones, hammers, and knives moved toward Daniel, Charles, and Beau. Their movements were slow and tired, and their bodies seemed to be nothing more than bones wrapped in thin skin.

Daniel stepped forward and slammed his foot against the chest of the first one. Bones crunched, and the weightless man fell back and toppled over several others behind him.

"They're frail," Charles said.

"Follow me." Beau marched past Daniel and slapped the oncoming hoarders to one side or the other.

He led the way into the mob. Most of them were still fighting for the stones that fell from the bag. Daniel and Charles stayed close to Beau, who easily manhandled anyone who impeded him. At one point, he slung a man into the air and several yards away.

There was a lot of noise and flailing arms, but these people seemed to weigh less than the stones in their hands. When anyone tried coming at Daniel, Charles, and Beau, they easily pushed them back. After a minute of plowing through the crowd, they were running across an open field toward the rising smoke.

Mammon stood on his ledge with his arms folded, watching them flee for a time. Eventually, he squatted down to all-fours and started barking at everyone who was still quarrelling over the spilled bag of dust.

The land bent downwards. The stench of burning sediment irritated Daniel's nose. He trotted to a walk, fighting a cough. Beau handed him the horn.

CHARLES

Hot smoke blasted against Charles's face. He inhaled it and sighed. Spurs and smoldering fissures riddled the hillside. Dark lava oozed and bubbled from fiery cracks. Ahead of him, Daniel and Beau kept low to the ground and took turns breathing through the horn. About a hundred feet from Stygian Lake, they entered a pocket of air.

The sinister glow of the boiling red waters whirled with sporadic flames. Golden embers burst and diffused across the blotted sky. Daniel turned to Charles. His blue eyes glistened in the dull light. Though distance drowned the effects of the Holy Spirit, Charles felt a strange need to be closer to Daniel. He didn't know why, but figured it was because of Daniel and Beau's ignorance of Hell's many dangers. As for Fortuna's promise, he wondered what was in it for him. If she said she would help them succeed, surely it meant he'd gain the power he desired.

He caught up with Daniel and Beau near the shores of the lake and loosened his necktie. "Where is she?"

Beau lifted a finger and squeezed his eyes shut. When he opened them, he pointed to a pier covered in slow-moving, molten rock. "She wants us to go on that." It stretched twenty feet into the simmering red waters of Stygian Lake.

"It's covered with lava," Daniel said.

Beau's eyes shifted about the sky. "She told me to use the horn."

Daniel took an exasperated breath. "Use it for what?"

"The horn just does what it wants, so I guess—" Beau shrugged. "We'll see."

He took a hesitant step toward the molten pier with the horn held out. Charles and Daniel crept behind him. The tarry path sank under the weight of their steps and clung to their soles. A hollow whistling sound escalated from the horn. Beau continued forward, groaning, and struggled with the horn, which sputtered and shook until a powerful wind blasted from it.

Beau fell back and knocked Daniel into Charles. Another memory came to him. Charles was beside his sobbing grandmother in front of a grave. His mother's name was etched on the tombstone. *Elaine Love Thorne.* His grandmother squeezed his hand. *I'm so sorry, Chip. You'll meet her someday.*

"No. No. No." Charles jerked away from Daniel. "Get off me."

Charles stumbled and fell to all fours, gasping. His eyes flooded with tears, and he closed them tight. His grandmother's face faded into the dark canvas of his mind, humming the lullaby. A chilly breeze reached his nostrils. The ground beneath him shimmered with a thick layer of ice.

"Gentlemen." A pleasant, feminine voice spoke from the pier. "Please. Join me."

A lady in an ivory-colored gown and yellow sash rested in a golden chair. A spinning tabletop sat before her. A soft smile blossomed between her blushing cheeks. A light-blue cloth covered her eyes and disappeared into her blonde hair, which was wrapped in a thick bun behind her head. She raised her hand and beckoned. "You must hurry."

The sight of this woman and her many colors evoked emotions Charles had never felt—even in life. Her smooth, unblemished face. Petite and confident. Sweet, yet promiscuous. A mysterious angel who cursed with her left and blessed with her right.

"You OK?" Beau asked Daniel as he helped him to his feet.

Daniel rolled his shoulder while nursing his wrist. "Yeah. How about you, Charles?"

"Fine." Charles leered at Fortuna while fixing his hat and tie.

Beau led the way onto the icy pier. A ghostly mist issued from it. Fortuna's smile never left her shining, youthful face. A light-green aura gleamed around her. They came to the opposite side of her table. Its top was a spinning ship's wheel. She placed her hand on one of the eight wooden handles and brought it to a stop.

"Have I earned your trust?" she asked.

Beau looked at Charles and Daniel and answered. "Yes."

"I've set a path in your favor, and it requires trust." Her smile faded. "The only way beyond this point is through my assistance alone. I will grant that if, and only if, you hand over my cornucopia."

"You mean—my horn." Beau squinted at Daniel. "We need it."

"It may pain you to let it go after keeping it for so long, but I'm afraid there's no other way. Give it to me, or else you'll fail."

"How can it be yours?" Tears welled in Beau's eyes. "I've had it for ages."

"I give cornucopias to the shadows to help them with their sad work," Fortuna said. "You are no longer a shadow, therefore, it should return to me."

"But I need it to stay alive," Daniel said.

"My cornucopias can't go beyond the isle of Greed. If you try to go forth with it, a great wind will propel you back here. It is the same wind that iced this pier. You must go on without it, or Azrael will find you. He arrives soon, so you mustn't delay."

"Can it take us back to Limbo?" Beau asked.

"Only by Charon can one return there." Fortuna shifted slightly in her seat. "Considering the arduous route you've taken, you must know he'd decline."

Daniel's face flushed red. "I'll die without it."

Fortuna's smile faded. "A man chased by Death, speaking with insolence to one who can help him." Fortuna pursed her lips. "Not wise. Impulsive. Maybe not worth my time."

"No," Beau cried, his voice cracking. "It's not his fault. It's mine."

"*Shh.*" Fortuna leaned over the table and caressed Beau's cheek. He hung his head in shame. "The cornucopia is the only price you'll have to pay. Daniel may live and return—but he alone must choose. And time is short. Too much delay will destroy all permutations of your survival."

"What will happen in the end if we do this?" Charles asked, gazing at Fortuna.

"You will succeed if you do not delay and Daniel doesn't give up."

"Do it, Beau," Charles said. "I trust her."

"Don't." Daniel's eyes shimmered warily. "We need it, Beau."

Beau clenched his teeth. "I trust her too."

Daniel glared at Beau. "Don't."

Beau frowned and sighed. He placed the horn on the pedestal of the ship's wheel and turned the handle clockwise.

Fortuna retrieved the horn and cupped a hand beneath its brim. Three golden arrowheads fell into her palm. She placed them on the pedestal and the wheel carried them around to Beau.

"One for each of you," Fortuna said as Beau picked them up. "When the ferry comes, offer them to Phlegyas, and he'll take you to the shores of Dis."

Beau handed an arrowhead to Daniel and Charles. Charles marveled at its craftsmanship. Near its tip, an emblazoned sun shot twisting, fiery rays from its arc, and stretched down the arrow spurring from its edges and base.

"Where do we go from there?" Beau asked.

Daniel folded his arms. "She's already gone.

The iced pier was empty. Charles moved past Daniel and Beau to look over the fiery waters. "Welcome to Wrath—the Fifth Hell."

Chapter Twelve

Fuming Across Stygian Lake

DANIEL

Cool vapors swaying from the pier relieved Daniel's burned skin and throat. It did nothing for the fire rising in his bones. Stygian Lake simmered and hissed beyond the frosted dock, and its heat dug into his skin and poked at his nerves.

He placed his palm inches from the icy surface. It showed no sign of compromise, but should he find it cracking or melting, he'd leave the pier despite Fortuna's promise. The scent of carbon heightened his bitterness toward Beau. Without the horn, there was no solace or reprieve from whatever horrors awaited him.

Something in his pocket dug into his thigh. He set the golden arrowhead aside and pulled the necklace from his pants pocket. Kristine had told him the faint purple crystal would bring him calmness and clarity. Daniel squeezed it and willed images of Kristine's smiling face to his mind. His arm shook and her face faded into the blackness. Frowning, he draped the necklace over his head and tucked it under his shirt.

He pulled out the engagement ring. Adorned with five small, sparkling diamonds, it shone even in the dim light of the sporadic fires that flared along the hillside and upon the frothy buildup in the waters. It reminded him of the promise he had broken. The scuffle he had gotten into the night before was mild compared to others, but he still had failed to control himself. Where all this anger came from, he didn't know. It had started well before he left home, but the first time he acted upon it was when he shoved his father to the floor.

Daniel placed the ring on his pinky finger and twisted it around, wondering if that was all the ring would ever be—a broken promise. "Most of my life, I thought very little of these things." He stared at the ring. "To me, they were just things you buy for a girl. Maybe for something in return. They're more than that, though, right?"

"I think so." Beau managed a thin smile. Slumping and sleepy-eyed, he rested his thick arms on his knees with his chin pressed upon his meaty shoulder. His hands hung with the arrowhead dangling by his fingertips.

Sitting at the end of the dock, Charles tethered the chain of his pocket watch to a buttonhole. "It's just jewelry. A little trinket wrapped around your finger like a bow."

"Is that how you see your watch?" Daniel asked.

Charles took out his pocket watch and rubbed his thumb over its golden shell. "This is no simple trinket."

"Not to you." Daniel shifted and crossed his legs. "An engagement ring means something. It unites two people. It brings people together."

"Never heard *that* before." Charles saw Daniel glaring at him and shrugged. "I've harvested generations of souls who bought rings and made vows, and half of them ended up in Lust over affairs. Shows how much their jewelry means to them."

Daniel took the ring off and put it back into his pocket. "Most people take off their rings before they cheat. Maybe if they'd keep it on and give it a long, hard look, they'd overcome the temptation."

"Believe what you want." Charles stood and placed his hands on his hips. "Phlegyas may be more tolerant than Charon, but he's definitely much slower."

"I don't think anybody's coming," Daniel said. "It was just a trick to get the horn."

Beau blinked and twisted his beard. "No. It wasn't a trick. Just be patient."

"Patience is no virtue of mine." Daniel half-smiled and picked up the arrowhead, turning it in his hand.

"I think I see him." Charles pointed over at the boiling lake.

A faint red glow shimmered against the dark smoke carpeting the sky. Flames sprouted along the horizon and revealed a large, shadowy figure using a pole to push a small skiff toward the pier. Several bodies clung to the stern, trying to capsize the boat. They screamed foul, outlandish curses as fire rolled over them. Phlegyas raised the pole and hammered at their bobbling heads until none remained. Once cleared, he returned to guiding his skiff toward the dock.

Phlegyas slowed the small boat to a stop beside the pier. A dark, heavy robe covered his enormous body. He was at least eight feet tall. His long fingers with thick, knobby knuckles clenched the log he used to push the boat. Although his cowl covered most of his face, his sneer revealed sharp black teeth.

"Why are you here?" Phlegyas growled.

Beau and Daniel came up and stood behind Charles. Beau trembled, while Daniel stood rigidly still.

Charles showed no visible signs of distress. "Take us to a safe place on the shore of Dis, and this," he said, raising his arrowhead, "and two others, just like it, will be yours."

The thick pole groaned in Phlegyas's tightening grasp. "Where did you get that?"

"Doesn't matter," Charles said. "They're yours if you take us to Dis."

"It matters to me." Phlegyas lifted his pole and slammed it on the pier. The icy layer shuddered. White cracks flourished over it.

"We got them from Fortuna," Beau cried. His eyes were wide, and he exhaled as if he had been holding his breath.

Charles cleared his throat and added, "She told us you'd carry us across Stygian Lake to Dis in an exchange."

Veins bulged from Phlegyas's swelling neck. "I'll let you board. Maybe halfway there, I rip you apart and scatter you across the lake to feed the filth residing within it."

Charles smiled down at his arrowhead. "I knew you didn't want these. Sorry to bother you." He turned and winked at Beau and Daniel. "Let's see who can throw the farthest."

"Stop!" Phlegyas yelled, slamming the pole to the pier again. Ice shattered. Bits of it grazed Daniel's arms.

"So, you do want them?" Charles asked.

"Give me the arrowheads, and I'll take you."

"You threatened to toss us overboard." Charles canted his bowler hat. "We'll give them to you once we reach Dis."

Phlegyas roared at the sky. His cowl flipped back, revealing his bony-gray head and empty eye sockets. His wrinkled face fluttered as if tiny insects scurried under his skin and about his skull. "Fine," he growled. "I'll take you. Hand them over before you disembark, or I'll break every bone in your skin sacks."

"We'll hand them over. In fact, here's mine." Charles handed Phlegyas his arrowhead and came aboard. "The others will be yours when we make it to Dis. Understand?"

"Don't patronize me," Phlegyas hissed. He held the arrowhead up and gazed at it. "The other two are like this one?"

"They're identical," Charles said.

Phlegyas turned his attention to Beau and Daniel. "Hear me clearly. This is my ship, and I won't hesitate to club you, should you disrespect me. Now get on."

The skiff wavered as Beau and Daniel came aboard. The boiling waters vibrated the boat. Its wooden surface was slick and dark red with blood. The smell of rot sickened Daniel. Hot steam rolled against his face from all directions. It was maddening. He covered his mouth and nose while taking a seat next to Beau near the boat's center.

"It won't take much to flip this over," Daniel said.

"We'll be OK if the boatman doesn't kill us." Beau brushed his hand over his shirt pocket, checking for the keystone.

Charles sat behind Daniel and Beau, clicking his pocket watch open and flipping it shut. At the stern, Phlegyas placed the arrowhead in a pocket of his robe. It occurred to Daniel that they each held on to something for different reasons. The engagement ring in Daniel's pocket gave him hope that he'd find his way back to Kristine. Beau kept the keystone out of some sense of duty. Charles's watch seemed to grant him some sort of authority over others. They needed their effects, but Phlegyas didn't seem to need these arrowheads.

"Why do you care about these arrowheads?" Daniel asked. Beau's body grew rigid beside him.

Pushing from the pier, Phlegyas grunted. "They're Apollo's!" He jammed the pole hard into the waters and reared the boat. "As I burned his temple to the ground, he shot me dead with these arrowheads. Having them will give me strength."

"Apollo?" Daniel cleared his throat. Phlegyas forced the boat out into the lake with surprising speed. Steam blasted into Daniel's face.

"Do you not know of Apollo, boy?" Phlegyas sneered.

"You mean the Greek god?" Daniel asked. "Didn't know he actually existed."

Charles cringed and palmed his face. Beau leaned closer with wary eyes and whispered, "Careful what you say."

"You see me standing here?" Phlegyas growled.

"Yes sir." Daniel averted his eyes to the bloody deck. A blend of fear and anger coursed through him. The steam rising from the lake pressed hard into his skin, coating it with a slick layer of sweat. It agitated him. He squeezed his fists, straining his arms.

"I am real, and I say that Apollo killed me."

Blistered hands slapped upon the gunwales of the skiff. Rust-colored beads sizzled upon the deck. A man, covered in sweltering boils, heaved his upper body up to come aboard. Phlegyas kicked him off, and from where he fell, flames burst from the water. The small boat quivered as four others tried to climb on. Phlegyas swung his pole like a baseball bat and sent them hurtling back into the fiery waters. "They're more insolent than usual because of *you* three." Phlegyas pushed harder through the lake. Heads knocked against the boat, and hands grasped and slipped from the gunwales.

Phlegyas cut a path straight through a warring mob cloaked in the dense steam. The sounds of combat enticed Daniel. He pulled his wet shirt from his sticky skin and eased near the side of the boat.

"Don't get too close." Beau gripped his arm. "Someone could grab you."

Daniel didn't say it, but he wanted someone to try. He could see himself swatting these maggots around like they were nothing—just like he did in Greed. *What am I thinking?*

He rubbed his eyes and looked straight ahead, trying not to look at the brawl that ensued around the boat. Lights flickered in the darkness. He pointed and asked, "Is that Dis?"

"One of its many towers." Phlegyas grunted as he pushed the boat forward with his pole. "See the parapets? Powerful warriors roam them. They'll torture you for the rest of your miserable existence when they find you."

Daniel turned to Beau and asked, "How are we supposed to get past them?"

"We'll find a way." Beau stared ahead, tugging on his beard. "Fortuna set a path for us."

"Fortuna isn't here." Daniel became aware of his rising anger. He took a breath, but the steam entered his lungs, filling him with more hostility. "If she set a path, we still have to find it!"

"There is no path," Phlegyas said. "No one can infiltrate the great city. These warriors fought alongside Satan in the Heavenly Battle. They cannot be defeated or deceived by inferior creatures such as you."

"Weren't Satan and his warriors *cast out* of Heaven?" Daniel glared at Phlegyas. "Sounds like they can be defeated to me."

Phlegyas kicked Daniel in the chest and he fell back. Beau shielded Daniel with his body while Phlegyas raised the pole over his head. "You pathetic insect."

CHARLES

Charles came between Phlegyas and Daniel. "If you hurt him, you're not getting the arrowheads."

Phlegyas scowled at Charles. Nothing seemed to move, except for the boat drifting through the waters. Phlegyas snarled and thrust the pole back into the lake, propelling the skiff forward.

Charles huffed and turned to Beau and Daniel. They returned to their original positions. "You're about to get us tossed overboard." Daniel had grown sullen and didn't respond. His jaws flexed. He stared back over the waters. "Just keep quiet. We're nearly there."

The steam dissipated, and the swimmers jostled the boat while they ripped, slashed, punched, plucked, and bit each other. No one attempted to board; they preferred the fighting. Beyond the fray sat dark, still waters. Fiery sconces set at ten-foot intervals glimmered from the stone parapets that stretched out along the horizon. The most important thing of note was the absence of guards standing watch.

"Where's the entrance to Dis?" Charles asked.

"Find it yourself," Phlegyas grumbled. "After I get my arrowheads."

Daniel's body jerked. He looked over his shoulder. His wary eyes passed over Charles and beyond Phlegyas.

"What is it?" Beau asked.

Daniel shook his head. "Nothing good."

As they neared the shore, a thick layer of tar covered the water. Smoke transcended the steam. Daniel and Beau heaved and coughed while Charles took deep breaths, savoring the carbonic scent. It pleased his lungs and warmed his coal-heart. A graveyard cloaked in a pale mist stretched along the exterior walls of Dis. Tombstones, mausoleums, ossuaries, and contorted statues of anthropomorphic beasts congested the strip of land in a jumbled display.

Elaine Love Thorne.

Phlegyas grunted and strained as he plowed through the clinging tar. Once he reached a dock of bones, he held out his massive hand. "The arrowheads now."

Since Charles had already given his up, he stepped onto the dock, which bent under his feet. Beau handed his arrowhead over and stepped off next. Daniel didn't move. The color in his face had drained. He surveyed Stygian Lake.

"Move it, boy," Phlegyas said.

Daniel came to his feet, nursing his back. He stepped toward Phlegyas and offered his arrowhead with a shaking hand. Phlegyas snatched it and grabbed Daniel by the throat.

"The life in you sickens me," Phlegyas growled.

Charles and Beau stood petrified. Daniel peered back over the dark waters, then at Beau and Charles. He rasped, "Azrael—he's crossing the lake right now."

"Azrael?" Phlegyas glared over the lake.

Charles nodded. "He's been following us."

Brown mucus oozed from Phlegyas's mouth. He snarled at Daniel. "He wants you, doesn't he? You will be my bait."

"He doesn't want him," Charles said. "He wants your arrowheads."

Phlegyas glared at Charles. "It's obvious he wants the boy."

Charles shook his head, looking skyward. "Fortuna told us Azrael wanted to steal the arrowheads back. He claims they are his and that he gave them to Apollo to kill you."

Phlegyas growled. He twisted his head in agitation before tossing Daniel off the boat and into Beau. “The warriors of Dis will deal with you. I’ll deal with Azrael.”

Phlegyas forced the pole into the black tar and pushed away. He shouted for Azrael while guiding his boat to the deep of Stygian Lake. Beau, Daniel, and Charles hiked a short incline to the edge of the graveyard. The foggy mist proved to be a thick gauntlet of cobwebs teeming with tiny black spiders.

Charles grimaced. “I hate spiders.” He took out his timepiece, opened it, and clamped it shut. All the nearby spiders scurried off. He looked about the graveyard and shuddered. “Nasty little buggers.”

Beau pointed at the parapets. “No one’s standing watch. We can follow the shore until we find the entrance.”

“I doubt it will stay that way for long.” Charles spotted a statue of Baphomet with a lit torch inserted into the back of its head. “Oh, Fortuna,” he sang with subtle laughter. He sauntered to the statue and clamped his watch to scare off the surrounding spiders. Using his hat, he brushed away webs and retrieved the torch.

“What are you doing?” Beau asked. “That will give away our position.”

“Oh, ye of so little faith.” Charles smiled while testing the weight of the torch. He lowered it to the web and burned a hole between a pair of gravestones. Spiders squealed as flames overcame them. “We’ll burn a path to the wall. From there, we’ll burn our way to the entrance. Catch.” Charles tossed the torch to Beau, who flinched when he caught it. “You’ll burn, and I’ll keep the spiders off us.”

“What do you think, Daniel?” Beau asked. “Shouldn’t we stick with the shoreline?”

Daniel’s attention remained on the lake.

“The shore isn’t safe,” Charles said. “Someone from Wrath could be lingering near the shallows, or a demon may spot us from the parapets—among them, the Furies, the fiercest warriors guarding Dis. Our best chance is to get close to the wall and use the graveyard for cover. We’ll slip in when no one’s looking.”

“They could just as easily spot us along the walls,” Beau said.

“How often do you think someone’s tried to enter Dis of their own free will?” Charles asked. “The demons here will be complacent, and their eyes will be on the lake, maybe the shore, but not right under their noses.”

“Just stop.” Daniel sat on the sandy hillside, pressing his forefingers to either side of his head. “It’s too late. Azrael is crossing the lake. It’s over.”

“You weren't bluffing?” Beau asked.

Daniel shook his head. “I had another vision. Azrael came onto the pier where we were and leaped from it.”

“He’s flying?” Beau asked.

Daniel surveyed the sky. “Can show up any moment now.”

“Well, Phlegyas will be upset about that.” Charles wiggled the knot of his tie. “Like he needs a reason.”

“Fortuna’s helping us,” Beau said. “We got through Greed and Wrath with no problems because of her.”

“She told us we can make if you don’t give up,” Charles said.

“I don’t trust her.” Daniel crossed his arms and leaned forward. He squeezed his eyes shut and let out a long breath.

“You’re giving up?” Charles asked. “This is Heresy. The Sixth Hell. We get into the city, and we’re safe. Azrael would have to fight an entire army of demons to follow us.”

“What army?” Daniel gestured to the empty parapets. He slapped his hands to his thighs and huffed. “I fell here for a reason. We all know that.

I'm not right with God, and at this point—after seeing all this—I doubt I'll ever be right with Him. This is who I am. This is where I belong."

"What's gotten into you?" Beau asked.

"I know what it is." Charles stepped closer to Daniel. "Wrath got to you. You're an angry person and that steam got into your head and pushed all your buttons. Didn't it?"

Daniel frowned at Beau. "Too bad we lost the horn then. It would've helped."

"You don't need it," Beau said. "Everything you need is already inside you."

"He's right." Charles loosened his necktie and cleared his throat. "The Holy Spirit is with you. It hasn't given up on you, so you shouldn't give up either."

Daniel folded his arms and rolled his eyes. "You'll say anything to get what you want."

Charles snapped his watch at a nearby crowd of spiders. "Regardless of what I want, it's in you. It affects me and Beau."

"It's true." Beau nodded. "I think it's why I'm remembering my daughter."

"And I'm seeing my grandmother." Charles removed his necktie and rubbed the impression left on his neck. He could breathe much better. "I lied about many things, but not this."

"Demons tell the truth when it suits them?" Daniel glanced up at Charles.

"That's right." Charles tossed his necktie into the tarry waters and offered Daniel a hand. "And I won't lie to you again."

Daniel sighed and grasped Charles's hand. Expecting another vision, Charles winced as he pulled Daniel up, but it never came. He opened his eyes.

"Well, ain't that somethin'," Beau said. "We told you, Daniel."

"What?" Charles asked.

"Your eyes." Daniel squinted. "They're—human."

Charles smiled. "They're my mother's."

Chapter Thirteen

The Heretics' Yard

BEAU

Since telling Daniel about the poor child who he had sent on to Heaven, Beau felt a strange connection to another child who had died more than a century ago. *Hurry Daddy.* The voice sounded familiar. Her face was identical to the little one who had died in the ditch. Her smile flashed in his head. He remembered how she'd dirty up her dress when running to a small shop in town. "Sugar cane," he whispered. "She loved it."

Something happened to this girl. He chased after her when she ran away, oblivious to the dangers lurking in the woods. She had looked back at him—laughing. Her big brown eyes beamed under waves of shaggy brown hair. After that came the screaming, harsh thuds, and then a dreadful, painful silence.

Beau burned a narrow path along the wall while Charles clicked his pocket watch open and snapped it shut repeatedly to scare off countless tiny spiders. Daniel crept between them, covering his mouth and nose to diminish the noxious gas that squeezed through the cracks of the mausoleums built into the walls surrounding Dis.

Beau turned and asked, "How are you holding up?"

Using the neckline of his shirt to shield his nose, Daniel shook his head. His eyes watered as he cleared his throat. "I could use the horn about now. The fumes—" He coughed. "—are killing me."

Beau grunted. He couldn't fault Daniel. The foul stench lingered over them like a cloud of death.

"These mausoleums lead to a catacomb under the city." Charles ran the tips of his fingers along the concrete walls. The gas seemed to have no effect on him. "It was built more than a half-century ago for a group called the Schutzstaffel."

"You mean the SS?" Daniel croaked.

Charles nodded. "Satan's generals forced them to dig under the city, creating a special chamber. Once completed, demons sealed them in and turned on the gas. They're stuck there forever, but hey, at least they'll never have to face another Jew."

"We won't have to go through there, will we?" Beau asked.

"No." Charles snapped his watch shut. "We'll travel through the Heretics' Yard to the center of the city and drop into the Seventh Hell."

"What sort of people are in the Heretics' Yard?" Daniel asked.

"Heretics, of course," Charles said. "They changed God's words to have it suit them. Some of them think they *are* gods."

Silently, they continued along the wall under flickering firelight. The line of mausoleums ended, giving them a sense of progress, and a reprieve from the noxious gas. The burning of the cobwebs and squealing spiders created hideous popping noises and high-pitched squeals. Daniel kept looking over Stygian Lake, expecting to see Azrael descending from the sky with his long, sharp scythe.

"See the bridge?" Charles pointed to the right. "The entrance isn't far. Keep that torch down."

They crouched behind a row of tombstones. Fiery red barrels stretched along the bridge. Men clad in armor faced inward along either side, with spears held to the sky. Through the center, four columns wide, marched a long procession of ragged men and women to and through the entrance to Dis.

"Move it." A guard swatted his spear upon a slower man, who crumpled to the ground. Those behind him fell, causing a hole in the formation.

"Halt!" another soldier shouted. He jabbed his spear at the trailing group until they stopped. He turned to those who fell. "Move out, you clumsy rats."

"They're not on the parapets because they're imprisoning new souls," Charles whispered. "Stay low, but keep burning the path."

They crept along the wall toward the entrance. Vicious lashings answered the tearful pleas of the marchers. Pained cries and maniacal laughter grew louder as they approached. The graveyard and the spiderwebs ended upon a long semi-circular stone platform. The entrance was centered at the back. Above it, upon a protruding archway, three blue-skinned women in dark robes stood guard. They wore bull skulls with metallic horns for helmets. Long skinny snakes curled from their heads, hissing and waving in all directions. They wielded bullwhips and observed the march with unblinking, pitch-black eyes.

Charles placed a hand on Beau's arm and whispered, "Back up before they see us."

"Are those snakes in their hair?" Daniel asked breathlessly.

"Yes. They're Furies," Charles whispered. "They can't turn you to stone if that's what you're worried about. But they are fierce and intelligent. We'll have to sneak past them somehow."

They backtracked about twenty feet and watched the marchers file through the entrance. Most had their faces buried in their hands and were convulsing with tears. The soldiers lining the bridge scowled and jabbed loafers in the back with their spears.

"If one of those Furies turns her head just a little more this way," Beau said, "we're done for."

"They're focused on the march." Charles snapped his watch at nearby spiders. "Maybe we can run along the wall and—"

"Shh." Beau gripped Charles's shirt and pulled him lower.

A Fury jumped from the archway to the right of the march. Another joined her. They didn't see the burned trail, but they stood just beyond the graveyard within ten feet of Beau, Daniel, and Charles.

"You sense it, too, Alecto?"

"Yes, something is off." Alecto sniffed the air.

The third Fury's robe sprouted into wings. Her body was covered in dark armor that glistened in the firelight. She glided to the others. "I feel so too." A man pleading for mercy broke rank and dashed after her. He was about two feet shorter than the Furies. A single backhand sent him sprawling to the ground. A long, serpent-like tongue came from between her teeth. She yelled. "Guards, let one more break rank, and I'll slit all your pathetic throats!"

Daniel covered his mouth and stifled a cough. A Fury jerked her head in their direction, then turned back to the sky over the lake. Charles held a finger over his lips.

"Whatever it is, it doesn't belong here," the same Fury said.

"It's powerful," Alecto shifted from one foot to the other, "and predatory."

A violent wind howled over the lake. The glowing red barrels on the bridge screeched like banshees as they crushed and flamed out. Guards fell to their knees, grasping their necks. Marchers ran in every direction. Some jumped from the bridge and splashed into the tarry waters. Frigid air rolled over Beau, Charles, and Daniel; with it came a sweet, flowery fragrance. The sconces on the wall, and even the torch in Beau's hand, flamed out. The only light remaining came from the orange glow rising from the walls of Dis.

Daniel shuddered.

"It's Azrael," a Fury growled. "How dare he come here!"

"Clear the bridge," Alecto said. "Guards, take your posts." Her robe sprouted into batlike wings. The snakes on her head coiled. "He's hiding in the sky—like a coward. Let's meet him there."

Alecto sprinted over the bridge and lunged into the air, beating her wings. The other two followed. Charles pulled Beau and Daniel by the sleeve. "This is our chance."

The three stayed crouched and kept a hand on the wall while running for the entrance. The Furies and the marchers had disappeared. Few guards remained, and they watched the skies over the lake. The Furies screamed from afar. No one noticed Charles leading Beau and Daniel under the archways and through the iron gates.

Oppressive heat stole Beau's breath when he entered the Heretics' Yard. Radiation pressed into his flesh like countless invisible knives. Shimmering red light emanated from countless fiery pits, stretching to their left and right at five-foot intervals. Farther ahead, stone buildings billowed smoke from windows and cracks. A few marchers ran about helplessly, seeking escape.

They were on a cobblestoned road that stretched deeper into the city. "We follow this?" Beau asked.

"Yes." Charles looked at the sky. Winged demons flew over them to the parapets. "Don't worry about them. They're after Azrael."

DANIEL

Despite the throbbing in his feet and head, Daniel limped alongside Charles. The intense heat and stench of carbon burned his lungs when he inhaled. It didn't fill him with anger like the steam that fumed over Stygian Lake, but it drained him of energy. Beau fell behind them, trudging like an old car on the verge of collapse.

"We're losing Beau," Daniel rasped.

They stopped and looked back to the wall, where demons shot flaming arrows that disappeared into the smoking black sky. Daniel propped his hands on his knees and panted. Sweat fell from his head like rain and sizzled on the road beneath him.

There was a metallic clatter. Flickering embers floated from a near-by pit. A man with a melted face pulled himself up and extended an ashy-white arm as far as his shackles allowed. Smoke fumed from exposed bones. When he saw Daniel, the hairless man's eyes went wide. He pleaded, "Please, please, please, set me free. Please."

Daniel looked away from the man, but that wouldn't erase the image seared into his mind. A hand touched his back, startling him. "It's me," Beau gasped. "Let's go."

The man jerked at his chains, and his pit roared with fire. "Come back," he cried. "Get me out!"

The ruckus stirred others from their pits. They were all burned in varying degrees. Some had strings of hair curled along the sides of their heads. They gazed at Daniel with wonder. *He's alive. Why is he here? He's shining. Can he help us?*

Daniel pretended not to notice them and focused on Charles's back. The heat irritated his scar. He scratched it. His throat was dry, and he felt dizzy. "How far do we have to go?"

"About two miles." Charles pointed ahead. "When we come across a lot of rubble, we're close to the next pit."

Daniel coughed and looked back. "Beau's falling behind again."

They stopped and allowed Beau to catch up.

"Sorry." Beau coughed and spat. "The heat, it's draining."

Something grabbed Daniel's shin. A woman with a charred face extended her grin to a menacing smile when they locked eyes. She had long, stringy gray hair and seemed unaffected by the fire. "Take heed, for I see your future, Daniel Strong."

He nudged her off.

The woman seemed taken aback. Her eyes went wide. "You will never escape death!" she shouted. "Listen to me, sweet child. Please. For your own sake, hear me."

Daniel looked down at the woman in the pit. Maybe he should listen. She seemed to know something he didn't.

When he started back toward her, Charles grabbed his shoulder. "We'll get out of here sooner if we don't entertain these people."

"She knows my name," Daniel said, "and about Azrael."

"Daniel, please." Beau coughed and cleared his throat. "Let's keep moving."

"You must listen, sweet boy," the woman cried. "Come. Hear what I have to say."

"It won't take long." Daniel stepped closer to the woman and squatted just beyond her reach. "What is it?"

"Choose death." She smiled and nodded. Daniel stood and moved back. Her expression softened with empathy. "Oh, you poor child. Choose death."

Charles grabbed Daniel's arm and pulled him away. "Why must we chat with everybody in this godforsaken place?"

As they hurried along the stone road, the woman cried out to them. "They're taking you the wrong way. Choose death."

"What if she's right?" Daniel looked back at the lady.

"Kristine wouldn't want you to choose death," Beau said.

Daniel massaged his forehead, and a terrible weightlessness made him sick to his stomach. For the first time, he longed for his father's pitiful last words. But all he could hear was the loud echoing of *Choose death... Choose life...* tolling in his mind.

They trotted deeper into Dis. Arrows still flitted through the sky beyond the wall behind them. Clattering chains and loud grunting turned Daniel's attention forward. To their right, a man pulled at his chains in vain to break them. When he locked eyes with Daniel, he hollered. "Hey! Help me break this. Come on."

Though he longed to help the man, he stayed in lock-step with Charles and passed him.

"Come back," the man pleaded. He yanked hard on his chain and issued a raspy yell. "Stinking bourgeoisie. Can't stop for nothing, can you? You're all cursed. You, the one who is alive—you reek of murder."

Daniel turned back. Beau grabbed his shirt. "Don't worry about him."

"I'm no murderer," Daniel growled at the man.

"It's in your bones." The man's smile revealed a mouth filled with blackness, a tar-like tongue, and inky gums.

Another man rose from his pit and pelted the instigator with a bright-orange lump of coal. "You contentious fool. Is Hell not enough for us? Must we suffer your endless blabbering as well?"

"The demons are gone," another shouted cheerfully. "Toss out your coals. Yank your chains. Free yourselves."

"Dear brethren!" A man in a dark gown waved his hands over his head. "Don't do that. There is no escaping. The demons will return and will beat us senseless should they find coal scattered everywhere."

"You're the reason I suffer, Reverend," another pit dweller jeered. "Preached Jim Crow to me and my family. We trusted you, but now we're here because of what *you* taught us. We all suffer separately and equally now."

"You owned a Bible," the preacher said. "Maybe if you read it, you could have saved yourself. Maybe you could have saved us all."

"Here's a blessing for you, Reverend." Another lady hurled a burning coal at him. Others joined her. The reverend retreated to his pit, which ignited into flames as more coals fell into it.

Charles pulled Daniel's sleeve. "Let's go before they start aiming for us."

"That was a preacher." Daniel didn't understand how a person who had dedicated their life to preaching the Bible could end up here. "Why is he here?"

"Preachers aren't exempt," Charles said. "There's no Get-out-of-Hell-Free cards just for getting through seminary."

The commotion behind them created a domino effect amongst the pit dwellers. Curious souls peered at Daniel, Beau, and Charles, who hurried by, keeping their sights on the road leading deeper into the city.

A bulky man with burns trailing down the left side of his body rose from a pit. The right side of his body seemed unscathed. He folded his arms and rested them on the edge of his pit. "You're American," he said to Daniel in a deep, gravelly voice. "And I can tell by the looks of you that you served. What branch?"

"Army, but not anymore." Daniel stopped, just out of reach of the man.

"Daniel?" Charles raised his hands, palms up, and shook his head incredulously.

"Give me a minute." Daniel turned back to the man in the pit. "You served too?"

"I did, but never mind me." The man waved off the importance of his military time. "What made you get out?"

"I wasn't happy," Daniel said. "Thought I'd try something different and go to college."

"Ha!" The man shook his head. "That's why the world's in such a mess. Young people want to prance around in their happy pants, rather than do what's best for them and their country. I saw it coming when I was alive. The United States will become a socialist welfare state, while everyone's running around like a bunch of chickens with their heads cut off, looking for happiness and handouts. See the irony in that, kid?"

"You don't know what the future holds," Beau said.

"We know more than you think," the man said.

Daniel kneeled down and locked eyes with the veteran in the pit. "Someone said I have murder inside me. What does that mean?"

"It means nothing coming from them," Beau said.

"It means something, but I can't outright say it." The man ran his hands along the edge of his pit. "But if you hear my story, maybe you can read between the lines."

Daniel shifted closer. "I'm listening."

"I married into the wrong family," the veteran snarled, shaking and nodding his head. "My wife's liberal parents kept feeding her lies about me. She believed them, so I divorced the empty-headed woman. Then she and her parents got my children, my own flesh and blood, to hate me. Since they'd have nothing to do with me, I disowned them all."

"What does that have to do with murder?" Daniel asked.

The man's eyes widened. He extended his neck, glaring at Daniel. "Read between the lines."

"You never tried to make amends with your family?" Beau asked.

"Oh! My kids wanted to make amends." The veteran laughed derisively. "For college money, of course. What they found was a bunch of nothing. That's one lesson their liberal professors can't teach 'em. Earn your keep."

Another man rose from a neighboring pit. Flames rolled from his eyes and mouth, but his decayed skin didn't burn. "Don't listen to him. He failed to transcend his human experience. Couldn't realize his own godliness. It's why his body burns, unlike mine."

"You're in the same hell as me, so how is that working for ya?" the veteran growled.

The man looked at the sky in awe and raised his hands. "Once I master this reality, I will enter into higher realms. My spirit will ascend beyond the smoke overhead, and I'll look down on you and laugh."

"Fools!" another man cried out. He rose from a pit holding a picket sign. It read: *Not Blessed Just Cursed*. "You're here because God hates you. God hates the USA and lukewarm Christians. Praise God for your suffering."

They talked over each other, making it impossible for Daniel to discern anything. The heat seemed to intensify. His head swam, and he stumbled. The surface of the road looked like it would be cool to his cheek if he'd lay down.

"Had enough of these guys yet?" Charles asked, breaking Daniel from his stupor.

Daniel nodded. He went to wipe his face. It was no longer sweaty, but dry and hot.

"Focus on getting to the pit." Charles continued down the road. The smoke thickened. Daniel and Beau slogged along behind him.

"No one's good enough," Daniel rasped. "Everybody's damned."

"That's not true." Beau cleared his throat. "Plenty of people go to Heaven."

Daniel kept his eyes down. The stones in the road were charred. Some glowed and emitted heat. "Everyone back there believed in God," Daniel said. "One was a preacher."

"They didn't believe in everything God said," Charles said. "They twisted His words into what they wanted."

Daniel was surprised to see Charles defend God. He wondered if it had something to do with the drunken preacher Charles had mentioned earlier. Maybe that preacher had hurt him. Daniel didn't push the issue. Everyone he had spoken to in Hell seemed to fit into Beau's theory. They were all selfish and prideful, but they shouldn't be stuck here for eternity. If they learn their lesson, shouldn't they be given another chance?

Keeping up with Charles became difficult now. *Murder in my bones. Choose death.... Choose life...* The darkness. The fire. The horrors. It all charred to black. He hit the ground. The road didn't cool his cheek. Beau patted him on the shoulder, encouraging him to get up, but Daniel closed his eyes and slept.

Chapter Fourteen

Lord of Violence

CHARLES

Long rows of burning sepulchers marked the end of the Heretics' Yard. Smoke engulfed the inner-city. Fire crackled and roared. Charles stopped and took it in. The smell brought him waves of euphoria, but the absence of footsteps gave him pause. Daniel and Beau had fallen behind. Farther back, he heard faint coughing.

Charles backtracked and found Beau tugging on Daniel, who had passed out. "I've got him." He pulled Beau aside, took Daniel's hands, and started dragging him. "Keep moving. We're right behind you."

Though Daniel weighed two times more than the souls Charles had to handle back in Limbo, he kept up well enough with Beau, who crawled on all fours, wheezing and hacking his way to the center of Dis. Progress was slow yet steady. A thin crack emerged at the center of the road. It extended and widened to the size of a trench, where folds of land and debris from fallen monuments blocked the road.

Beau sat up and scratched his head. "Now what?"

Charles dropped Daniel's arms. "We get in the trench."

Carefully, they dropped themselves into the ditch. It was cooler and about five feet deep. Together, they lowered Daniel to the bottom of the trench and propped him along the wall.

Beau squeezed his magic rock. Light flashed, and Charles flinched, shielding his face. He expected it to trouble him as it had before, but it didn't. Its radiance soothed his skin and eyes.

Daniel's head shifted. The light cast ominous shadows upon his dirty face. When he opened them, his eyes glimmered with tears drawn from the smoke. "It's hot," he croaked, rubbing his chest.

"The pit to Violence is just ahead," Charles said. "Ready?"

"I saw him." Daniel coughed to clear his throat. "Azrael—he's still outside Dis."

"Good." Charles checked his watch. "The Furies are holding him off."

"Not really," Daniel said. "I saw the last one falling to the lake. The arrows they've been shooting—not even close. He's up too high."

"We'd better move then." Charles pushed his hat down on his head. "Azrael isn't coming this deep into Hell for nothing."

Crawling through the trench, Charles led them under the rubble. The soft light emanating from Beau's fist revealed the sharp rugged edges along the wall that could slice unwary flesh. After a few minutes, they reached a six-foot-wide pit where a stream of smoke jetted upward, as if the sky were sucking it through a straw.

"This is it," Charles said, sitting up.

Daniel shifted with unease. "How bad is this next Hell?"

"The Seventh Hell has three parts," Charles said. "This first one is the most brutal. It's an underground nest with hundreds of tunnels leading into different chambers. This drop should take us to the main tunnel. A boiling river of blood runs through it. The souls sentenced there are in the river, trying to reach the end, where they'll earn horns. When they do, they join the demonic army that occupies the nest."

"How many demons are in there?" Beau asked.

Charles shrugged. "Thousands, at least."

"Just like a colony of ants." Daniel stared at the smoke zipping skyward. "They're going to swarm us, aren't they?"

Charles fumbled for his pocket watch and clicked it open. He swallowed. "It's called Violence for a reason."

"I'll show them some violence," Daniel grumbled. "This is worse than the snake-infested dog—Wait. Did they all come from the river?"

Charles nodded. "I believe so."

"Then maybe they're weaker than us, like the squanderers and hoarders were in Greed," Daniel said. "We could just bowl right over them. Fight fire with fire."

"A lot of them will be armed with bows and arrows," Charles said.

"What about the keystone?" Beau raised his glowing fist. "It could be useful."

"It doesn't bother me anymore, Beau," Charles said. "It may have lost some of its energy. I'll drop first and let you know when it's clear."

Daniel and Beau helped Charles climb into the pit. He gripped the edge, lowering himself. Heat shot up from underneath him. When he let go, the air rising from the pit slowed his fall. His fingers trailed down the wall until he slammed onto a stone surface.

The tunnel was an equilateral triangle, six feet wide on all sides. Smoke rolled along the narrow roof and jetted into the overhead pit. Thirty feet away, the next tunnel shimmered with light. The raucous noise indicated that it was the tunnel that would lead them out.

Charles stood up and shouted upward into the pit, "Drop!"

Charles went to a prone position, crept to the other side of the tunnel, and peered into the wide fiery chamber. Fifty or more people waded in a boiling crimson river, gnashing their teeth in pain or anger. Torches leaned out from the rock wall behind them in black sconces. The embankment was stone. Rust-colored steam emitted from the river, ran up the stony embankment walls, and lingered overhead, shrouding the ceiling.

About thirty feet away, a crowd of demons in dark loincloths taunted the swimmers. With red skin and yellow eyes, they looked like caricature versions of demons. After reaching the river's end, a general in Satan's army had hammered two shiny-black horns into either side of their skulls. They held longbows and carried quivers filled with arrows over their shoulders.

Beau and Daniel thudded behind him. Groaning, Daniel grabbed his knee and writhed. Charles put his finger to his lips, warning them to keep quiet. Beau whispered the message to Daniel.

"Don't squeeze the rock," Charles said. "It'll give away our position."

Beau nodded and tucked it into his shirt.

"You've marinated well enough," a demon squealed from the main tunnel. "Come to your feet, my darlings."

When the swimmers stood, the river proved to be waist deep. Their blistered skin was a lighter shade of red than the demons'. They flexed their arms and bared their teeth to intimidate each other.

"The last one standing gets moved a hundred yards downstream. That's a hundred yards closer to joining us. The losers will stay put. If you're a coward and choose not to participate, move upstream now." They must've known better than to show any cowardice. All of them remained, snarling at each other like mad beasts.

"Very well." A demon came to the edge of the embankment and raised his arm. He balled a fist and jerked it down. "Begin."

Splashing blood and steam obscured the chaotic brawl. Battle cries and anguished screams reverberated throughout the cavern. The demons congregated and pointed to different individuals, placing their bets.

Daniel and Beau came to either side of Charles and watched.

“What’s your plan?” Beau asked.

Charles had no idea. There was no easy way to get through the tunnel without being seen. “When the brawl is over, they’ll clear out,” Charles said. “We can try to make it to the next tunnel and stay hidden. It’s not much, but it’s a start.”

The brawl had already thinned out. Fighters gave up and waded off. The last man roared and beat his chest.

“Winner,” a demon announced, “step forward. We’ll fish you out and move you downstream.”

Another demon nocked an arrow to his bow and aimed. A chain was fixed to the end of the arrow and tied around the demon’s waist.

The victor went wide-eyed and shouted, “Come on! Shoot me! I’ll pull you in, you privileged weakling.”

The demon released, and the arrow pierced the winner’s rib cage. The man groaned. With shaking hands, he grabbed the chain and yanked. The demon lurched forward, but followed up with a tug that brought the man ashore. Other demons surrounded and beat him until he was still.

“This is ridiculous,” Daniel said. “You really think we can sneak out of here?”

“Got any better ideas?” Charles asked.

“I got one.” Daniel crawled into the main chamber and hobbled to his feet. “Hey. I wanna talk to whoever’s in charge?”

Several demons turned. One launched an arrow that zipped by Daniel’s head and clanged against the cavern wall.

Beau buried his face in his hand. “What is he thinking?”

“He told us,” Charles said, “patience—”

“—isn’t his best virtue. I know.”

The gang of demons started after Daniel. He didn't back down, but limped straight at the oncoming mob. "Did you hear me? I wanna talk to whoever's in charge!"

A loud shot rang out, followed by a booming voice blaring from the right, "Halt!"

A rugged man wearing a goat's skull upon his head pointed a sawed-off shotgun at the band of demons. High on his upper back, between his shoulder blades and spine, sprouted twelve fused bones; six to either side. They were the skeletal frames for the dark scaly wings folded down his back. He was nine feet tall, with thick arms and legs.

"I've got this one," he said, "so move on out."

The demons obeyed, dragging the unconscious man downstream about twenty-five yards before tossing him back into the river.

"This isn't good," Charles grumbled.

"Who is this?" Beau asked.

"A Fallen One," Charles said, "like Asmodeus, Lilith, and Mammon. But worse."

The ancient demon lowered his weapon into a holster attached to the tactical belt around his waist and brought a cigar to his mouth. Forcing smoke from his nose, he snarled, "You two best come on out from there."

Charles and Beau crawled into the main tunnel. Upstream, past the demon general, flecks of fire issued from a cave glowing with lava that oozed into the bloody river. The smell of iron and decay lingered like moisture in the air; hot fumes swelled and rolled in the shimmering light. The heat didn't bother Charles, but he wished there was more smoke. Daniel, however, took heaving breaths and staggered.

"We need you to give us safe passage out of here," Daniel said.

"Safe passage?" The demon jerked his cigar from his mouth and smoke wafted over his massive head. He wore metal bracers on his forearms and a leather breastplate. His dark pants were thick with padding. Metal claws protruded from the toecap of his boots.

"Master." Charles bowed. "Your presence—"

"Save your venerations for someone who cares," the demon growled. He stroked his thick goatee and pointed his cigar at Daniel. "As for you. If you want safe passage, come 'ere."

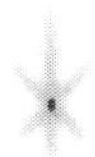

DANIEL

Drained. Lightheaded and thirsty. Burned and aching. Daniel wavered on the brink of collapse. Sheer determination kept his feet under him. His thoughts trailed from him like the fumes issuing from the boiling river. Despite dire signs of heat exhaustion and heat stroke, he felt he couldn't die even if he wanted to. Why else would the Angel of Death be coming to kill him? Why else would Fortuna say he could make it back home if he chose to? If Hell couldn't kill him, it would make him stronger.

Daniel said, "Are you going to help us or not?"

The demon puffed on his cigar, glaring at Daniel. His eyes became bright red. A V-shaped vein emerged from the center of his forehead. "Don't make me tell you again."

Pain throbbed from Daniel's knee as he limped toward the demon. The collar of his t-shirt tore when he pulled it to release the tightness irritating his neck. He flexed his jittery arms and huffed through his nose.

"Who are you anyway?" He could almost sense Charles and Beau cowering behind him on account of his tone, but Daniel didn't care. This heat filled him with a rage that begged to be unleashed.

The demon curled his lip and coiled like a spring, ready to bounce. "I'm Azazel."

His voice rumbled through the cave. The ground seemed to wobble, and Daniel sank to a knee. After gathering his bearings, he continued toward Azazel. The demon's face had darkened to purple. His eyes and veins glowed with inward fire. "This is my world. Yer disrespect will not serve you well."

Daniel stopped where Azazel had pointed. Glowering, the demon growled. He took a long drag from his cigar and exhaled. His face returned to its original state. "This is where you belong. I'm yer master, but Satan—he wants to see you. I'll let you pass," he pointed the cigar at Daniel's chest, "once I know that thing inside you is dead."

"You can't kill me," Daniel said.

"You know what I'm talking about." Azazel tossed the remainder of the cigar in his mouth, chewed, and swallowed. "The Holy Spirit doesn't belong here or in you, son."

"There's nothing in here," Daniel gestured to his heart. The heat of the chamber intensified. His eyes stung, and he burned with rage.

Azazel put his hands behind his back and lifted his chin. "We've watched you for a time. You've done well, but the parasite needs to go. It's holding you back. Yer better off without it."

Behind Daniel, Beau said, "The Angel of Death—"

"—isn't here and couldn't stop me if he tried." Azazel's face swelled with each word he spoke. "Let's exorcise that little pest."

There was a flash of light. A massive force struck Daniel's face, and he fell back.

"The righteousness of that Spirit," Azazel growled, "makes me sick!"

Daniel groaned. The left side of his face stung. His head swam in a haze of throbbing pain. He tried to regain his feet, but fell forward. Azazel pushed him over with his foot. "It wants to leave you, Daniel. Stop clinging to it. Let it go."

Beau lunged, but Azazel caught him by the arm and slammed him hard to his back, enough to shake the floor. Daniel tried to get up, but Azazel stomped on him and forced him back to the floor.

Charles stepped forward. "If you inadvertently kill him, it would ruin everything."

"Come here, you skinny twig."

Charles blinked like a lost forest creature and did as he was told. Once within reach, Azazel gripped Charles's collar and slung him to the far side of the cave against the wall, where he crumpled.

Azazel scowled at Daniel. Saliva oozed from his teeth. "Take up yer rage. It swells within you, son. But that Spirit..." Azazel sniffed deeply. "It's still in there."

Seeing Azazel with his eyes closed, Daniel hobbled to his feet. Pain whirled around his knee. He supported it with his hand, while gaining some distance between him and Azazel. "There's nothing inside me."

"That will soon be true." Azazel stepped after him.

Knowing he couldn't leave Charles and Beau behind, Daniel braced himself against a wall and watched Azazel approach. The demon removed a sword with a curved blade from a leather sheath. With it, he lifted Daniel's chin to observe the scar. The sharp blade pressed into his skin and relieved the itch. Daniel whimpered. Tears darted from his eyes.

"Within your weak carcass, blood boils like the river before you. You'll make a fine lieutenant." Azazel stooped and whispered. "Just need the proper push."

Daniel's voice trembled. "I don't belong here."

"Not yet. You need to earn it, but you will." Azazel pulled the sword from Daniel's scar. Heat and wetness reinvigorated the itch. Daniel applied pressure to his wound. He slunk past Azazel and stumbled toward Beau, who lay twisting weakly where Azazel had planted him. "Stop cowering," the demon said. "You serve me. Always have. Nothing's changed."

"I don't know you." Daniel fell and kept crawling toward Beau.

"But you do," the demon growled. "You call upon me each time you boil over with anger. Every time you lash out, I am there. Violence comes to you naturally. You partake of it shamelessly. It has made you what you are. Accept this and you'll be free from that spirit."

A massive weight, like a sledgehammer, struck Daniel's lower back. He rolled and tried to shimmy toward Beau. Azazel pressed a heavy boot on his chest. The claws protruding from the toe cap pierced his skin. Azazel glared with a menacing smile and spat onto Daniel's burned cheek. It sizzled against his skin. Unable to breathe or scream, he slapped at his face, squirming.

He grabbed Azazel's foot and twisted it. The claws dug four crescents into his chest, tearing his shirt. Fearful, Daniel kicked at the demon's knee repeatedly.

Charles leaped on Azazel's back and wrapped his arms tight around his thick throat. "Get Beau's rock," he cried.

With one swift motion, Azazel wrenched Charles off and slung him against the wall a second time. A loud thud rolled like thunder through the cavern. Dust fell from the steam-covered ceiling. Charles lay on the floor, coughing and groaning. Daniel hastened to Beau, but Azazel cut him off and pinned him.

"It's almost done," the demon grumbled, slamming a hard fist against Daniel's face. The back of his head struck the ground. Everything blurred. An oscillating ring chimed in his ears. Large, powerful hands gripped his throat. Daniel pulled at the demon's thumbs, but Azazel was immovable. Daniel weakened. The cavern darkened. Shadows wavered in the thick fog overhead. Croaking for a final breath, his hands slipped from Azazel's grip and dropped to the floor.

"Azrael is here," Beau murmured.

Azazel released Daniel's neck and stood, looking about. Daniel gasped for air, which burned his lungs. Hatred coursed through him. It had replaced the oxygen in his blood. He wanted to fight more than ever, but could barely move.

"Is that supposed to frighten me?" Azazel asked. "Even if he were, he's no match. I'm far more powerful than any of those subservient to the Almighty Pretender."

Beau reached into his front pocket and cupped the keystone with both hands. "Then why are you here and not there?"

"Time for a swim, little man." Azazel marched to Beau, who squeezed the keystone. Azazel recoiled and turned away. Black wings sprouted and shielded him from the light. The sight of it sent chills through Daniel. Beau came to his feet and approached Azazel, squeezing it tighter.

Azazel stepped back. "Too late. It's done." He jumped into the steam overhead. It rippled over Beau, down the tunnel, and into the cave oozing with lava.

Grimacing and grunting, Beau held the keystone firmly and limped over to Daniel. "I would've done it sooner, but my head—everything's muddled."

Daniel dropped his head to the stone floor. "Me too. I can't think straight, and my face hurts where he spit on me."

"Don't touch it." Beau frowned. "Is the light helping at all?"

Daniel shrugged. "A little, maybe."

The light from the keystone cooled Daniel's skin. Beads of sweat prickled along his forehead. The air had thinned, and the stench of molten rock and the boiling river had diminished. Beau helped him to his feet. Charles came over with his arms wrapped around his ribs, as if holding himself together.

Daniel looked downstream where the embankment followed the river. Demons stood along it, glaring.

"If Azazel can't stand the light," Charles said, "then they can't either."

"The light helps, but I don't feel right." Daniel stumbled.

Beau steadied him. "I'll carry you if I have to."

"I don't need to be coddled. Just hold on to that light," Daniel said. "The brighter it is, the better."

Eyeing the scars on Daniel's chest, Charles said, "The second chamber is cold, so it will heal us." He glanced at his vest and found the buttons had been torn off. With a look of disgust, he unclasped the watch's chain from the buttonhole, placed it in his pants pocket, and then tossed the vest into the simmering river.

"The Holy Spirit—" Daniel massaged his throat and winced. "Do you still see it?"

Charles stared into Daniel's eyes.

"You said you wouldn't lie," Daniel rasped.

Charles shook his head. "It comes and goes."

"It's gone." Daniel glared back at the violent demons crowding the embankment. "All I feel is a need to cause pain."

"It's the heat," Beau said. "You'll feel better once we're out of here."

"You're so sure of that," Daniel said brusquely.

He took a strange pleasure in how Beau averted his eyes and shrank away. Somehow, it allowed him to bear the misery he felt in this world. If he asserted himself a little more—lash out and dominate those who crossed him in any way—he'd hold dominion over all of them.

Beau's face looked pained. "I'm sorry."

"You're still alive," Charles said. "That's what matters."

"It matters to you." Daniel peered into the boiling river. "You want to use me for your own gain. I don't have to go anywhere. I can stay right here and jump into this river if I want."

"Choose life, Daniel," Beau said timidly.

Daniel swallowed and closed his eyes. Fury caused his body to quiver. A deep breath helped it to subside. Another brought tears. "We need to hurry before I change my mind."

Chapter Fifteen

Hot-Blooded and Coldhearted

BEAU

Demons of Violence grumbled empty threats while scrambling into nearby tunnels to avoid the light emanating from Beau's fist. Though the light helped to dampen his pain, no matter how hard Beau squeezed the keystone, his back ached, and it felt like someone had inserted razor blades at his knees. This chamber was insufferable. The heat and the stench alone made him reluctant to breathe.

The farther they followed the simmering river of blood, the worse Daniel fared. He hissed and grimaced almost constantly. Azazel had swelled his eyes shut and burned a hole through his cheek with spittle. The scar on his neck trickled with blood.

Just behind them, Charles trudged along with his head down and arms wrapped around his ribs. He said little, even though scurrying demons ridiculed him, calling him a deserter and traitor. Beau doubted any of their words mattered much to Charles. Hard to tell, since his bowler hat shielded most of his face.

Daniel tripped and staggered. Afraid that he might slip into the river, Beau grabbed his arm.

"I don't need your help." Daniel righted his footing and jerked away.

Daniel's suffering went beyond flesh and bone. His manner had darkened and festered. He moved like a predator seeking prey. Beau had to mind his words and his gaze. The slightest thing set Daniel off. *Maybe Azazel was right. Maybe it was too late for Daniel.*

The cave narrowed, and the river shallowed. Demons lingered along the embankment behind them. The path ahead was clear. The few souls in the river lay supine, as if to stay warm. Their skin was dark red, but they had no horns hammered into their heads yet. They shielded their eyes from the keystone's light and bellowed curses.

Daniel yelled back at them. His voice had grown hoarse, making his words sound more like snarls and roars. He touched the side of his head, slowed to a stop, and collapsed. With no attempt to catch himself, his head thudded against the stone floor. Beau squatted by him and patted his back. "Daniel?"

Charles knelt on the other side, shaking his head. "I wish he'd stop passing out."

"Do you think he's dead?"

"No, I don't think he can die unless Azrael catches him." Charles flicked his bowler higher onto his head. "Why else would he come after him?"

"Maybe it's better if we let it happen."

Charles frowned. "Then all this would be for nothing."

"Can you see what's happening to him? His temper is worse. He's losing hope. Besides, maybe Azrael is coming to help."

"You know Azrael wants him dead." Charles sighed and peered down the tunnel. "His temper will settle once we get him out of here. Come on."

They draped Daniel's arms behind their necks and carried him. The river retreated to a stream and pressed against the opposing wall of the cave. The embankment descended and merged with the riverbed.

Ahead, they heard a deep voice echoing, "... therefore you have reached the end of subservience. Transcended your human nature and evolved into something greater." They rounded a curve, which revealed an assembly of about two dozen people crowded before a row of fiery spears less than fifty yards away. "You each have earned... Who's that?"

The congregants turned. Red shimmering eyes gleamed at them.

"Squeeze that rock tighter," Charles whispered.

"What are they doing?" Beau raised his clenched fist and squeezed. Angry, bloodstained faces squinted and snarled.

"It's a ceremony for their horns." Charles shifted to get a better hold on Daniel. "If that light doesn't move them, be ready to fight."

When they were less than ten feet from the crowd, the same voice announced, "Let them come forward." The crowd scowled at Beau, Charles, and Daniel, but allowed them to pass. Beau's hand and forearm trembled with muscle fatigue and fear. They came to a line of six horned demons in dark robes. Their six-foot-long spears had metal tips that burned and glowed.

Charles canted his hat. "Let us through. Azazel already told us that Satan is expecting us."

"I know," said a figure, who paced slowly behind the line of armed demons. "But who's this light-bearer?"

"I'm Beau."

"A shadow spirit, yes?" The figure continued to pace.

Beau stood taller, feeling Daniel's weight bearing against his side. "Not anymore."

The figure stopped. "We'll let you pass, but only if the Holy Spirit has left your undead friend. Kill the light so I can verify that it's gone."

"We don't have time for that," Charles said. "Azrael is coming after him."

"Azrael is your problem." The figure moved closer to the line of demons that shielded him. "I couldn't care less if you make it to the Ninth Hell. Satan is merely amused and can do without your company, so do as I say."

Fear rose from Beau's gut, but he managed to swallow it and say one word. "No."

Murmurs and hisses erupted from those gathered. Claws scraped down Beau's back. He grunted. A searing pain trailed where his skin had ripped. He turned and extended his lighted fist. The attackers backed away.

"Everyone, stop." The demon pushed through the line of soldiers and revealed himself. His leathery red skin rippled as if his blood boiled beneath the surface. Unlike the others, his goat-like horns were a dull, earthy gold. He entered the light, and pus leaked from his pink eyes. An iron war hammer rested against his shoulder. In his other hand, he carried a satchel full of small, black horns.

Charles nodded to the demon. "We are at your mercy."

"Mercy?" the demon looked bemused. A chorus of voices seemed to come from his mouth when he spoke. "You've lost your jacket, your tie, and vest." Beau squeezed the stone tighter and more pus flowed from the demon's eyes, though it didn't seem to faze him. "Even your eyes have devolved. Soon, you'll be left with nothing."

"What would you know?" Beau growled.

"I'm Abaddon," the demon snarled. "With one word, I could have these demons destroy you. Azrael will find you and your man splattered along the walls and scattered across this floor in fleshy pieces should he somehow breach our home. Now put out the light, or your journey ends here."

Charles adjusted his grip on Daniel and righted his posture. Beau brought his lit fist closer to his chest and shook his head.

"So be it." Abaddon circled them and addressed the assembly. "No one gets their horns until that light is out, and these maggots are torn to shreds. Fail and you all return upriver."

Abaddon left through a side tunnel. Those with spears blocked their way out, while the others closed in behind them.

"I got Daniel," Charles said. "Squeeze that rock."

Beau kneeled and squeezed with both hands over his head. The crowd backed away, but a fiery spear stabbed his forearm. The light shrank. He moved the keystone to his good hand.

"Make the light brighter. Keep moving!" Charles shouted while he dragged Daniel.

Beau strained his arms, but his strength was depleting. He focused the light on the armed demons. Claws, fists, and feet reached Beau's back, where there was no light protecting him. Another demon jabbed his weapon at Beau's face. He dodged it, grabbing the pole just beneath the steaming hot spear, and with a grunt, yanked the weapon from the demon's grip.

Charles attempted to do the same, but cried out when a fiery tip penetrated his palm. Other tips jabbed into his arm and torso. He bent over Daniel, clutching his wounded hand. The other demons poked at Charles's back repeatedly while other unarmed demons kicked at his ribs and head.

Another blade stabbed into Beau's shoulder and became lodged. He dropped the weapon he had beside Charles and removed the one stuck in his shoulder. *Mind over matter.* Snapping to his feet, he snarled and tightened his lit fist. The demons backed away. Beau stabbed at a demon that had lunged toward him. It backed off while others dashed toward him. Beau whirled the spear in a wide circle, slicing the attackers.

Another spear came down at Charles, and he swatted it away. His bowler hat fell from his head. He picked it up and pulled Daniel away from demons who were tugging at his feet. Beau kicked one of the armed demons into another and sent them both to the walls of the cave. With another wave of his spear, Beau knocked the remaining armed demons out of their path.

They were no longer surrounded. Those remaining were hesitant to attack. They followed Beau, Charles, and Daniel, perhaps waiting for an opportunity to strike. Backing away, Beau held the keystone in one hand and a spear in the other.

Charles gasped, "We're almost there."

Two demons lunged after them and Beau swung the spear hard enough to launch one into the other. "They're weak like everyone in Greed," Beau growled.

Charles dragged Daniel farther ahead. "I see the exit."

Beau followed, while keeping his eyes on the few remaining demons. A thin, icy wind pressed into his aching back and entered his wounded shoulder. A tingling sensation seized him. His skin hissed as if burning and stole his breath. He dropped to a knee. The keystone slipped from his fingers and rolled behind him. He heard the demons sprinting toward him. Unable to see, he came to his feet and swung the spear in an X pattern. His foot bumped into what he hoped was the keystone. He threw the weapon toward the attackers and grabbed the rock. He squeezed. His fist lit like a lantern and the attackers fled. Someone pulled on the back of his shirt. Beau slung his lighted fist rearwards.

"It's me," Charles said. "Oh look. The hornless ones are *running away*. Enjoy the river, cowards!"

"Where's Daniel?" Beau panted.

"Just outside. Already healing."

A hard blast of frosty air jarred them when they exited the cave. Thick frozen weeds crunched under their feet. The frosted land smelled like preserved cadavers. The gray overcast was much like the sky over Gluttony, except colder and drier. Curving right, the thin, red stream descended across a valley and emptied into a lake roaring with flames.

In a pocket of hard sand between mounds of tall frozen grass, Daniel lay shivering in a fetal position. Charles dropped beside him and stretched his wounded hand skyward. "Just lay down, Beau. It's gonna hurt, but we'll be healed."

The cold penetrated Beau's aching bones. He stumbled and fell on the other side of Daniel, gripping the gaping wound in his shoulder. Icy air slipped under his hand and pressed into his gash. White frost expanded over his injury and dug into his flesh, issuing horrible snapping and crackling noises. It felt like a fire ignited within the wound. He writhed and cried out, thinking that he'd burst into flames, until he felt the sensation of hammers beating thousands of nails all over him. Then, with sudden relief, the cold released him.

Beau came to his knees. Curious, he pulled open the tear in his shirt sleeve. Frost covered his skin. Carefully, he grazed his forefingers over the place where his cut was, and numb tingles flourished. Just feet away, Charles examined his hand, which now had a dab of frost on the palm and backside.

"Let's try not to get sliced up anymore on the road ahead," Charles said.

"I thought I was dying," Beau gasped. "But I'm healed—like you said."

"Beau? Charles?" Daniel croaked. Frost covered his eyes and half his face. "I can't see."

"We made it to the forest," Beau said.

"Why can't I see?" Daniel touched his face. "My face..."

"Your eyes are covered in ice," Beau said. "We're in the cold. That's supposed to heal everything."

"But I'm blind."

"No, you're not," Charles said. "You need to warm up. Luckily, there's a lake of fire nearby. Take him closer to it, Beau."

Beau stood. His feet and hands ached from the cold. Though his shoulder and back were stiff, he felt fine. He took Daniel's hands and helped him up. Charles remained on the ground.

"Aren't you coming?" Beau asked him.

"Give me some time," Charles said. "I won't be long."

Daniel and Beau lumbered across the valley. The hardness of the ground loosened into soft dirt. The frost covering Daniel's eyes thawed and leaked down his face as they neared the fire. About twenty yards from the lake, they sat down. Daniel propped his elbows on his knees and rested his head on his arms. Beau massaged his shoulder, wiping away the remaining ice crystals that melted against his reddened skin.

He sighed while listening to the whooshing flames. Not long ago, the sight of such a blaze would cause him to shrink away into the shadows, but now he couldn't be more thankful for it. An anguished scream disturbed the silence. It was Charles.

Daniel tried to get up, but Beau caught his arm. "Give him a minute."

"He's never screamed before." Daniel looked down at the holes in his shirt. The cuts in his chest were gone.

"He'll be all right." Beau noticed Daniel still had the same angry look in his eyes. "Feeling any better?"

Daniel sat down and drew a circle in the sand with his finger. "I don't know, Beau."

"I imagine most people would have quit by now." Beau pocketed his keystone and massaged his forearms. "You're not like most people."

"This place is rubbing off on me." Daniel drew a larger circle around the smaller one. He rested his arms on his knees and stared at the fire. "I feel infected. That getting out of here will be like sneaking out of quarantine. Maybe I'll damage everyone who comes close to me. Maybe that's what Satan wants."

"You're not diseased. There's so much good in you."

"I don't think so." Daniel's face shimmered with light from the fire. "This isn't going away. It's always going to be in my head. In my heart. Some things can't be fixed, Beau."

Behind them, Charles approached. He was studying his bowler hat and clicking his tongue. "This ol' hat's done for." He flung it into the flames with a side-arm throw. "Lost my coat. My tie. My vest. And now my hat. Abaddon told me I'd end up with nothing, but I still have my watch." He pulled it out and rolled it in his fingers.

"Who's Abaddon?" Daniel asked.

"Another ancient demon. While you were out, he sicced a band of demons on us." Charles placed his hands on his hips and took a deep breath. "We ended up having to fight 'em off. You should've seen Beau. He took one of their weapons and beat 'em with it."

Daniel wiped away his drawing. "Congratulations."

Beau looked toward the forest. The leafless trees stretched and swayed in a steadfast wind. "We're heading through there next?"

"Pretty much." Charles pointed along the shore. "We'll follow the lake until we find a thin, red stream, which will lead us to and through the last part of Violence." He clapped his hands together. When he saw Daniel sulking, he asked, "Are you thinking about giving up again?"

Daniel smacked his lips. "I don't want to. It's just that I don't think I can let any of this go. I'm already haunted by lesser things. My father. Iraq. Everything. And the Holy Spirit—I think Azazel got rid of it."

"It's not something that can be taken from you," Charles said. "You would have to let it go, and I don't think you've done that. Not yet, at least."

"I don't see why it would stick around," Daniel said. "It's given up on every soul down here. Tossed them out like trash, and look where I am. Why would it care about me?"

Beau shrugged. "You're still alive, and I figure it'll keep helping you."

"Maybe that's what was trying to tell me to go back to Azrael." Daniel looked at Beau. "Maybe that's what I should do. Stop pushing deeper into Hell and end this?"

"Check this out." Charles unbuttoned his shirt and revealed a vague half-moon scar under his chest. "I was famous for being heartless, but I'm not heartless anymore."

"You let the cold heal your heart?" Beau asked. "Why?"

Charles buttoned his shirt back up and pulled a lump of coal from his pocket. "I'm carrying around a rock of my own, because I remember who I am. The Holy Spirit is stronger than you think. No one can coax it out of you or kill it. Not me, Azazel, or anybody else. Maybe not even you."

"I never felt it," Daniel said. "It's pretty much been useless all my life."

"You're blind to it, but I'm not." Charles pointed at his green eyes. "I'm probably the only soul in Hell who's felt it. It may ruin me, but it's worth feeling alive again."

"That doesn't help you." Daniel stared out into the fire. "You're stuck here no matter what."

"Look at it this way." Charles pocketed his coal. "If I can change, then you can too. Now. How about a stroll through the woods?"

Chapter Sixteen

The Sad End of an Old Friend

DANIEL

The urge for violence ebbed like a receding wave. In its wake remained the skeletons that refused to stay buried in the shallow graves of Daniel's mind. Snapshots of his parents flashed through his thoughts. Their voices and words seemed too distant to remember. His memories were silent, but he could see and feel everything he felt when he shoved his father over the coffee table. Shame had washed over him while he watched his mother drop to the floor, crying into her husband's chest. In that very brief moment, which he'd visualized countless times since, he saw them take each other's hand. Then came the last words his father said to him.

Just go then.

At the time, Daniel heard only rejection in those words. *"We don't want you."* A weak retort from the man everyone still saw as the town drunk even after years of sobriety. But over time, the words had evolved into question after question. *Why? Is this what you want? Is this who you are? Are you ready to come home? Will you repent?*

The questions seeped into the soil of his mind and sprouted all sorts of thoughts. Some grew. Others died. These last words from his father mattered, but he didn't know why.

Just go then.

"It's not that simple," Daniel muttered.

The breeze settled when they entered the dense forest. With no path, they kept the fiery lake to their right just far enough to keep them warm. Large black ants infested tree trunks and scurried into the soft powdery soil. Milky fog tore between skinny, contorted branches. They slouched under long slivers of cobwebs drifting like ghostly banners. Like the one on Grandfather Mountain, these trees were dead, depleted, and disfigured.

Beau failed to duck under a low, brittle branch and broke it. An anguished cry came from a hole in the tree and startled them. Blood dribbled from where the tree splintered. "Oh," it whimpered. "You cruel beast. How could you?"

Charles grimaced at the fractured limb. "Try not to touch them." He squatted lower, treading deeper.

"They bleed?" Beau's face wrinkled. With a shaking hand, he placed his palm on the trunk. "I'm so sorry. I didn't mean to."

"Don't beat yourself up," Charles said. "Just be careful not to disturb any others."

"Are people trapped inside 'em?" Daniel asked.

"No," Charles said. "The people are the trees."

Daniel noticed the trees surrounding him had no bark. The exposed wood was gray, like the flesh of those in other hells. Daniel brushed his fingers along a trunk. It felt cool, dry, and smooth. Thin black veins ran just beneath the surface. A wide knot looked like a gaping mouth lined with greenish teeth. Two sunken eyes faced skyward.

"Why trees?" Daniel asked.

Charles shrugged. "They destroyed their bodies. The forest is dense because they destroyed themselves to hurt others. Whenever the wind blows, they smother and break each other."

"Because they committed suicide?" Daniel asked.

"It involves more than that," Charles said. "Many of these people murdered others and then turned around and murdered themselves."

"What if they weren't in their right mind because of drugs or something?"

"I don't know," Charles said.

"What about refusing medical treatment because they're sick of suffering?" Daniel asked.

"Then they aren't trying to hurt others, are they?"

Daniel had so many questions. He already felt the punishment of eternal damnation was heavy-handed and unfair. The thought that anyone was put here because they felt a need to escape a painful world saddened him. "What if they were afraid?"

Charles stopped and turned. "What's with you?"

Daniel stepped up to him. "You were there when they were sentenced here. You should know."

"I told you," Charles said, "they hurt themselves to hurt others. That's why they're here. They weren't trying to escape pain. They weren't depressed. They wanted others to be hurt by their actions. Many times, they killed others before doing it to themselves." He eyed Beau. "Wanna speak up? You should know more about this than me."

Lines deepened along Beau's brow. He seemed disgusted. "When demons provoked people to take their own lives, I'd blow my horn. It helped some, but those who had been oppressed much longer..." Beau shook his head and sighed. "In the end, families suffer from the sin of suicide, but we all have sinned. And we can all be forgiven, including them. Not everyone who took their lives was sent here. That much, I know."

Fresh tears rolled down Daniel's cheek. He scratched them off. "A friend of mine killed himself recently. Captain Jones. I say he's a friend, but he's more like a brother. He was my commander. Never thought he'd do something like that. He believed in things, went to church, and all that. I told 'im I'd keep in touch, but—you know me enough by now to know how that went."

"Don't blame yourself for whatever he did," Beau said.

"How could I?" Daniel asked defensively. "I had no idea what was up with him—been too busy. Maybe things would have been different if I had, though, but I can't help but see that I did him like I did my parents. Just left and never looked back. Pretty selfish of me."

Charles took out his watch and started opening and clicking. "Everyone's selfish. I bet a majority of those in Heaven are too."

"You're not thinking selfishly, though," Beau said. "Sounds like you care to me."

"I never reached out to my parents." Daniel caressed the scar on his neck. It didn't heal like everything else did. "They could be dead for all I know."

"You can fix that when you get back home," Beau said.

"I've had that chance for years, but I never did," Daniel said. "If it takes falling into Hell for me to care, then maybe I'm doing it for the wrong reasons. I shouldn't care because I fear repercussions. I should care because I want to."

"We're all victims here." Charles stepped over several roots and ducked under low branches. "No one in Hell takes responsibility for their actions. No one repents. We give elaborate discourses on the wonderful things we've done, and why we shouldn't be here, but we don't repent. It's everybody else's fault. I stole from rich folks. I still think they could afford to lose a priceless painting or an expensive pair of trousers."

"What we're trying to say is," Beau said, "at least, you're willing to admit you have a problem. That's a start."

They shifted farther from the lake for easier terrain. Daniel kept an eye on the blades of fire that danced beyond the thicket of trees beneath wavering fumes that rose into the gray sky. Wood cracked and several branches dropped twenty yards from them. Painful groans cried out as blood poured from the trees. A large bird leaped and disappeared high into the fog.

"See that?" Charles pointed. "It's a harpy. Part bird. Part human. All female."

"Are they going to be a problem?" Beau asked.

"They won't bother us," Charles said, "but they'll peck and scratch at the trees."

"Never hurts to be ready." Beau patted his front pocket.

"There's a clearing." Daniel nodded ahead. "Looks like a path."

"Wait here. I'll check it out." Charles walked to the clearing. When he got there, he grabbed a handful of dirt and let it sift through his fingers. He looked around and waved for Daniel and Beau to join him. "It looks as if someone made this path recently. It curves with the lake."

Daniel and Beau took great care not to break any hanging limbs on their way to Charles. When they came to the trail, an eerie whisper prickled Daniel's ear. *Strong.*

Daniel looked at Beau and Charles. "Did one of you say something?"

Beau looked at Charles.

"Are you kidding me?" Charles rolled his eyes. "I'm standing right here. Why would I—oh, never mind."

Strong.

"Neither of you heard that?" Daniel turned in the sound's direction.

"Hear what?" Beau asked.

"Strong."

"Someone's calling my name." Daniel started in the direction he heard the voice.

Beau got in front of him. "Remember where you are?"

"He's right, Daniel," Charles said. "It's leading you away from where we need to go. It could be Azrael."

"It's not him." Daniel heard it again and pulled Beau aside. More certain of where it came from, he sprinted. The voice grew louder and clearer. The path ended at a tree that was strangled by a single spiraling vine. Its pale, gray wood seemed shiny, as if it were younger and more vibrant than its neighbors. He focused on the trunk in search of a familiar face.

"You are—really fast." Charles bent down and propped his hands on his knees. "What are you doing?"

Please, Sergeant Strong—help me.

Daniel grabbed the vine wrapped around the tree and pulled until it broke with a soft thud.

Beau came trudging up and panting. "What's going on?"

The voice said, "Thank you, Sergeant Strong."

"I heard it that time. It called you sergeant." Charles straightened his back and scratched his head. "Is this—"

"Captain Jones?" Daniel gazed at the trunk again and saw a horrifying version of his former team leader. An elongated face with hollow eyes and a gaping, displaced jaw made Daniel sick to his stomach. He looked away. "Is that you, sir?"

"It's me," the tree said. "Why are you here?"

"I was about to ask you the same thing," Daniel said.

Captain Jones groaned. "I messed up."

Daniel hung his head and rubbed his fingers through his hair. Unable to bear the contorted face of his former commander, he stared at the ground. "What happened?"

Captain Jones said, "My wife left me for my brother. Took the boys and blamed me for getting deployed. She told me she had needs, and the boys needed a father."

"It was your job, though," Daniel said.

"That didn't matter to her," Captain Jones said. "My brother and my wife. Not able to see my kids or do anything about it. I couldn't live with that."

Daniel squatted and ran his fingers through the loose sand. "What did you do?"

"I did what my parents said. Focused on what *I* had to do. I drove to *my* house and went into *my* bedroom, where *my* brother slept with *my* wife. Shot him. My wife bawled her eyes out. I relished her screams and turned that gun on myself." Captain Jones cried. "I didn't know my oldest son was watching me."

Daniel covered his face. "That's terrible."

"I know," Captain Jones said. "I keep telling myself it never happened. That at some point, I'll wake up. But what's done is done."

"If you had to do it over again," Charles leaned against another tree, "would you?"

"My brother and my wife with my kids!" Captain Jones sobbed. "I'd never let that be. Never."

Daniel swallowed. "Your kids..."

"My boys will always hurt because of what I did, but they'll get by," Captain Jones said. "Though nothing's set in stone, I see they'll live good lives. While they're young, the slightest actions, the tiniest things, can change them. What I did will haunt my oldest son, but I already see him and his brother overcoming it. I'm proud of them. If they stick with their current path, they'll be fine. The older they get, the more predictable their journeys become. It's the same with all of us. We stay in our lane, driving north or south, rounding curves, taking back roads—but all the while we know where we intend to go."

"What about me then?" Immediately, Daniel felt selfish for asking.

"You already know where you're heading," Captain Jones said harshly.

"I'm trying to escape this place. If you know something that'll help, please tell me."

After a lengthy pause, Captain Jones said, "I can't tell you what I see. The one who woke me told me I couldn't."

"Who woke you?" Daniel demanded.

"I forgot, Sergeant."

"That doesn't make sense." Daniel folded his arms. "How could you forget?"

"He did something to my memory," Captain Jones said. "When he said I couldn't tell you what I see in your future, I couldn't see it anymore."

Daniel rubbed his face. "What can you tell me then?"

"The one you're running from—what is his name?" Captain Jones asked.

Beau perked up and said, "Azrael."

"Names have meanings. Do you know what that name means?" Captain Jones asked.

Daniel looked at Beau and Charles. Neither of them seemed to know. "I don't know."

"It means *One whom God helps*," Captain Jones said. "If Azrael is here, he's here to help you."

An invisible weight that had been lingering over Daniel dropped upon him. He sank to a knee. In a way, it was validating. He *knew* Azrael was there to help him. *But I ran away anyway.* Daniel felt a need to head back the way they came, but he wasn't sure if he'd be running to Azrael or to the violent nest of demons where he had fought a desperate desire to jump into the river.

"That heretic told me to choose death." Daniel turned to Charles and Beau. "Is it true? Is that what his name means?"

"Your friend's mistaken. He's the Angel of Death," Charles said. "His purpose is to take life."

"Why are you still worried about what those heretics said?" Beau asked. "They don't care about you."

"They called me a murderer—even though I haven't murdered anybody yet." Daniel turned back to the tree. "Sir—"

"I'm tired," Captain Jones said. "You have a lot of questions. I don't have the answers, so listen carefully to what I say. We gravitate to the ones we serve. Those who serve themselves will be left to themselves. But those who are humble will be exalted."

"What does that even mean?" Daniel shouted. "Just tell me what I need to do, sir!"

A chilling breeze came from the tree. The gnarled image of his commander's face stared past him. Daniel balled his fists and left the way he came. "You wasted my time."

They silently walked along the dirt path with the fiery lake sitting to their right. Daniel scratched the scar on his neck. After a half-mile of silence, Daniel asked the question burning in his mind. "Why are we running from an angel whose name means *One whom God helps*?"

"Ever hear of Sodom and Gomorrah?" Charles hissed. "Should I remind you of the death of the firstborn in Egypt again?"

"What are you getting at?" Daniel asked.

"Let me say it once more, so you'll get it this time," Charles said. "Azrael isn't some sweet angel strumming a harp on a puffy white cloud. He's the destroyer. Anything foul to God is foul to him. He'll blot out whatever *He*"—Charles pointed to the sky—"finds unclean. *You* are here because *you're* unclean. We're running away for that reason."

The trees moaned as their trunks and canopies creaked and swayed in a brisk wind. Shrieks erupted from overhead. Daniel crouched as three harpies flew from a large conical nest high overhead. Limbs and branches dropped, and blood dripped like the start of a light rain. The broken trees sobbed. Another harpy peeked from the nest. It twisted its head and stared at Daniel with beady, black eyes. Though it had a long, pointed beak, its face looked human. The cawing of the fleeing harpies caught the stragglers' attention. It leaped into the air, revealing a feathered underside and wide wings as it fled.

"I'm glad they're skittish," Charles said.

"Me too." Beau returned the keystone to his pocket.

Daniel had nothing to add, so he moved on. He took the ring from his pocket and stared into the central diamond. Though he may escape Hell with his mind stained with misery and horrors, he longed to see Kristine's soft eyes again. A glimmer through the trees caught his attention. A thin red stream flowed from the lake and cut through the forest.

Chapter Seventeen

Canteen of Tears

DANIEL

The pale-red stream cut a thin line through the forest. It widened to about two feet wide, but was only an inch deep. Eventually, trees tapered off and dead grass gave way to hard sand. Once the forest was behind them, the fog slowly dissipated. Black smoke rose along the horizon and blanketed the sky. Glowing embers drifted and twinkled like fireflies. The air warmed and thickened, and a steady wind blew against their faces. The stench of carbon and sulfur irritated Daniel and brought on a cough. Beau took out the keystone, and it helped a little.

Ambient light glimmered against the underside of coal-colored clouds that belched flakes of fire upon a vast plain. Multitudes of people scurried over and between sand dunes, flailing and leaping about in a maniacal dance. Near the creek, charred bodies lay on their backs screaming while glaring at the sky; others sat and counted with their fingers while mumbling. Unable or unwilling to protect themselves, they remained still as burning cinders fell onto their skin. Wide-eyed and grimacing, they trembled and muttered to themselves.

"This is the last chamber of Violence," Charles said.

"I don't get it," Daniel said. "Why don't they get up and run to the forest?"

"We're paralyzed," growled someone from the crowd.

A man, scorched and smoking, lifted his head from the ground. "The Almighty Comforter saves some, but damns others. He forgives cowards and despises those who dare to think for themselves."

"But those running around aren't paralyzed," Daniel said. "They could make it."

"All who try fail," another soul wailed. "The wind would force them back, and they'd end up stuck in the sand, like the rest of us."

"Thanks to the All-Powerful, All-Loving Creator who put us here," another growled. "The Almighty Oppressor who rules with an iron fist and hides His failures by punishing those with the gall to criticize Him."

"As you can tell, they have a grudge." Charles gestured down the small stream. "Shall we skip the pleasantries and move along?"

The incapacitated sufferers were three yards from the stream that Daniel, Charles, and Beau had followed into this desert. Burning flakes of ash dissolved in the keystone's light. Far to the left, runners sprinted toward the forest, and, like the man had said, a wind swept them from their feet and raked them across the hard sands until they were stuck.

Beau relaxed his grip for a moment and small cinders poked into Daniel's arms and singed his hair. He swatted them off.

"Sorry." Beau moved the stone to his other hand. "My hand is sore from all the squeezing. Maybe you should try holding it."

"I told you before, it burned me once already," Daniel said.

Charles sniffed the air and cupped his ear. "Wait here a minute. Think there's a shortcut." He hiked to the top of a large dune to their right and peered out. When he waved for Beau and Daniel to join him, they started up the slope. The sand was hard, slippery, and abrasive, but they made the climb with little difficulty. When they reached the summit, Charles pointed to a bright crack in the low-lying clouds about a thousand yards away. From it, rain fell into a silvery lake that waxed and waned against a brown shore. "The stream we've been following will take us to that."

Daniel licked his cracked lips and swallowed. "Is that water?"

"It's the source of Hell's rivers," Charles said. "It's the heart of all suffering—tears from the living world." Charles held his hand out and caught an ember. "The fire can't touch it. The ashes flame out in its lingering mist. It'll shield us all the way to the Eighth Hell."

"A lake of tears?" Daniel asked.

Charles nodded. "Earthly spirits gather the tears and drop them over a ruined shrine that sits concealed within a mountain. The tears sink from there and pour into here."

"If they can't make it to the woods, why not run to the lake?" Beau asked.

"Everyone in Violence is repulsed by its odor," Charles said.

A hot cinder burned the back of Daniel's neck. He brushed it off. "If that's where we're heading next, I'll meet you there."

Daniel trotted down the dune. His momentum caused him to stumble once the slope leveled. His tired, heavy legs didn't want to cooperate, but he set a quick pace that kept the drifting cinders from catching him. Gasping and pushing, his dash diminished. More flakes of fire stung his skin. Although his feet burned, he pushed harder, groaning and coughing, until the vague smell of water and salt caught his nose.

Falling softly, drizzling tears distorted the lake's surface and splattered quietly. Steam waved over it like a hot pot of coffee. Daniel collapsed and crawled to the shore. His rippling reflection glistened in the tears as he plunged his hands in. Dirt plumed within the lake and trailed to the right. He drank from his palms and lapped at his fingers. Millions of visions flipped through his head. Every image contained sorrow from the young and old, from fears and hardships. Their pain had remained with these tears. So many unfamiliar faces—all of them suffering… Feeling their sadness, Daniel wept.

After a moment, he regained control and drank some more. The images didn't occur this time, and for that, Daniel was grateful. Though the tears were salty and warm, he had an empty stomach and a dried-out throat. It felt wrong to drink the tears of all humanity, but it satisfied his thirst.

Footsteps came from behind. Daniel recognized it was Charles's gait by its cadence. "Drink while you can. There won't be another opportunity like this."

Beau gasped as he trudged toward the lake. He dropped beside Daniel and drank. After a few slurps, he sobbed too. "I feel—their sadness."

"Don't get caught up in all that." Charles looked down the lake's shore. "Just give yourself a little to drink before we go."

"It only happens with the first sip," Daniel said. "It's like whatever pain they were feeling stayed with their tears."

"It's better than nothing," Charles said. "Take advantage of it while you can."

Daniel washed his hands and arms. Its oily texture relieved his dried skin. Leaning closer, he splashed his hot face, and his scar twinged.

Behind him, Charles shouted. "Who are you?"

"Pardon us," a voice said. "We're just three distinctly different kinds of people, though we do share one commonality, being pyromaniac vandals. Collectively, we have set fires to forests, cars, and buildings."

"Sounds like you're very proud of yourself." Charles folded his arms.

Twenty yards away, three men danced in circles. Whirling their arms over their burned faces, they twirled, kicked, and jumped to keep the drifting ashes from touching them. Their energy seemed fleeting. They snarled and sneered with tired, drooping movements.

"There are many like us, but they have done far less than us," one said. He leaped about on his tiptoes, waving his arms around in circles. "In a way, we are the greatest of our kind."

"We don't care," Charles said. "So go."

"Forgive our sudden approach," another gasped. This one twirled and skipped about, rubbing his body frantically with his hands and arms. "But I must ask—how do you bear the stench of those repulsive waters?"

"We're not prisoners here." Charles took out his coal and looked like he may throw it at one of them. "It's not repulsive to us."

"You don't smell that God-awful stench?" the third one rasped. This one leaped side to side, clutching something close to his chest.

"Actually," Daniel came to his feet, "it smells better than everything else down here."

"Interesting." The man looked down at whatever he was holding onto. "We've come here many times, but none of us could bring ourselves to get any closer than we are now. May I ask how you have come here?"

"From the forest," Daniel said.

"Through the previous chamber?"

Beau eyed them suspiciously. "What do you want?"

"Just a friendly chat," the same one said. "I'm sorry. I'm being rude. My name is Marcus. You're an American? From the South?"

Daniel nodded. "I'm from Georgia."

"I've been through Atlanta," Marcus replied. "I was born and raised in California."

"That's good to know." Daniel glanced at Beau and Charles. "You guys ready?"

"Wait," Marcus said. "I can help you."

Charles pocketed his lump of coal. "What could you possibly do for us?"

"I can give you this." Marcus revealed what he was holding. Something metallic. Daniel couldn't see it well because of Marcus's strange movements. "But I want something in exchange."

"What is that?" Daniel asked.

"This, my friend," Marcus knocked his knuckles against it, "is a stainless-steel flask. No holes or leaks. Uncompromised. I was told that if I bring it here, I'd come across travelers from a different world, and if I give it to you, I'd receive something valuable in return. Considering we've never seen an outsider around here before, this flask is meant for you."

Charles squinted at Daniel, then back at Marcus. "Who told you this?"

Marcus continued his strange dance. "I'm not sure. I can't remember much about him, but he was friendly enough, I suppose."

"I don't think so. Let's go." Beau started to leave.

"Wait a second." Daniel eyed the flask and then the lake.

Having a flask full of tears for whatever remained ahead seemed like a godsend. He understood Beau's caution, but thought no harm could come from making a fair exchange. It gleamed in the light, piercing the clouds over the lake. He pulled his necklace from under his shirt and held out the crystal. Kristine would forgive him.

"My fiancée gave this to me last Christmas. It's a crystal."

Marcus cringed. "Tell me you have something better than that."

"Don't give him anything," Charles said. "We don't have far to go. Just two more hells."

"More than I'd like." Daniel reached into his pocket and retrieved the ring. "How about this?"

Marcus smiled. "I can work with that, friend."

"Have you lost your mind?" Beau asked. "Don't trade that."

"Toss it and we have a deal," Marcus said.

"I can buy another, Beau." Daniel nodded to Marcus. "Toss on the count of three?"

"Stop," Charles sneered. "Just stop."

"Charles—I can buy another ring," Daniel said.

Charles turned to Marcus and heaved a sigh. "I have something you'll value over the ring."

"There's not much else I can value more than a ring like that."

Charles reached into his pocket and produced his prized possession. "How about a harvester's watch?" He clicked it open and slapped it shut. "This will give you demonic status."

Marcus chuckled. "Are you sure you want to part with that?"

Charles's lips curled with contempt, but he nodded. "For the flask."

"On my count. One... two... three..." Marcus tossed his flask, and it landed by Charles's feet. Charles held fast to his timepiece. He caressed its smooth shell with his thumb and clicked it open. Slowly, he closed it.

"We had a deal," Marcus said.

"Give me a minute." Charles opened it one last time. His solemn face wrinkled. He closed it and tossed it yards short of Marcus. "Earn it," he growled, marching down the shore.

Beau retrieved the flask and made for the watch. "I'll get it for you."

"Don't touch it. It's mine." Marcus tried to lunge at it, but he recoiled, gagging and spitting. After wiping his mouth, he leaped and landed on his stomach. After fumbling around it, he grasped the watch and laughed. The ground beneath him sizzled and smoked. He screamed as he tried to push up. His skin stretched and peeled while fiery flakes of ash fell upon his backside.

He twisted his head to his companions and whimpered, "Go. Forget about me."

They ran away twirling and leaping. "We'll come back," one shouted.

Daniel shook his head. "I'm sorry he did that to you, Marcus."

Marcus groaned. "You don't understand." He shrieked with laughter. His head flamed. "This will forever change me." He clicked it open and gazed at its face.

"It does something when you clamp it hard," Daniel said.

Marcus didn't respond. His body became rigid. He froze as embers floated down and burned his skin. Beau pulled Daniel's shoulder and placed the warm flask in his hand. "It's full. Let's go."

Ahead, Charles waited along the shore, staring at the tears raining from the sky. Daniel said, "Why would he give up his watch like that?"

"I don't know," Beau said. "I'm glad he did. That ring isn't just something you bought from a jeweler. It's helped you get through this and will help you when you get home."

The lake's current traveled along the bank with increasing speed. Standing at the start of a river, Charles pointed. "This leads to the next pit."

"Why did you do that?" Daniel asked.

Charles glared back. His green eyes shimmered with tears. "Not too long ago, you went on a tangent about wedding rings. If people kept them on, they'd overcome adultery. Remember that? Now, look at you. You're ready to toss it out for something as pathetic as a flask."

Daniel stepped up to Charles. "I can get another ring."

"You could get another girl too," Charles said.

Daniel swung his fist and struck Charles's jaw. The demon stumbled back, holding his face.

"Kristine is worth more than any ring," Daniel snarled. He rubbed his eyes. "I've got to get back. I'll give anything to make it happen—even the ring."

Charles rubbed his cheek. He looked at Daniel and laughed.

"You find this funny?" Daniel squeezed the flask to keep from slinging it. "Best choose your words wisely."

"That Holy Spirit you thought was gone—it's all over you right now." Charles winced as he stood and backed up. "It's stronger, too. If you weren't so angry—I'd probably burst into flames or something."

"Shut up!" a voice shouted. A man sat with his knees to his chest twenty feet away from the waters. His blistered head smoked, and he seemed to count his fingers repeatedly. His eyes spun as if he were tracking a fly. "Look around you. You're shielded by that foul mist. Surely you can do what others can't, which is leave, so get to it, why don't you?"

"What are you counting?" Daniel asked.

"Just going over the numbers, you see," the man said. "Trying to figure how many fools caused me to end up here. I need an accurate account of them in order to regain my footing."

"Why are you stuck there?" Daniel asked.

The man's mouth stopped. He gritted his teeth and balled a fist and shook it furiously. "I created revenue for my employer. Attractive loans with simple terms. The customers could afford it." The man licked his finger and seemed to resume counting. "It's not my fault they couldn't keep up with their money. Seems the so-called good Lord required I follow 'em around and remind them of their financial obligations. Ha!"

"You took advantage of people, is what you did," Daniel said.

The old man stopped counting and grimaced at Daniel. Long, crooked teeth spread out as if a blind man had plugged them in haphazardly. "Why don't you *just go then*?"

Daniel's head became light and seemed to drift away from his body like a balloon. Everything swayed beneath him. His throat locked and he couldn't breathe. Beau took his arm and pulled. He spoke, but Daniel couldn't discern the words. They were following Charles along the river.

Lava burst and oozed from geysers along the desert plain. Bright flecks flickered in the sky, and the hardened sand glowed orangish-red.

Daniel dwelled on his father's words. *Just go then. Today in class we will discuss what that means to you. Daniel, look at me.*

"Daniel, look at me." Beau was looking right into Daniel's face. "Do you need a minute?"

"I'm fine." Something prickled in his clenched fist. Daniel opened it and saw the ring sitting in the center of his palm. He thought he had put it back in his pocket.

Beau gave Daniel's shoulder a squeeze. "Best put it away for now."

Daniel held the metal flask in his other hand. It didn't shine like the ring. If it were empty, Daniel wouldn't find it valuable at all. Charles had done him a huge favor, and in return, Daniel struck him.

"I should have thanked him," Daniel said. "What was I thinking?"

"You still can—when you're ready." Beau nodded ahead, where Charles treaded along the riverbank.

"I guess I'd better add an apology, too."

"That's simple enough."

"Not for me."

"Well, look at the bright side," Beau said. "The Holy Spirit is still with you."

"I'm not sure why." Daniel started after Charles. "Hey, Charles, hold on a second."

Charles turned and folded his arms, waiting for Daniel and Beau to catch up.

Daniel rubbed the back of his neck and looked at the river of tears. "Sorry for hitting you."

Charles smiled and resumed walking. "Don't be. I'm not."

"You stopped me from losing Kristine's ring. I wasn't thinking right and—anyway, thanks."

Charles reached into his pocket but came out empty. He scratched his chin. "What that old man said back there bothered you. Why?"

"The last thing my dad said to me before I ran away from home was 'Just go then'. It's been stuck in my head ever since."

"So you've thought about it over and over again. Going around and around in a circle. In your own Hell. Punishing yourself." Charles took out his piece of coal, tossed it in the air, and caught it. "A vicious cycle is hard to break, but my grandmother once told me something that may help you. If you keep failing at the same thing," Charles paused and looked into Daniel's eyes, "try another way. Running away isn't working for you, so try something else."

Daniel nodded. "Tell me about the next hell."

Charles resumed the walk. "The Eighth Hell is called Malebolge. It's for frauds. I was sentenced there and know it very well. Unfortunately, it knows me too. It's far worse than every hell we've been through so far."

"It's worse than this?" Beau looked around in disbelief.

Charles looked out into the desert, where fire descended from the sky. "Oh, this place is a dream vacation in comparison."

"You were sentenced there because you were a thief?" Daniel asked.

"A very good thief." Charles smiled proudly.

"A good thief who got caught," Daniel said.

"Yeah, they caught me." Charles's smile deflated. "It also led to my eventual death. Something I spent decades forgetting, so I appreciate the reminder."

"No problem." Daniel suppressed a laugh. "Look. I know that watch meant a lot to you, so again—thank you."

"Enough of that," Charles said. "Listen, before we get to the Malebolge, we have to deal with a monster called Geryon. It guards the pit. We'll need its permission to enter."

"What if it says no?" Beau asked.

"Satan is expecting us. Remember?" Charles asked. "If we're lucky, it'll give us a ride to the bottom. This pit is the deepest yet."

The river narrowed and strengthened the farther they went. The grade descended slightly until they reached the bottom, where waters eddied and drained into a large hole. The sound of falling water hushed everything. Beau patted Daniel on the back and gave a nod. When they looked into the pit, watery, purple eyes emerged.

Chapter Eighteen

Into the Malebolge

DANIEL

A broad body ascended from the murky depths of the pit and burst into the fiery sky. A mighty wind, reeking of sewage, forced Daniel to take several steps back. Geryon expanded its fleshy wings overhead and landed hard on the desert floor.

The surface rippled and cracked under Geryon's enormous paws. Its four legs were covered in thick, mangy fur, but it had a massive body that was green and scaly. A scorpion's tail with a bulbous stinger curled over its shaggy head as it turned toward them.

The beast had the face of a man. He scowled with disapproval at Daniel and Beau, but when he turned to Charles, a low guttural sound echoed from its throat. Long, prong-like teeth protruded from its slobbering mouth.

Beau stood in front of Daniel as Geryon stomped toward Charles. It stopped feet from him and glared down his nose.

Charles raised his hands submissively and pointed at Daniel. "I am taking this man to Treachery. Satan is expecting us."

Geryon didn't seem to care. "You lost what we gave you," he said. "Your suit—"

"We came all the way from Limbo," Charles said, laughing nervously.

Geryon grimaced. "Where's your watch?"

Charles gasped. “The journey has been harsh. Did you hear me when I said Satan is expecting us?”

The monster extended its scaly neck and squinted. “Your eyes are like a man’s again.”

“I couldn’t help that.”

Geryon sniffed Charles’s chest and grinned menacingly. “You’ve regained your heart.”

Charles winced. “You knew about that?”

Geryon’s stinger dropped and pierced just under Charles’s left shoulder. He groaned as the beast lifted him overhead. To keep from sliding, he grasped the stinger’s globular base.

Beau held the keystone toward Geryon and squeezed it tighter.

Geryon backed away and snarled, “What is that?”

“Drop him now.” Beau stepped forward and spoke with a commanding voice. “I’m taking these men to the bottom of Hell.”

“On what authority?” Geryon growled.

“On my own authority.” Beau swallowed and said, “I’m Azrael.”

Geryon’s eyes widened with fear. His jaw hung open. “Are you here to destroy me?”

“Release the harvester and take us to the Malebolge,” Beau said, “and I’ll leave you be.”

“So be it.” Geryon lowered its stinger. Charles thudded to the ground, grabbing the far-left side of his chest.

“Let’s not test his patience,” Beau whispered to Daniel. He pulled Charles to his feet and ushered him to Geryon’s side. Turning back, he gave Daniel a curt nod. “Get over here now.”

Daniel willed himself to creep closer to the strange beast and did as he was told. He and Beau set Charles onto Geryon’s muscular back so that his legs straddled the monster's neck under its folded wings. Daniel sat behind Charles, and Beau climbed on last.

Beau clasped Daniel's shoulder and whispered, "Ready?"

Daniel nodded.

"Let's move, Geryon." Beau said.

The enormous beast lurched forward. Its shoulder blades oscillated as it approached the pit. Daniel grasped fistfuls of loose skin where its wings met the beast's back. Geryon nosedived into the stinking hole. Daniel pushed his body against the monster and tightened his legs around its ribs. Charles's weight slid against him. Daniel gritted his teeth. The freefall weakened his grip until Geryon spread his wings and began gliding downward in a spiral around a loud waterfall.

Overhead, a metal gate clanged shut. Beyond it, the scarlet sky of the Seventh Hell diminished to a red speck in growing darkness. Slowly, they drifted into a large cavern lit with columns of shimmering torches. A rotten sulfuric stench thickened the deeper they went. Daniel held his breath and pressed his nose into his shoulder, but a sudden twist by Geryon made him gasp. The noxious fumes brought a fit of coughing. He grabbed his throat and slipped from the monster's back.

He fell a hundred yards before he struck the reeking waters below. The swamp was two feet deep. He pushed himself up, hacking and heaving. His hands sank and slid into the gooey muck. Everything burned, especially his eyes. His left knee twinged when he stood.

Feet sloshed toward him. "Beau, is that you?" Daniel rubbed his face.

"It's us," Beau's voice echoed. The warmth of the keystone crawled over his irritated skin and caused him to shudder. The burning subsided, and the air improved somewhat. Beau took Daniel by the shoulder. "Are you OK?"

"Think so," Daniel said between breaths. "Where did that thing go?"

"It's gone," Charles croaked. He pressed his right palm hard against his gaping wound.

"Are you going to be all right?" Daniel asked Charles.

"Did you hit your head when you fell, or did you forget that I'm already dead?" Charles trudged past Daniel. "This way."

The cavern had a high ceiling, shrouded by wavering shadows. The slimy stone walls stood about fifty yards apart. Broken columns hung and sprouted like fangs. The muddy surface sank with every step they made. Daniel braced his knee with a hand to dampen the pain.

"How far does this go?" Daniel asked.

"Not sure," Charles said. "We'll know when we're close because it's much louder than the other hells."

"They sentenced you here, right?" Daniel asked.

"Yes," Charles said. "I spent several years in the seventh trench."

"How many trenches are there?" Beau asked.

"Ten. And we'll walk over most of 'em," Charles said. "The bridge has collapsed in some places. Went down two thousand years ago. I met a person who witnessed it. He told me a man floated toward the Ninth Hell, and wherever his shadow touched, walls and bridges fell. The demons hid for days after that."

"Was it—you know," Daniel said, "Jesus?"

"Lines up with the timeframe." Charles pulled out his lump of coal and rotated it around in his hand.

"I never believed in Him," Daniel said. "It's still hard to imagine He's real."

"I didn't either," Charles said. "I went to church with my grandmother. She often read and quoted the Bible. Admired that drunken preacher I mentioned earlier. But when she died, I let it go."

"Where the bridge is down, do we need to climb down and back up?" Beau asked.

"That or follow a trench wall to another bridge," Charles said.

The water receded to their ankles, and the ground hardened. Daniel's knee improved. He limped along well enough without supporting his knee. The cavern narrowed to the size of a hallway. Beau took the lead while Charles took up the rear. Green smoke billowed up the walls and accumulated overhead. The roar of an unseen crowd intensified. An orange light shimmered from a passageway that led to the right.

"That's it," Charles said. "The entrance to the Malebolge."

Beau halted near the mouth of the cave and took a deep breath. He rubbed the back of his neck. "What's the plan?" he asked.

Charles shrugged. "There are thousands of demons here. We can't just sneak by them."

"What about the keystone?" Daniel asked.

"It may help in a pinch," Beau pulled on his beard, "but it barely got us by a few demons in the first chamber in Violence."

"They weren't even real demons," Charles added. "They're wannabes like me."

"Can't we just tell them that Satan is expecting us?" Beau asked.

"No one cares," Charles said. "Azazel and Abaddon didn't. Not even Geryon. These demons won't either."

"Fine." Daniel cleared his throat. "We don't have many options, so we'll evade as much as we can, but when we come across any demons, Beau will tell them he's Azrael and that he's taking us to the Ninth Hell—unless either of you have a better idea."

They looked at each other, but no one said anything.

"That'll have to do, I guess." Charles pocketed his lump of coal. "Remember this, Beau. Azrael would command authority. If your voice cracks or you show any sign of weakness with these demons, they'll know you aren't him."

Beau righted his posture and nodded. "I'll keep that in mind." He marched through the threshold and into the Malebolge and stopped immediately.

From outside, a strained voice snarled, "Put out that light."

A sick feeling rose in Daniel's stomach. "Already?"

Charles wiped his forehead and said, "They must've sensed you somehow."

"You do not tell me what to do, demon!" Beau shouted.

"Defy me again and you'll regret it," the same voice growled.

Beau grabbed Charles by the wrist and jerked him forward, and did the same with Daniel. Hot, musky air burned Daniel's skin when he came into the Malebolge. The keystone must have been helping, but it didn't feel like it. Along the ridge, demons with purple skin and dark-green horns crowded around them. They convulsed and grimaced like football players rallied to play. Their noses and chins were long and pointed. All of their eyes were black and red.

"Who are you and why are you here?" the same demon asked.

"I'm Azrael," Beau said with a deeper voice than usual. He gestured to Charles and Daniel with stiff movements. "I'm taking these two to the Ninth Hell."

Beau had done a much better job pretending to be Azrael with Geryon. If Daniel could tell he was putting on an act, certainly these demons could. They mumbled amongst themselves. The speaker relaxed his arms and twitched his ear to the crowd.

"Move," another voice commanded. The crowd parted, and a lavender-skinned demon with leathery, black wings approached. It sneered at Beau, revealing two rows of fangs. "Azrael, you say?"

Beau nodded sheepishly. "That's right." His voice held a slight tremor. He glanced at Charles, then back at the winged demon. Daniel sucked his lips in and closed his eyes, trying not to shake his head. "We're p-passing through."

"I recognize the tall, skinny one," someone shouted. "Charles was a thief granted the rank of harvester."

The winged demon turned to the crowd. "Sounds like you're in love." The gaggle of demons laughed. "Silence. All of you have somewhere else to be, so get there."

The demons dispersed and the world of the Malebolge opened. From a mountain ridge overlooking rust-colored terrain, Daniel counted six deep trenches bending and stretching left and right below the horizon. Like a thriving colony of cockroaches, countless demons inundated the stone bridge and the ledges in-between.

"Oh, wise Azrael." The wing demon bowed his head. "Why are you escorting these maggots to Treachery?"

"I don't need to explain my actions to you, demon." Beau glanced at Daniel, who gave him a slight nod of encouragement.

The demon didn't look up but said in the sweetest voice a demon could muster, "Please be gracious, mighty Azrael. It's unprecedented to have an angel, especially one as great as you, enter our world."

"I am taking them to the Ninth Hell. There is nothing else you need to know." Beau bowed his chest a little too much, but thankfully, the demon still wasn't looking.

"You are welcome to pass as you need, most powerful of angels." The demon grinned at Beau and bowed again.

"Good." Beau placed his hand on the small of Daniel's back and ushered him toward the ledge of the cliff. "We'll be on our way then."

Daniel was certain that Beau was going to walk them right off the cliff. He closed his eyes and prepared for the worst.

"Before you go..." The demon hunched in front of Beau with his hands folded near his heart.

"Get out of my way, demon." Beau managed to make his acting even worse. Daniel felt his hand shaking at the small of his back.

"My aim is not to hinder you, wise angel." The demon came to his feet, pretending to be meek. "Please, allow me to guide you through the Malebolge." He pointed to the bridge below. "My kind overcrowds the bridge. I have authority to clear it, so your journey is less encumbered."

"I don't need an escort," Beau growled.

"I know you can handle yourself," the demon nodded with an affirming finger, "but your master, the Nazarene, passed through ages ago and damaged our infrastructure. We've yet to repair all His damage. Allow me to usher you through to prevent further impairments."

"Fine," Beau said. "But do not test me, demon."

"I would never do so." The demon bowed again with a sly smile that revealed many fangs. "I'll show you a path that'll take you down to the bridge."

When the demon turned his back, Charles glared at Beau, shaking his head. Daniel didn't like this either, but at least they were making progress. Their demonic guide ushered them to a crag that hung out from the cliff and stretched his arms like a ringmaster presenting a circus. "Behold the Malebolge." He twisted around to face them. "If the Almighty looked down upon us from His high place, He'd see a dazzling eye where the pit to the Ninth Hell is an ice-blue pupil. Each of the ten ditches surrounding it represents every Hell."

"But there are only nine hells," Beau said.

"Ah, but for us, Heaven is Hell. You just haven't figured that out yet." The demon smiled harshly. When Beau didn't respond, it cackled. "You obviously don't share my belief. So be it. Shall we continue, wise angel?"

Beau nodded.

The demon walked from the crag to where it met the cliff and pointed to a thin path. "Take this. It snakes to the bottom. Meet me at the bridge." The demon leaped from the ledge and spread its leathery wings. It soared downward in a circle until landing in stride.

The path was a skinny crevice that zigzagged down the slanted cliff. This first stretch led to a spear-shaped rock jutting from the rock face. The next path curled back beneath them. Considering the height of the cliff and the hazard of the winding path, Daniel imagined they'd be sidestepping their way to the base for what might amount to a mile, maybe more.

Beau whispered, "I think he knows I'm not Azrael."

"We'll deal with it when we need to," Charles said. "Just get moving."

Beau led the way. Facing the Malebolge, they sidestepped to the first bend. The decline was slight, but the height made Daniel weak-kneed and dizzy. He focused on breathing and took careful steps. When they rounded the first bend, it steepened.

They went from one bend to another several times over. The path slowly widened as they followed it down. The knot in Daniel's stomach loosened. Their guide watched with his arms crossed at the base of the cliff. After ten bends, they reached the bottom.

Shifting his weight from one leg to the other, Beau gasped. He stooped over, panting. Extreme heat gave Daniel the impression that his brain was boiling inside his skull. Blisters burned inside his boots, and his knee still troubled him. Charles's wound had hardened into a tarry mess, but he appeared to be faring better than Daniel and Beau.

Ahead of them, the guide spoke with a squad of six unwinged demons standing at the foot of the crowded bridge.

"Get control of yourself," Charles grumbled to Beau. "Stop fidgeting, breathe normally, and stand tall."

Beau heaved a sigh and straightened his back. "Let's go."

Wearing mischievous smiles, the demons watched them approach. The guide raised a hand and said, "Clear the bridge for the mighty Azrael." Without a word, the squad marched onto the crowded bridge and shouted for everyone to move. They tossed anyone who didn't comply swiftly enough into the trenches.

The guide sauntered to Beau. "As promised, you will be unobstructed on your journey through the Malebolge. I ordered them to clear the entire bridge for *you*, most stupefying Azrael." The guide strolled onto the bridge and peered over the edge. "Don't be shy. Come along."

When Beau stood rooted in place, Charles whispered, "Move it."

They came onto the bridge, and the demon said, "The first ditch is filled with panderers and seducers." He licked his lips and fluttered his eyelashes. After a hearty cackle, he spat into the trench. "Pimps on the left. Whores on the right. I can point out some noteworthy ones if you like."

"We aren't here for a tour," Beau said. His disgust came off naturally.

"Suit yourself," the guide said, moving along.

Daniel didn't want to look but couldn't help peeking. Demons stood on ledges. Hundreds on either side of the trench whipped those walking along the base in two single-file lines. Leering at the ground, the seducers and panderers trembled and pressed against each other to shield themselves from the harsh lashings.

One man crumpled after a whip slashed his face. A demon rushed from a nearby cave and dragged him inside while jeers erupted from the ledge.

"The living one looks interested," the guide said. "Tormentors drag those who fall into nearby chambers. There, they have creative reign over the weak prey. In time, the prey will become predators—lest they prefer the suffering. It is, after all, through suffering that we become stronger."

"Enough. Stall anymore and you'll regret it, demon," Beau growled.

The guide recoiled and bowed. "Forgive me, most confounding of angels. I'll delay no more. Come along."

Charles whispered, "Stop looking unless you want nightmares."

Daniel turned away, but he couldn't do anything to escape the screams. He scratched the scab off his scar. The sting exhilarated him, but it brought tears to his eyes.

The guide chuckled. "No need to cry. The next trench is more interesting, anyway."

When they reached the end of the first ditch and came upon the first plateau, a stale and putrid stench seized Daniel's stomach. He gagged and shielded his nose.

"Smell that?" The demon asked. "Behold! The home of the flatterers. The scent issuing from this garden derives from their many, many, many tainted words. Ha! Ha!"

Beau squeezed the stone harder. To Daniel's relief, the stench diminished. Chaotic noise, louder than in the first ditch, roared from underneath as they crossed the bridge. Daniel kept his eyes forward to keep from looking.

The guide paused and gazed into the trench. "I can't pass up on this." He smiled at Charles and said, "I'll rejoin you shortly." He leaped in.

Chapter Nineteen

The Malebranche

BEAU

When the demon guide leaped from the bridge, Beau doubled over. His body fluttered with numbness. The terrible sound of souls suffering and warring over each other was too much for him. How many souls did he send here? After a quivering inhalation, tears fell, and he couldn't stop them.

Daniel placed a hand on Beau's shoulder. "We've got to go."

Beau wiped his eyes. "Give me a minute."

"Have you lost your mind?" Charles asked. "Everyone can see you. If one demon catches sight of you blubbering, we're through."

"I'm sorry." Beau stood upright and squeezed the keystone a little tighter. "That demon knows I'm not Azrael."

"Don't worry about it." Daniel took Beau's arm and gave him a slight tug to hurry him along. "If we get moving, we may not even see him again."

Beau walked on. He masked his emotions with a stony gaze. "What do you think that monster is up to?"

"Who cares?" Charles reached for his tie, but it wasn't there. He huffed. "You shouldn't have allowed him to guide us."

"Where would we be if he didn't?" Daniel asked. "This bridge was full of demons. It's empty now."

"We get a small window when we can lose him," Charles said, "and Beau decides to have a mental breakdown."

"I don't think we can lose him." Daniel looked down into the pit. "Do you know who that demon is?"

"No, but he's winged, so he outranks everyone without wings," Charles said.

Beau peeked into the trench. Demons carried buckets of brown sludge to an iron ledge that overlooked the deep ditch. Within it, souls fought with no apparent alliances. A bald spot emerged in the thick mob. Their demon guide gripped a female by her matted hair while a party of other demons guarded him. He gazed up at Beau and pushed through the crowd toward a nearby wall with the woman in tow.

"That demon's coming back with a lady."

"He's going to test you," Charles said. "Tell him we're moving on without him. And don't show any sympathy for whoever he's bringing."

The demon bounded up the wall and leaped into the air, pounding his wings. Flying under the bridge, he emerged on the other side and landed five feet from them. He flung the filthy woman before him. Her head slapped against the bridge.

The guide raised his arms in grandiose fashion. "Behold, most factitious of angels. I present to you, Elaine Love Thorne, Charles's stinking mother. Woman, raise your worthless head and meet your child."

CHARLES

"Can't be," Charles muttered.

But demons speak the truth when it suits them. This woman, caked in excrement, had the same frame and face as his grandmother. When her eyes met his, the truth beamed from her maniacal smile and joyful tears. He gasped and stepped back. *It can't be true.*

"Oh, my sweet Baby Chip." Her ragged voice clawed at his heart. "Look at how beautiful you are." She reached for him and he stepped back. "Oh, how I longed to see you with my own eyes. Come to Mummy."

Panting, Charles said, "This is a trick. You found someone who favors me, is all you did."

The demonic guide grinned mischievously. "Oh, it's her. I know all who writhe in my trenches, Baby Chip."

"I named you after your daddy." The woman nodded absently. "He must have taken good care of you, bless his sweet soul."

"I never knew my father," Charles retorted. "Grandmother raised me—'til she died."

"What game are you playing, demon?" Beau growled.

"Oh, this is a rare opportunity for Baby Chip to meet his mummy. And for Mummy to meet her little Chippy." Pouting his lips, the guide folded his hands together and made puppy dog eyes. "Certainly, an angel can allow a brief sabbatical for family."

"I met your father at Mum's church." The woman smiled widely. "A handsome man, and well-to-do. I knew in time he'd leave his wife for me.

He just needed a nudge. One night, we managed to be alone together, and on that night, you were conceived. Once you were born, we would live a life of comfort and luxury. If he denied us, he'd have to provide to keep my silence. Extramarital affairs would ruin a preacher's career."

"Reverend Wilfred," Charles said under his breath. He staggered into Daniel, who steadied him.

"Charles P. Wilfred." His mother's toothless grin stretched to the orange sky. She flipped her disheveled long hair over her bare shoulder. "Such a lovely man. Oh, and you favor him as I imagined you would. He promised we'd run away when you were born and start anew. But I was so tired, so weak. When I woke here, I took solace in knowing that my Baby Chip would grow up a preacher's son bound for Heaven."

"He was nothing but a drunk," Charles hissed, glaring at his mother while she raised her eyes dreamily. "He denied me. When grandmother died, he took me to an orphanage. Told them I was a bastard with no family. I never saw him again. I fell here and now—I'm a demon!"

Nothing Charles said seemed to register with his mother. She gazed at him in a daze. "Did Granny sing to you? She used to sing me to sleep when I was a child. *This little light of mine. I'm gonna let it shine. This little light of mine...*"

"Stop it," Charles said.

"Sweet Chip, don't be so contrary. Come, give Mummy a hug, please. It would mean so much." She brought her hand over her heart. Her jaw tremored. "I had you for such a short while, but you were my everything in those last moments."

"Didn't you see my future while you were—no!"

The guide had yanked Elaine by the hair and tossed her back into the fray below. Charles dropped to his knees and sobbed. His mother's screams were swallowed by the ruckus. The demon cackled loudly. "Her words were as thick as the slop on her skin! Were they not, Baby Chip?"

"We don't need any more delays," Beau croaked. "Find some other business to carry out and leave us."

"I wouldn't have delayed if it hadn't been so necessary." The guide frowned while blinking with mock innocence. "Chippy never knew his mummy. Didn't your master once say the truth shall set you free?" The demon lost his frown and broke into a chuckle. "Oh, come on. Charles is one of us, even though he's been shifting back to his weaker state. He can be primitive if he likes. This was merely a parting gift. Please, allow me to guide you. There'll be no more delays, I swear."

"Go away," Beau said firmly.

"Very well," the demon took a deep bow, "blubbery angel."

The demon stepped aside and allowed Beau to march past him. Daniel tugged Charles's sleeve until he came afoot. Still, his eyes scanned the mob inside the second trench; his mother lost in the rabble. *The Reverend Charles P. Wilfred. Probably living in Paradise through remitted sins.* Charles's body shook with sadness and rage.

The demon winked at him when he passed. "Welcome home, Baby Chip."

"Are you OK?" Daniel asked. His face was drained of color.

"That demon's still watching us." Charles glowered at Beau's back. His eyes shimmered with tears, but he didn't care. The Holy Spirit had weakened him, and now he suffered for it. "We'll deal with him when the time comes."

Beau spoke over his shoulder. "Was that really your mother?"

"I don't care, so don't ask," Charles said, unable to stop his chin from trembling.

They crossed the next plateau and over the third ditch. Smoke and flames rose from evenly spaced cylindrical holes in the ground. Feet stuck from them like stems. Demons walked about sprinkling powder to ignite flames from where the feet sprouted. One stopped at a hole framed in purple and red stones and said, "Almighty Pope, I'd like to buy God, but this is all I have." He slung a fistful of powder. Flames and screams rose. "Oh no. You must be all out of God. How about the Spirit?" The demon dumped the contents of his bag into the hole. A flaring green torch hissed and the protruding feet writhed.

"The Pope?" Daniel asked.

"Not even they get a free pass to Heaven," Charles said. An image of the reverend, his supposed father, came to mind. He longed to see the pathetic drunk abiding and suffering in Hell. "When so-called holy men worship power and money, they end up in this ditch."

They came to another long sliver of land and continued over the fourth trench. Charles looked back and saw the winged demon following from a distance. He gnashed his teeth. *I'll rip those wings from your back and make you eat them.*

Below, the fortune-tellers suffered. Their heads were twisted to their backsides. With shocked expressions, they stumbled about, mumbling and groaning. A few used stones to make markings on the iron walls of the ditch. Unlike the other trenches, no demons oversaw this one. Demons controlled these witches and sorcerers the same way they had during their lifetime—through their minds.

"I bet they didn't see this coming." Charles forced a laugh. Tears escaped his eyes.

Daniel shook his head. "It's the fourth one. That's all I need to know."

A shadow passed over them, but all Charles saw overhead was an empty, bright orange sky. He peered over his shoulder. "No one's following us. So be ready."

DANIEL

They kept moving. Dark wisps of smoke rose from the next ditch. Tar staining the air made it hard and detrimental to breathe. A thick band of persistent pain tightened around Daniel's stomach. His head throbbed and burned inside and out.

Beau turned about, looking in every direction. "No sign of him anywhere."

"He'll be back," Charles said. "Likely with others."

About two hundred yards from the next trench, Daniel's ears erupted with a high-pitched ring. He dropped to his knees, clutching his head to keep it from bursting. Beau pulled on his arm. Daniel jerked away and lowered to a fetal position, pressing his forehead to the bridge.

"What's wrong?" Beau sounded distant.

"My head—it's going nuts," Daniel said. "Everything's spinning."

"We'll have to carry him," Beau muttered.

Pain seized Daniel when they tried to lift him by the arm. The noise in his ears sprang higher. He pulled away and bowed his head forward. "I can't move. Not now."

"Oh, great." Charles stood up straight. "Our friend is back with members of the Malebranche."

Although it felt like bombs were exploding in his head, Daniel lifted his gaze. The winged demon had returned and waited at the next ridge with three other winged demons. The ringing in his head jumped several octaves higher, and he rolled to his side. Charles and Beau tried to lift him again, but Daniel pushed their hands away.

"Every time we need you to fight, you're incapacitated," Charles grumbled.

"We can handle them," Beau said.

"You don't understand," Charles said. "This is the Malebranche."

"There are only four of them, and I have the keystone."

Charles grimaced at Beau. His body trembled. "You have no idea. I've seen them at work, and they are brutal." He looked back at the Malebranche standing on the ridge. "Get up, Daniel. We need you for this one."

Trembling with fear and weakness, Daniel pushed from the bridge. Despite the war in his head, he slouched to his feet but remained hunched and high-shouldered. Certain that a toddler could knock him over with a playful slap, he knew he'd be worthless in a fight right now.

Another winged demon ascended from the smoking trench with a tarred man impaled on its spear. A gush of methane-laced air wafted in his wake. The stench, so horrible, debilitated Daniel. He almost fell back to the ground. The demon slung the man back into the depths. Glaring at Daniel, it whirled the spear to an overhand position and was ready to throw.

"Malecoda!" their former guide shouted. "Not yet."

Malecoda's mouth curled, and he pitched the spear. It struck and pierced the ground near the guide's feet. Malecoda flew to the ridge and took back his weapon. They huddled around the guide and glared at Beau, Daniel, and Charles.

"Keep walking," Charles said. "They sense fear."

"No way," Beau said. "Let them come to us."

"Then we'll be in for a fight, for sure," Charles snarled.

"We have the keystone. And Fortuna's promise."

Charles and Beau continued to argue. The sound of static blared in Daniel's head. He doubled over and dropped to a knee. Charles attempted to lift him by the arm, but Daniel refused to move. "Stop. My head..."

"If you thought Azazel was bad," Charles said, "imagine four just like him."

"It's not them I'm worried about," Daniel grunted. "Something else is coming."

"Most fictitious of angels," Malecoda hollered, "come and join us in a most interesting of discussions."

Charles poked Daniel with his foot. "You need to get over whatever it is and get up."

The ringing in his ears changed tones. It was as if a pianist ran scales along a keyboard, increasing speed with each pass. Everything else slowed down. Charles and Beau tugged on him, but Daniel remained rigid. Their mouths moved, but he heard nothing. Their wrinkled, wide-eyed faces looked animated and demanding.

Charles and Beau turned. Ahead of them, the Malebranche stormed the bridge. Beau interlaced his fingers over the keystone. His glowing fist blinded Daniel. Stench gave way to the scent of spring. Hot air turned lukewarm.

An overpowering, staticky voice occurred within. *Your choice, Daniel.* The pain was gone. Daniel knew who spoke these words in his head and it frightened him more than the oncoming attackers.

"Azrael," he uttered. Tears streamed from his eyes.

The light of the stone dimmed. The orange sky over the Malebolge became red. The pianist dropped his hands and head on the lowest keys. An icy breeze cracked the sky.

The Malebranche stopped.

The demon guide looked about. "What's happening?"

"Azrael is here," Daniel whispered. No one heard him.

"Drop whatever's in your hand," Malecoda growled.

"Never," Beau said.

"You're going into the pitch, fatso. With or without your hand attached. Grab him."

Two demons became limp and thudded upon the bridge. The remaining Malebranche members readied their weapons and looked about.

Daniel's head fluttered. *Concede or proceed. But know that I'm here for you. Wherever you go, I'll follow.* Feeling Azrael's presence, Daniel turned. At the ridge where they first entered the Malebolge, Azrael stood wearing an illuminated white gown with a glittering black shawl resting over his head and shoulders. Scores of unconscious demons lay around him along the ledge.

Daniel gasped and pointed.

"Everyone to the real angel." The guide flew from the bridge and passed Beau, Charles, and Daniel. Azrael waved his hand, and the guide went limp and fell into the trench below.

"To Alastor!" shouted Malecoda. The remaining members of the Malebranche dropped into the tarry ditch to retrieve him.

Charles tugged Daniel's shirt. "Run." They sprinted to the next ridge. The bridge for this sixth trench had collapsed. They turned back to Azrael, who hadn't moved.

"What's he doing?" Beau asked.

"He told me it's my choice," Daniel said. "I can continue or go to him."

Charles folded his arms. "We've come too far for you to give up now."

Daniel shook his head and wiped his face. "I'm tired, and I don't see the point in trying."

"You *are* selfish," Charles sneered.

"Charles—"

"Stop, Beau. He thinks everything's about him." Charles glared and gestured at Daniel. "What about me and Beau? Kristine? Your father? Your family? You're giving up on everybody because *you're* afraid?"

Daniel winced. "I'm not being selfish about this."

"It's his choice," Beau said. "Fortuna said so."

"Everything's been his choice." Charles turned to Daniel. "You just want to give up because that's all you ever do. Isn't it? It's not only pride and selfishness that gets people here. Many of us just gave up on life. Is that what you want?"

Beau balled his fists. "Stop!"

"No, he's right, Beau." Daniel pulled out the ring and gazed at it. Gripping it in his fist, he shouted at Azrael. "I choose life!" A rush of energy swelled within his head. Feeling faint, he blinked to stay awake. He buried the ring back in his pocket. "No matter what, I'll always choose life."

Chapter Twenty

The Unchained Giant

DANIEL

The sky remained red and cracked. Demons of the Malebolge were nowhere to be seen. The bridge to the sixth trench was down, but getting down into the trench didn't look too arduous. The hillside wasn't too steep or deep for Daniel, Beau, and Charles to climb down. At the bottom, a line of monks in golden robes inched along a path, maintaining six feet of space as they toddled to an unheard cadence. All of them were stooped, some worse than others. A few had toppled and lay along the path, begging others for help.

On their way down, Beau asked, "Do you think the Malebranche will be back?"

"They'll be busy for a time," Charles said. "Once they fish their leader from the tar pit, they'll have to wash off in a petroleum basin."

"They're also more concerned with Azrael," Daniel added.

A monk, who collapsed on the path, spotted them and reached out. "Please. Help me up. The weight—it's too much for me to do on my own."

"What good would it do?" Charles came off the hill and picked dried blood from his shirt. "You'll just fall again."

Daniel took the man's hands and pulled. "My gosh. You're heavier than you look. Help me, Beau."

Together, they pulled the old man to his feet, but he struggled to keep upright without help.

"Turn me loose," the old man rasped. His hood had fallen back and exposed his bald head. His face was bony, with sagging gray skin.

When they let him go, the old man buckled and fell. Daniel and Beau went to lift him again, and Charles palmed his face. "Have either of you learned anything about these people yet?"

Coming to his feet, the old man smiled with wide eyes. "I haven't stood in ages. May take some time getting used to it again."

"How is someone as little as you, so heavy?" Daniel asked.

"Everyone in this trench is forced to wear these robes lined with lead." He grimaced while taking a tentative step.

Charles folded his arms. "Because they're hypocrites."

The old monk scowled at Charles. "I did nothing wrong. I gave to charities. Preached the gospel. Everyone who knew me saw I was a righteous man, but I had no choice but to do what I was told or else get beaten by the demons."

"Go figure," Charles sneered, "a righteous man here in Hell."

"I swear on my life that I am." The old man lifted his arms slightly for balance as he took a tiny step forward.

"Truly, he's worse than most of us," groaned another monk, trudging along the path. "Got off easy, I'd say."

"You lousy hypocrite." The old man raised a shaky arm and pointed. "You slandered your brother over an affair while you slept with his wife behind his back."

"Ha, like you can talk." Someone else pointed at the old man. "The only charity you gave to was your wallet."

"Oh quiet, all of you." A monk farther down the line said, flailing an arm. "Neither of you tithed like you should have."

"Oh! Like you're some beacon of integrity?" the monk in front of him snarled. "You stole money right out of the offering plate."

All the nearby hypocrites bickered over each other. The old man pointed to one and then another, exposing their misdeeds until he lost his balance and fell. He reached for Daniel. "Help me, please."

"Just leave him," Charles said. "He can't stand on his own anyway."

Another monk who had fallen along the path said, "I bet he could. He's just lazy. Ow!"

The monk walking by him had stepped on his foot. "You've been sprawled along the path for *four years*, and you call him lazy?"

"But I can't get up, you imbecile."

Someone else in the line shouted, "But you make sport of tripping people!"

"Only if they call me lazy."

"You *are* lazy," several others said together.

Daniel had enough and broke through the line of hypocrites and started up the opposing embankment. Charles and Beau caught up soon after. The arguments continued behind them. Loose dirt caused a lot of slipping, but they eventually reached the next ledge. Beau and Daniel sprawled out, gasping while Charles brushed himself off, looking along the plateau.

Beau peered into the seventh trench. "It's too dark to see anything."

"It's deeper than others," Charles said. "Best we follow this ledge to another bridge."

Daniel came to his knees. The ledge was only five feet wide and rough. One misstep would send him into either trench. "Which way?"

"Just follow me and try not to slip." Charles started to the left.

CHARLES

Afraid they would fall, Beau and Daniel crawled along the narrow stretch of land. Charles crept along on foot, knowing the evils lurking in the darkness of his former trench. Snakes wrapped and bit, while lizards scurried and licked, spreading a disease that caused mutation; the very thing that had changed Charles's eyes.

Somewhere in the depths, a large centaur called Cacus and a fire-breathing dragon chased and incinerated thieves. When Charles was there, he had learned the dragon was blind and avoided its wrath by squeezing into a crevice in the wall. He cut it deeper and hid there for years until a demon found him. After a lengthy punishment, that demon's commander had offered Charles a special position in Satan's Army. He would only have to harvest fallen souls. Far better than the prospect of getting burned to a crisp or bitten by another poisonous reptile, Charles accepted.

Charles no longer cared for thieving. He thirsted for revenge. Knowing that his biological father suffered would never suffice; he'd prefer to see him tortured in the vilest of ways. Unfortunately, the drunk could have weaseled his way into Heaven somehow.

"Finally, a bridge," Daniel gasped. He pulled the flask from his back pocket and drank. When he was finished, he grimaced and offered it to Beau.

"Keep it," Beau said.

Though the ridge widened as they neared the bridge, Daniel crawled at a snail's pace. His arms shook, and he breathed heavily. No doubt the undead man was tired, but his real problem was much deeper. If not for Charles and Beau, he would have given up already. Fear was leading the man to stagnation.

Once on the bridge, Beau helped Daniel to his feet, and the two hobbled over the seventh trench, ignorant of the glories below. Charles felt nostalgic. He had suffered a great deal there, so much that it made him proud.

"Snakes," he hissed, remembering how one had breached into his hiding place and bit his arm. He had smashed its head with a rock and ate it raw.

Daniel narrowed his eyes. "What about them?"

"I was bitten once." Charles grunted and grabbed his chest. A numb spot at his heart expanded in all directions. When it reached his solar plexus, he gasped and fell to his side, writhing. An unrelenting pressure squeezed within.

Daniel dropped beside him. "What's wrong?"

"The second death," Charles groaned.

Daniel took his hand. "I'm here for you."

Charles felt and heard a massive pop behind his chest and coughed up blood. The worst of it was over, but a horrible cramp would grip him until they entered the cold. He released Daniel's hand. Trembling and aching, he clambered to his feet. Clenching the wound on his chest, he hobbled on without addressing the undead man or the shadow.

He heard Beau calling out from behind him. "Charles?"

"We don't need to discuss every little thing," Charles snapped.

DANIEL

The pains throbbing throughout his body, the hunger, the thirst—none of it deterred Daniel. None of it kept him from worrying about what lay ahead, either. His imagination went to dark places—places he'd rather not go. What would Satan do to him? Would he be imprisoned and tortured? Maybe they'd hammer horns into his temples years or decades after getting tossed into the headwaters of the subterranean river of blood that runs in the first chamber of Violence.

"Can somebody say something already?" Daniel asked. "The silence is killing me."

"Evil counselors are in the next trench." Charles tossed his lump of coal in the air and caught it. "They emboldened others to do evil, and for that, they are often sent back to Earth as spirits to whisper evil thoughts into human minds."

"Did you ever see demons talking to people?" Daniel asked Beau.

Beau squinted and pulled on the end of his beard. "You can't always tell the difference. Demons can sometimes seem like angels." Beau brought his hands to his head and chuckled. "I can't believe it. I remember my daughter's name. It's Angela."

Beau's skin and clothes were no longer soiled like they were back in Limbo. Everything about him seemed gray, like the sadness he brought with him into Hell. It was nice to see a smile on his face upon remembering his daughter's name. Daniel worried about what would come of his new friend, who had sacrificed everything to help him.

The next bridge arched over the trench of evil counselors. Crackling and hissing noises rose from either side as they walked over it. Smoke billowed from a multitude of people burning in separate flames. Most of them convulsed and flailed about in a futile effort to escape. Some, however, stood still and stared stoically at Daniel as he crossed the bridge.

Screams rose from the next pit. When they came onto the bridge, Charles gazed down with a fake smile. It seemed the fate of his mother weighed on him heavily. His demeanor had darkened since seeing her. He tried to hide his pain by pretending to enjoy the horrors of this world, but Daniel saw through the façade. Daniel didn't blame him, though. What else could Charles possibly do? He was stuck in Hell even if he succeeded in gaining power.

Charles clapped his hands and shouted at the souls below. "Everyone is a bloody mess. Well done! You earned it."

Daniel looked at Beau, who frowned and lowered his head.

Charles beckoned to Daniel with his hand. "Come and have a look. They are all quite grotesque."

"Why would anyone want to see that?"

"You don't get it." Charles glared at Daniel. "It is through suffering that we get stronger. It's why I can rip out my heart when others can't."

Daniel didn't respond. He looked down upon his lengthening shadow and thought of his father. Running away from home was a mistake. He knew that the moment he walked out the door. It ate at him endlessly, stinging more and more over time, but the thought of going back terrified him. One thing was clear though, if Daniel could go through Hell and look the Devil in the eyes, the greatest enemy of humankind, then certainly he could look into the eyes of his father and apologize.

The stench of decay and the screaming from the ninth trench gave way to the loud wails and weeping in the final trench. They crossed the last ridge and started over the bridge. Daniel shielded his nose from a potent odor that prickled his flesh. Charles shouted over the noise and pointed into the pit. "Falsifiers. Thirsting and diseased."

"I can barely hear you," Daniel rasped.

Charles nodded. "Toss your flask in."

"Why?"

"You'll see." Charles folded his arms and waited.

Daniel got the flask and took one last swig. The tears were hot and bitter. He cringed at the taste. His stomach groaned. He tossed the flask into the pit and the wails subsided.

"Better?" Charles tossed his lump of coal in the air, caught it, and then shoved it into his pocket. "It's going to get mighty cold from here on out." Charles headed over the bridge. "Your little stone may help, but brace yourselves."

"Will it heal your chest wound?" Daniel asked.

"It'll heal all of us," Charles said.

As they walked away from the tenth trench, an icy-blue fog thickened around them. Winds strengthened, and they trudged at a slant, heading farther away from the Malebolge. The frosted ground crunched under their feet and provided enough traction to keep them afoot. The cold burned Daniel's arms and face, stifling his breathing and stiffening his limbs. If not for the keystone glowing in Beau's hand, he was sure he'd be a pillar of ice by now.

A distant droning occurred, like a horn. "We're getting close to the final pit," Charles said over the noise.

Beau's light dissipated in the swirling fog. Daniel tucked his chin and hunched toward the low, bellowing noise. Minutes, maybe hours, passed as they bunched together, pushing against the wind. The light flickered in Beau's faltering grip. The warmth it provided was more invaluable than ever.

Charles shouted into his ear. "Look up."

Large shadows broke through the fog. First, Daniel thought they were buildings, but one shifted and the obnoxious horn ceased. Daniel stopped and stared. The enormous figures continued to move ever so slightly.

Charles pushed him at the small of his back. "Keep moving or you'll freeze."

Daniel leaned toward Beau. "Can you tighten up on the keystone?"

Beau squeezed it with both hands. "Any better?"

Tingles shot through Daniel. A wave of warmth crawled over his skin like spiders. "Good enough."

"The winds will settle when we reach the pit," Charles said.

"What's that moving up there?" Daniel asked.

"Giants," Charles said. "They're all chained—except one. We'll need to find him so he can let us down into the pit."

Daniel huddled close to Beau, rubbing his exposed arms. "Why not just climb down or jump?"

"It's too cold," Charles said. "We'll get stuck."

Daniel looked at the giant. Large, bulky features emerged. He was pale blue, bald, and had a long, frosted beard that pressed against his bare chest. It could wrap a large hand around Daniel and pop his head back as if he were a Pez dispenser. "These things could squash us like bugs."

"They won't," Charles said.

The winds eventually settled. Warmth from the keystone improved Daniel's motor movements. The giant's wrists were shackled to a chain that was anchored to the surface. It provided enough slack to allow the giant to bring the large conical horn to his lips. From the waist up, he was at least forty feet tall.

He stared at them with blank, white eyes. His voice thundered. "One more step, and I'll beat you into a broth."

Though they were well out of range from the giant, the three stopped. Charles shouted to him. "We're looking for Antaeus?"

The giant stooped toward them, grimacing. "You want my brother to help you down, little man?"

"He's the only one who isn't chained," Charles said. "Where is he?"

"Antaeus hasn't stood in ages. Others came well before you, promising fame in return for his help. Fame did nothing for him. Fame faded fast. He won't be privy to tricks or games. Now turn back the way you came and go."

"Enough of this!" Daniel shouted. "I'm climbing down." Despite the cold, he felt hot all over. Inside and out. He walked up to the ledge, and the giant slammed a fist down, the surface exploding. Icy beads sprayed, and the land quaked and cracked.

"Don't you try, little man," the old giant rumbled.

"You can't stop me." Daniel's throat burned.

Roaring, the giant jerked at his restraints, pounding his fists, but to no avail. Daniel peered down the cliff. Charles and Beau came up to either side of him.

"We can do this." Daniel pointed down the cliff. "There are a lot of cracks we can use to get down."

The giant slammed a knee against the rock face and shouted, "Antaeus, you coward! Do your job and destroy these fools!" From the pit rolled a series of thuds. The horn-wielding giant chuckled. "Best leave or become our lunch."

Chapter Twenty-One

Where Traitors Lie

DANIEL

Daniel gripped the ledge and slid his feet down the icy wall to a small crease. The shackled giant raised his hands and pounded the ground. Ice rained on Daniel's head. His feet slipped, but he didn't fall because his palms and arms were stuck to the surface.

Beau and Charles tried pulling him up, but Daniel shifted away.

"Have you lost your mind?" Beau asked.

"Antaeus hasn't stood in ages. No reason to wait around." Daniel looked down the rock wall. He could do this. "We can climb down it and use the light to keep us from getting stuck."

Beau strained and squeezed the stone, but it didn't help Daniel get free. He relaxed and panted, "It's not working. We're pulling you back up here. There's gotta be a better way."

Daniel found his foothold and tried to jerk his arms free. Stinging pain flared from where his skin pulled and stretched from the frosted ground. The giant kept beating the ground while Beau and Charles wrestled with Daniel.

Beau shouted, "Stop this!"

Daniel wrenched one arm free. His forearm scabbed and frosted over, but his other arm was still stuck. The cold cut its way up to his shoulder. He blinked. Consciousness began to slip.

Beau grabbed Daniel by his shirt. "Get up here."

"Just pull my arm free and let me fall," Daniel said weakly. "It'll be fine. The cold—will heal me."

Charles stood up and backed away. A shadow came over him. Beau's frightful eyes lifted to the sky, and he fell back, gasping. Daniel realized the thuds had stopped. A reeking breath warmed him and dampened his back.

Charles raised his hands. "Antaeus, we need your help."

"Antaeus," the chained giant growled. "These tiny people fooled you once. Don't let them do it again. Squash them."

"They never fooled me, Otus." His voice was large like his brother's, but milder. Daniel looked over his shoulder. The giant was built like an athlete. His pure white eyes discerned him solemnly. Unlike his brother, he had dark, frozen hair that was knotted and matted. He ran his knuckles under his nose and snorted. "My name is immortalized in their literature."

"And what has fame ever done for you?" Otus asked, jerking on his chains. "You crawl the floor staring into the depths of Cocytus."

Antaeus's massive hand wrapped around Daniel's torso, and he breathed on him. His warm, rancid breath freed Daniel's stuck arm, and Antaeus lifted him from the cliff.

Daniel groaned as frost formed over his torn arms. Stinging pain gripped him, and he folded them close to his chest. Antaeus's thick fingers obscured the pit below. When he looked up, he was staring into Antaeus's massive eyes. His hand could squeeze the life out of him, but didn't.

"I've been listening." Daniel hid his nose from Antaeus's foul breath. "I won't help you enter Treachery. It's in your best interest to turn back. Azrael is waiting in the distance."

"If you help us," Charles called out from the ledge below, "you'll gain more fame."

"I don't need it," Antaeus replied.

"Maybe we can have you restored on Earth," Charles said.

Antaeus tightened his grip. "Even if that were possible, I do not care to return. I belong here with my brothers. I want for nothing."

"Please, let me down." Daniel thought his bones would pop if the giant squeezed any tighter.

Antaeus placed Daniel between Beau and Charles. "Go to Azrael. Treachery is no place for you."

Daniel stepped forward until Antaeus pushed him back with his index finger. He stumbled back into Beau. "If you don't let us down, we'll just jump."

"Don't test my patience, little one," Antaeus said. "Leave. It's for your own good."

"Why did you let others pass before?" Charles asked.

The giant shrugged. "They offered me something I didn't have."

"What if I give you something?" Daniel stepped closer to the ledge, cupping the pendant through his shirt. "Not something abstract, like fame. Something you can hold on to."

"Why would I want to carry something for eternity?" Antaeus asked.

"You can wear it." Daniel removed his necklace and presented the crystal pendant. "The person who gave it to me said it would help me. It might be the reason I'm still alive, I don't know. Maybe it'll help you in some small way too."

Antaeus lowered his head, squinting. "What color is this?"

"Purple," Daniel said.

Antaeus smiled. "I haven't seen such a color in ages."

"You could wear it like a ring," Daniel suggested.

"Let me hold it," Antaeus said.

"Not yet." Charles wagged a finger at the giant. "It should be a fair exchange."

"Very well." Antaeus came closer. "Hold it higher so that I may see it better."

Daniel's back and arms ached as he raised the necklace overhead. Antaeus's nose grazed the side of Daniel's face.

"Is it easily broken?" Antaeus asked.

Daniel shrugged. "I've gone through almost all of Hell without breaking it. It's pretty tough, I'd say."

Antaeus's mouth opened with a wide grin. He came up straight and nodded. "It pleases me. I will let you down in exchange for the amulet."

"You coward." Otus turned and picked up his horn. "They'll punish you for this."

"I'd be punished regardless," Antaeus said, "but I'll have an amulet for my trouble."

Antaeus scooped the three men into his arms and brought them over the ledge. The giant twisted around and lowered to a knee, causing everything to whirl in Daniel's vision. Carefully, he placed them on the floor of the pit.

"Just ahead in the face of the cliff, you'll find the passage you seek." Antaeus set them on the ground. "Enter there, but don't blame me for what is coming to you."

An icy wind blasted from a cracked entrance in the wall. It resembled the upper half of a lightning bolt, reminding Daniel of the dead tree and the barren ledge back on Grandfather Mountain. Everything seemed to fall into place as if this were his destiny, but a horrible weight swelled in his bones, making it difficult for him to move his limbs.

Antaeus said, "The amulet."

Daniel gazed into the crystal pendant dangling from the thin silver chain one last time and then raised it to Antaeus. The giant pinched it with his thumb and forefinger and threaded his pinky through the hollow place.

"It fits well." Forming a fist, the giant raised the crystal to his eye and admired it.

His gaping smile pleased Daniel. "Thank you, Antaeus."

The giant looked solemnly at Daniel. "You won't be thanking me for long."

"I'm thanking you now."

CHARLES

Charles looked at his scuffed-up leather shoes. Within them, his feet tingled. Since regaining his heart, he had felt sensations he had long forgotten. He had sacrificed everything for this—his office as a harvester, his belongings, even his reptilian eyes. Gazing at the spot where a straight-line wind blasted from the scar within the cliff face, he felt redeemed for all he had done.

"We've made it," he muttered.

The ground shook while Antaeus crawled across the pit and disappeared into the snowy fog with his new trinket. Beau's light dissipated and diffused as the wind whipped around him. Daniel shielded his face with his shoulder and appeared rigid with his hands tucked under his armpits.

"Beau," Daniel said with a quivering voice. "I can't move."

Beau came closer, squeezing the keystone.

Bits of ice clung to Daniel's face and arms. "It's not helping."

Beau squeezed the stone with both hands, but it had no effect on Daniel. Beau heaved a sigh. "You need to hold it yourself."

Daniel's eyes glazed. His body shook less as he began to freeze. "But it burned me last time."

"You have to try," Beau insisted.

Fog fumed from Daniel's clinched teeth. "I can't move."

Beau placed his glowing fist between Daniel's chest and right hand. "Try."

Daniel twisted his forearm until his fingers and palm were exposed to the icy wind. Everything darkened when Beau handed the stone over to Daniel. When the light returned, it burned brighter and hotter than it had before. The wind receded and warmed. The ground became slippery. Daniel shuddered with relief. His posture eased, and he breathed deeply.

"Well." Charles reached for his necktie, but it wasn't there. "Looks like you are ready to go."

Daniel closed his eyes and passed his glowing hand over his body. He shuddered. "This is the best I've felt since coming here."

"Should be an easy finish, then," Charles said.

Daniel frowned. "What makes you say that?"

"There're no demons in Treachery." Charles dug into his pocket and squeezed his lump of coal. "Only Satan. Everybody else is stuck in the ice."

Daniel and Beau looked past Charles at the cave. They looked hesitant and fearful. If Charles didn't get them going soon, they may lose their nerve.

"Let's finish this." Charles turned and trudged to the fissure while massaging dull pain in the center of his chest. The cold had caused his heart to return, and it felt as if it may erupt again. His shadow shrank and stretched as Daniel and Beau followed him. At the threshold of the crack, a rotten odor blasted into his face. A whispering voice followed. "*Bring Daniel to me.*"

Charles nodded at the dark void. "We're coming, Master."

"Who are you talking to?" Beau asked.

"Just thinking aloud," Charles said.

They entered the tall crevice, and a continuous wind pressed against them. The keystone in Daniel's hand warmed him while an occasional cool gust whipped about them.

When Charles glanced over his shoulder at Daniel, a strange sadness crossed his thoughts. He'd never felt close to anyone since his grandmother died. Never wanted to, either. With eternity ahead of him, he feared the memory of his grandmother and Daniel would remain with him forever—and Beau, too. Without them, he wouldn't be here. Through them, he'd achieved far more than a mere chance at power. Because of them, he knew the truth about his mother and father. He worried this newfound sympathy of his would make him unworthy of the power he expected to gain.

The passage curved left at a slight descent. The light in Daniel's hand caused the frosted walls to melt, surrounding them in smooth, translucent-blue ice. The surface became slippery. It compromised their footing until they reached an open chamber with a level floor. Countless frosted columns twinkling in the light hung from the ceiling and stabbed into the floor. Pale mist whipped about as if lost in this vast, symmetrical labyrinth.

"This is Caina." Charles looked about the vast chamber, unsure of where to go. "Home to those who betrayed family."

I have a special gift for you.

"Wait." Daniel cocked his head and listened intently. "Do you hear that?"

They all stopped and listened. Someone was whimpering ahead. Charles followed the sound and called out. "Who's there?"

The whimpering ceased. "I'm no one. Master woke me to speak with you. You must hurry before I freeze over again."

Beau pointed ahead.

Between two frozen pillars, a head protruded from the floor. Steam rolled off of it like blades of fire. Charles walked toward it. Frozen heads bowing to the wind came into view on either side of them as they neared the steaming head. Shiny tear tracks trailed from their squinting eyes and glued their mouths shut or opened, depending on however they were when they froze. Their stiffened, windblown hair sprawled behind their heads.

As they came around to face the steaming head, it grimaced and turned away. "The light burns. Put it away." Fumes rolled from his long, narrow face. It looked familiar—too familiar. *It can't be.*

Oh, but it is, Charles.

"Put out the light," the man whimpered. "It stings."

"Say something if you have something to say," Charles hissed, curling his lips.

"Very well." The old man groaned. "I have a message."

"You're my father, aren't you?" Charles sneered. "The drunken preacher." The man didn't respond but looked away sullenly in shame. "Answer me!"

"I am," the man sobbed. "I was a coward, and I betrayed you, my own flesh and blood. My only child and namesake Charles Pierce Thorne."

Hearing this invigorated Charles. He wanted to savor this. Punish his father. "A bit late for a confession, don't you think?"

"The truth would have set me free, but I would have lost everything I had worked for." His father's voice diminished to a whisper. "My silence cost me my soul."

"You were alive when I died," Charles said. "Did you even bother to attend my funeral?"

"I did. I felt ashamed for failing you and your mother."

He's lying, Charles. He wasn't there.

Charles huffed. Tears threatened his eyes. "Mother's in the Malebolge. The Trench of Flatterers. Maybe a decent minister would have helped her. You're more than treacherous. You're a failure. She suffers because of you."

"I loved your mother," he said. "I would have taken her if she'd lived."

We know he's a liar, Charles.

"But you wouldn't have me." Charles laughed. "Oh, no—you wouldn't accept me."

"I'm so sorry," Charles's father sobbed. "I never said it, but I do love you."

"You called me a bastard!" Charles screamed. His body was trembling. He took a deep breath. "You love nothing, you fake. We all burn because of you."

"Your mother would have burned no matter what I did," the Reverend said. "What would Paradise be without her? We're where we need to be, Chip. This is where we belong."

Charles kicked his father's nose, and it broke off. His father screeched like an injured bird.

Beau and Daniel pulled Charles back, but he jerked away. "You shouldn't have slept with her. You should have helped her."

"At least you know the truth." Blood trickled and froze around his father's mouth and chin. Frost accumulated where his nose broke off. "Find peace in that."

"Peace?" Charles kicked his father in the ear.

Daniel pulled him away again. "Calm down."

"Don't tell me to calm down, you pathetic—" Charles bit his bottom lip. He opened and closed his fists. Unwilling to finish his sentence, he glowered at his father's broken face. He reached into his pocket for his pocket watch but instead found a single lump of coal.

"I'm proud of you, son," his father rasped. "You've made something of yourself. Heartless Charles. Satan will reward you for what you've achieved. He told me he would. That's the message he wanted me to give to you."

Charles scowled at his father with all the disgust he could muster. "I'm a bastard, remember? I have no father. This time—I abandon you."

Charles turned and walked away. Daniel and Beau caught up to him.

"Do you know where you're going?" Beau asked.

Head into the wind.

Charles nodded and looked at Daniel. "Sorry I called you pathetic. Seeing him filled me with rage. I wouldn't have said it if it wasn't for him. Everything is *his* fault."

Daniel looked deeper into the chamber. "I won't hold it against you."

"I thought I'd be glad knowing he suffered." Charles shook the tension from his hands. "I thought hitting him would make me feel better, but I just want to hit him more." Tears ran down his cheeks. "My mother's in Hell. My father. Grandmother—she may be in Heaven—either oblivious to my suffering or not caring at all."

She knows, but she doesn't care, Charles.

"How can Heaven be Heaven for her without me?" Charles asked. "Without my mum?" He looked at Daniel. "Your father and mine were the same."

"My father didn't abandon me, though." Daniel looked at the ground, rubbing his neck. "I abandoned him."

"He told you to go," Charles said. "You had every right to walk out. If that pains him, then good. He deserves it."

The winds picked up when they came to a narrow passage. They stooped and filed through. When they came to another chamber, heads were submerged to their chins. Their gnarled faces were frozen in perpetual grimaces.

"This is the second chamber. Antenora. For traitors to their countries." Charles continued to follow the wind.

The surface declined, and the winds increased. Daniel, Beau, and Charles used the heads of those on the icy floor as footholds. Hair crunched beneath their feet. Unable to speak, the Antenorans groaned and gazed upward, unable to blink or move their faces. The width of the chamber shrank to thirty feet, and they reached level ground, where bodies lay flat on their backs, encased in clear mounds of ice. Their eyes were glued open by tears. Frost collected in their lashes and brows.

"Ptolomaea," Charles said. "They betrayed their guests."

"How much farther?" Daniel asked nervously.

"Just one more," Charles said.

They walked through the chamber, between rows of supine bodies. The clear icy walls narrowed to ten feet. Deep within stood contorted, frozen bodies.

"And this is it." Charles raised a hand and brushed a wall with his fingers.

Daniel stopped. Trembling, he squatted against a wall. The light in his hand flickered, and Beau knelt before him, cupping Daniel's hand with his and squeezing.

"I can't do this," Daniel said between frantic breaths. "I can't."

"This was always part of the plan," Charles growled. "Would you rather face Death?"

Beau stood between them and faced Charles. "What's gotten into you?"

The voice spoke again. *He must come to me, Charles. Not Azrael.*

"Choose life, Daniel," Charles said. "Remember?"

"Choose life?" Daniel raised his head. His blue eyes shimmered. "After everything I've seen here, I don't know if I want to."

"You have so much to live for," Beau said. "Kristine, your parents—your future."

"What comes here stays," Daniel said tearfully.

"Others got out, though," Charles said. "Antaeus helped them. Remember?"

"And there's the one who tore down bridges in the Malebolge," Beau added.

"You mean Jesus." Daniel looked up at Beau. "I'm not him, Beau."

Enough talk, the voice inside Charles's head declared. *Come to me.*

"Get control of yourself," Charles snarled. "It doesn't matter who's made it out before. You're about to escape yourself."

"Give him a minute," Beau said.

"I miss Kristine." Daniel's words stung Charles's heart. "I miss my parents too. You hate your father, and maybe for a good reason. For years, I thought I hated mine. But really, I hated myself for what I did to him and Mom. I'm tired of hating. I'm tired of running. It's time to make things right." He came to his feet, wiping his eyes. "Save them from the hell I put them through."

"You can't save them." A whispering voice echoed ahead.

Daniel's face paled as he looked past Charles deeper into this icy tunnel, where a foggy mist lingered overhead. This voice was different from the one Charles had heard in his head. This wasn't Satan speaking. Weak and broken, it sounded like another sufferer. "Who said that?" he asked.

"I am"—the voice strained— "Judas Iscariot."

Chapter Twenty-Two

The Hanging Disciple and Satan

DANIEL

Daniel's heart pounded against his ribs like a prisoner longing to escape. All through his body, alarms blared. His ears rang. Thousands of thoughts slammed around in his mind. Every inch of him wanted to flee, but there was no safe place. He needed to get himself together and come to terms with the things that loomed in the darkness.

He looked at Charles. "Judas?"

Charles's lips curled into contempt and nodded.

Beau placed a hand on Daniel's shoulder. "You should talk to him."

"There's no time for that," Charles said. "We need to get this over with."

"He walked with *Jesus*," Beau pressed Daniel. "You have to talk to him."

"Are you ready to get out of here?" Charles gestured deeper. "It's right there. Just a few steps away."

Daniel's head swam underneath an ocean of surreality. He touched the wall of ice with his free hand. Those encased within seemed to stare at him like submerged statues. Mouths stretched into soundless screams.

Gritted teeth bared pain Daniel couldn't see. Squinting, grimacing, fearful expressions filled Daniel's imagination of the nightmares that may come.

"Daniel?" Beau asked, his hand still resting on Daniel's shoulder.

His legs felt like wobbly wooden pegs. He touched the scar on his neck, feeling the pulse beneath it. He had more questions than he knew what to do with. Maybe Judas had some answers. "I'll talk to him."

Charles shook his head in disbelief. "Make it quick then. Satan knows we're here, and you're making him wait."

Daniel crept through the tunnel, with Beau by his side. Charles trailed behind them, mumbling to himself. Judas couldn't be within the walls, but there was no sign of anyone ahead.

The silence exaggerated the quiver in his breath. "Where are you?" he asked desperately.

"Here." The voice was thin and close.

Overhead, the mist parted in the light. Daniel craned his neck, and a pale-blue body dangling from the end of an icy rope emerged. Judas wore a sackcloth that stretched down to his knees. A dark, frozen beard obscured his face. Frosted hair hung from his head and was caught under the noose wrapped around his neck. His unblinking eyes bulged when he saw Daniel. Thin wisps of fog steamed from his swollen lips and nostrils.

Daniel stumbled into Beau. "Y-you said I can't save my parents?"

"Only Yeshua Nasraya can." Judas swayed slightly when he spoke.

"How can you say that when you betrayed Him?" Daniel asked.

Judas groaned. His eyes cracked like glass. "At Passover, we feared He would cause a riot. The Romans would have killed indiscriminately. I led them to Jesus, and they arrested him. I thought our friends in the Sanhedrin would've helped Him and the unbelievers would hear Him, but He was turned over to Pilate, who had Him crucified."

"It was His destiny," Charles said. "Without your betrayal, there is no crucifixion."

"No," Judas croaked. "My growing contempt of Him made me easily deceived. Though I loved Him, I betrayed Him."

Daniel dropped his head. "Is there anything I can do for my parents?"

"Honor them." Judas's eyebrows flexed wide, as if struggling to remain awake. "Forgive them. Forgive yourself."

Daniel didn't like this answer, but it brought on his anger, which alleviated his fear. "Do that or else end up down here to suffer forever, even though God loves us?"

"Without forgiveness," Judas whispered, "hatred hardens our hearts. Like a heavy chain, it drags us from God. He calls to us, but we don't answer to spite him. In our bitter ignorance, we enter Hell on our own accord."

"How is it ignorant to be angry with the people who've wronged us?" Daniel shoved Beau's hand off his shoulder. "People who were raped shouldn't have to forgive their rapist. Murderers shouldn't be forgiven, either. What's ignorant is letting it go. Saying it's OK."

"Forgiveness is—not—ignorance," Judas rasped.

Daniel huffed and bowed his head. "If forgiveness isn't ignorance, then I don't know what it is."

"Mercy," Judas croaked. Fog ceased from his mouth. The second death had taken him. An icy wind gushed from the tunnel ahead.

"It's time," Charles said. He no longer presented the air of impatience. In his gaze was a paternal kind of sadness.

Daniel shuddered and nodded.

They walked silently until they reached a passageway shrouded in darkness so deep that the light emitting from Daniel's fist provided no trace of what lay within. Daniel's stomach rolled, and his head whirled like a spotlight searching a clouded sky. A presence waited in that darkness. And it smelled of death and rot.

Charles stepped off first, but stopped short of the last chamber. "I..." He turned and his eyes trailed away. "When you're ready, Daniel."

Tearfully, Beau whispered, "I'm so sorry."

Daniel wrapped his arms around Beau's wide frame and squeezed. Though he hadn't known Beau for long, he felt as if he were losing a dear friend. "Stop blaming yourself," he said. "You've done everything you could to help me."

Beau smiled a sad smile. He nodded and let Daniel slip away. They both looked at Charles, who scratched his head and bent down to wipe bits of frost from his shoes.

"You tricked me, Charles," Daniel said. "Used me for your own personal gain."

"I did what I had to." Charles folded his arms and shuffled his feet. Unable to look Daniel in the eye, he looked to the left and right.

"I forgive you." Daniel walked up to Charles and hugged him.

Charles didn't hug him back, but that was OK. When Daniel let him go, Charles squinted and swallowed. "And now, we're here." He gestured to the darkest, lowest place in Hell.

Holding the keystone out to ward off unseen evils, Daniel led them into the last chamber. The ceiling and walls stretched out and disappeared into the darkness. Carefully, they walked deeper into this wide void, upon a translucent floor. A brisk chill whipped about and diminished the light already flickering in his trembling hand. With it came the scent of sulfur that burned his eyes and nostrils. His stomach howled like a pack of wolves.

"You've come so far for so long," a silky-smooth voice said. It sounded familiar—like an old friend. "You suffered Hell to reach me, and your persistence has rewarded you with my presence. Come forward."

The wind pressed harder against them and twisted around Daniel like a vine on a tree. His insides writhed as if he had swallowed snakes. Sickness welled up in his throat, and he felt feverish.

A vague silhouette shimmered in the black. It emerged into the shape of a man beckoning with his left arm while his right arm hung to his side. Within seven feet of the shape, Daniel realized it was an ice statue. Its youthful face looked past them toward the entrance to the chamber. Its hair was sculpted to curl like fire, troubled by the wind. Back straight, shoulders squared, eyes forward. The posture of a powerful leader.

Daniel felt himself fainting, but a jet of air forced him upright. He looked at the clear eyes of the statue, clinging to the keystone. This statue, most certainly of Satan, seemed to lower its gaze upon him. Its head seemed to shift slightly to the right.

Satan's voice whispered. "I am not your adversary, Daniel."

There had been times when Daniel felt powerless. He'd stomached his fear and pressed through whatever it was, but this dark, expansive cavern unnerved him far beyond anything he had ever experienced. His ears pulsed. His body shook like a ragged diesel engine. Better men had failed in the face of fear—in moments of temptation. Captain Jones, for example. Daniel wondered if he could somehow do what Satan required and then make amends with God.

"Can't serve two masters," he muttered to himself.

"You serve me." The head of Satan's statue shifted to the left. "Charles, come before my monument."

Charles stepped forward and dropped to a knee, bowing his head. "I'm here, lord,"

The ice statue's chin rose and looked down its nose at Charles. "You had ripped your heart from your chest. Became the envy of Limbo. Why have you let it return?"

"A moment of weakness, lord." Fog puffed from his mouth as he spoke. "The life in Daniel brought back memories of my grandmother. Foolishly, I thought that having a heart would bring me closer to her. Instead, it weakened me."

"Of course it did." A wind blasted from the statue. The tone in Satan's voice had an edge to it. "Your grandmother basks in the light of God while you're left to suffer. Do you think she cares if you want to be closer to her?"

Charles shook his head. "No, lord. I'm sure she's forgotten me."

"She has," Satan said, "but I haven't. You sacrificed everything you have and have proven your worth. Do you still desire the power you sought when you were heartless?"

Charles looked up at the statue's face. "Yes, lord."

"Then give me your heart," Satan said. "Place it in the left hand of my statue. Become heartless once again."

"Of course, my lord." Charles came to his feet and started unbuttoning his shirt.

The icy fingers of the statue's outstretched hand widened. The thin, apathetic lips of its face slanted into a slight grin. Daniel closed his eyes and turned away. Charles grunted to stifle his screams. Flesh tore. Bones shifted and broke. Quiet tears streamed down Daniel's cheeks.

Charles's voice was weak. "Don't cry for me."

"Well done," Satan said. "Now return your chunk of coal to its rightful place, then go back the way you came. My closest ally, Beelzebub, is waiting for you."

“Thank you, lord.” Charles pulled out his lump of coal and looked at Daniel. His wide eyes seemed fearful and ashamed. “Goodbye, Daniel—Beau.”

“Do not delay, Heartless Charles,” Satan said.

Charles’s arm jerked inward. He groaned and winced. After clearing his throat, he turned and hobbled past Daniel and Beau without a second glance. Daniel watched the darkness swallow him. When he turned back to the statue, blood trickled down the forearm of its beckoning hand. Charles’s heart steamed in its palm.

A booming thud shook the floor. Charles screamed, and it echoed in silence.

“What was that?” Daniel squatted and looked about, seeing nothing.

“Heartless is receiving what he asked for,” Satan said. “It’s that easy. Now—Beau, it’s your turn.”

Beau said, “I’m here to see that Daniel—”

A cacophony of screeches descended from overhead. Something with many voices and many arms, unseen and massive, reeking of carbon and sulfur, knocked Daniel to the floor. The noise ended swiftly, and Beau was gone.

Daniel stared into the black for a time, then looked at his glowing hand. A thunderous thud jolted the floor. The wind stilled. Utter silence followed. His skin felt hot, as if warmed by a fire after ages in the cold. The thick stench of sulfur and carbon hung over him like a haze. He feared looking up, for he knew who was there.

“I could have had him taken away any time,” Satan said in a consoling tone, “but I gave him what he wanted. He saw you here. Now, he goes back to Limbo. It’s where he belongs. See how willingly I give, Daniel?”

Daniel couldn’t speak. All he could manage was a nod. He squeezed out tears for Charles and Beau. He was alone in the presence of Satan—The Satan. Daniel desperately wanted to sink into the floor and freeze forever rather than be in this position. He lowered his forehead to the ice and tried to will it to happen.

"I heard you speaking with the traitor in the hall," Satan said. "You showed a lot of wisdom in what you said. Mercy for rapists and murderers? Those who suffer in our world are evil and deceiving, yet no different from those basking in Father's light. Angels. Demons. They're all the same. Just like God and I are the same."

Satan stepped closer. His massive hand came underneath Daniel's arm and pulled him off the floor to his feet. Daniel stepped back. Satan's curly hair was shining gold in the dark. His eyes glowed like moons as his drab face drifted back into the darkness. "The only difference between Him and me is that I am not a tyrant. I empower those who call on me. I give more than what is necessary. Who would you rather serve, Daniel?"

"You haven't empowered anybody." Daniel's voice shook with fear. "They're all suffering."

"Suffering breeds power." Satan placed his hands at the small of his back and began to circle Daniel. "It is why Jesus suffered on the cross. We suffer Hell because we choose to. Basking in Heaven's light is for fools. They weaken while we grow stronger. That's why you're here. You choose us. You choose to suffer."

"That's not what I want."

"You came to me." Satan glared with eyes that Daniel would never forget, then pointed upward. "Not Him."

"I was told there was no other way," Daniel said.

"No." Satan stopped. His expression darkened even more. "You came to me because you wanted to be free. It's the same reason you left your parents."

"But I want to make things right with them."

"They told you to go." Satan walked over to his statue. "You've honored their wish by staying away, and they haven't changed their thoughts about you. They haven't reached out to find you. They're glad you're gone. You know it's true."

Daniel rubbed the side of his neck. "I have to try."

"Try if you must." Satan ran his hand up his statue's arm to its shoulder. "But first, you need to toss the stone and give me the ring."

With stiff, tingling hands, Daniel retrieved the ring. He was so willing to give it up earlier, but not anymore. It was smooth and shining in his hardened fingers. Closing his eyes, Kristine's face flashed through his mind.

"Ah, you think you're in love." Satan laughed as he began circling Daniel again. "You should know what love is by now. What it brings. You loved your parents and look what they did. Love her and she'll ruin you. It's a poison that Father uses to weaken us. Don't drink from that cup."

"I already love her, and that won't change with or without the ring."

Satan grimaced and shook his head. "You don't love her. You want to snare her. Control her. Own her. Like she's a dog!" Winds whipped against Daniel, knocking him to the floor. "You'll feed and pet her, but one day she'll escape the leash, likely the moment you go looking for a younger, more vibrant, and obedient pup."

"That's not how I see her at all." Daniel stood back up.

"You're naïve." Satan folded his arms over his chest, looking up into the darkness. "Easily deceived. I don't blame you. You, like everyone else, spent too many years hearing how good Father is, how love can set you free, but truly, you're too much like me and shouldn't fall for that nonsense."

"I'm nothing like you."

"You left the reign of an overbearing father," Satan said, "and found your own way. Be proud."

Dust and ash hovered in the light of Daniel's shaking grip. A flowery scent wafted in from the entrance. Daniel turned from Satan and heard a familiar voice in the darkness. "It is time for you to make your choice."

"In a hurry, Azrael?" Satan asked. "Want the boy to make a hasty decision? He is my guest, and I won't let you kill him."

From the black, the angel's pale white robe emerged. His dark cowl sparkled like stars in the night. Unable to see Azrael's face, Daniel dropped to his knees, breathing heavily. "I don't want to die. I want to go home."

Satan walked to Daniel and stood over him. "Then toss the stone and give me the ring."

Daniel looked at Azrael. "Are you going to kill me?"

"I won't let him," Satan said.

"Why won't you tell me?" Daniel pleaded to Azrael.

"Make your choice," Azrael said.

Daniel opened his numb hand and flipped the ring from his fingers to his palm. He looked at the bloodied hand of the ice statue. Red tendrils flowed down the outstretched arm. Lowering his head, he closed his eyes. The light of his other hand brought a rosy canvas behind his eyelids. "Lord, I'm so afraid."

The wind lashed out at Daniel, slashing his face.

"This is what you do after everything I've done for you?" Satan growled. A second blast of wind slapped against Daniel, and he skidded toward Azrael.

"Jesus." Fighting the wind, Daniel rose to his knees. "If you hear me, please forgive me. I know I've been selfish, and I'm sorry." He didn't know what else to say. "Amen."

The winds ceased.

"He denied you just like your parents did," Satan said. "I won't let you make this mistake. I'll steal you from Him. I'll steal you from death."

"Rise," Azrael said. Beads of static electricity crawled over Daniel's skin.

Daniel opened his eyes. A golden hue had diffused through the darkness. He came to his feet. His shallow breath spiraled in faint streams from his mouth. Tears had hardened and constricted his face. The statue of Satan glistened and dripped with water.

Beside it, Satan glared at him. His hair shimmered gold. "Don't kill him, Azrael. Take him home. I've got plans for my new friend."

Daniel looked at Azrael. His face was still hidden under the sparkling black shawl. Azrael took his hands, and Daniel flinched and turned.

Satan stepped closer. "You'll come to find that the one you prayed to—the one they call Almighty—is pained by me."

"Look at me." Azrael's voice sent tingles through Daniel. "Don't be afraid."

"Know why they called you a murderer?" Satan asked. "Because of your hatred. Hatred that is justified. He punishes the oppressed, but I liberate them."

"Daniel," Azrael said. "Look at me."

It took all of Daniel's will for him to lift his eyes from the floor. Though the angel had followed Daniel through Hell, his white gown smelled clean and appeared spotless. When he peered into the depths of the shimmering cowl, he found the silhouette of a somber face. Azrael's skin was pale and smooth. His eyes were dark and hollow. The mystery of what lay within swelled Daniel's fear—he closed his eyes. But the Angel of Death's face remained locked at the center of his vision. Daniel recoiled, but Azrael steadied him.

Daniel relaxed and opened his eyes. A thin smile stretched on the angel's face.

"I won't let him kill you, Daniel," Satan said again. The winds increased. "I'm sending you home."

Daniel tried to speak, but words refused to stir. His body refused to move. Slowly, Azrael came closer. His forehead touched Daniel's. Their eyes became one. A brilliant light flared into a tunnel of spiraling blue. He screamed as he felt himself getting sucked in. Something took his arm. He jerked away, and dirt fell on his face. The smell of the earth filled his lungs, and he coughed.

"We got you." A man in a bright orange vest, wrapped in a harness, stood over him and called to the top of the hole. "He's OK!"

Chapter Twenty-Three

The Scars

DANIEL

It took him a moment to gather himself. The day was warm. Sunlight beamed down from a blue sky. This was home, but he was so cold. Colder than he had ever been. Colder than Treachery even. Like his bones were made of ice. Maybe he was no longer meant for this world, but he was here regardless.

"You're lucky, kid." The ranger knelt in front of him, twisting the top off a canteen.

"Not feeling very lucky right now." Daniel sat up, shivering.

The ranger chuckled. "Lift your head for me."

Icy water poured onto Daniel's face. He shoved the ranger's hand away.

"Sorry, kid." The ranger handed him a freezing rag. "You're scraped up pretty bad."

Daniel pressed the rag to his forehead and eyes. "How bad?"

"Hold out your arms."

Daniel's arms were covered in countless long red scratches that ran down and across his triceps, biceps, and forearms. It looked as if a very frightened cat had scribbled all over them with its claws. "Is this what my face looks like?"

"It's not as bad." The ranger poured water over his arms.

Daniel gritted his teeth through the cold and the stinging, but let the man finish.

"What's your name?"

"Daniel Strong."

"Listen, Daniel." He wrapped a cloth bandage around Daniel's right arm. "You were out when I found you, but I think you'll be fine. How's your head? Any dizziness? Headache?"

Daniel shook his head. "Just cold."

The ranger taped Daniel's bandage and started wrapping Daniel's left arm. "Do you think you can climb out on your own?"

Daniel nodded.

The ranger helped Daniel into a harness. Others pulled on the belay rope as he walked up a wall of dirt. Cheers erupted from the mountain trail when he surfaced. Golden light beamed through the canopies of trees and dazzled his eyes. The sky. Distant rolling hills. Sounds of nature. Sheer beauty. A stark contrast of the Hell still looming in his mind. He felt out of place. A breeze scented with spring seized him and he sat down, shaking.

A rescue worker offered him a cold bottle of water. He refused it. Another tried to give him a blanket, but it was coarse and thin. They wanted to take him to a hospital, but the black-and-white checkered floor of the emergency room back in Grayton was too fresh in his memory.

"I am fine," Daniel told them, his teeth chattering. "Just let me go."

The rangers looked at each other, then back at him. One let out an exasperated sigh. "OK, but we're helping you down this hill whether you like it or not. From now on, stick with the trail, you hear me?"

Daniel nodded. "Thank you. For everything."

They trudged downhill to the crowd lining the trail, and Daniel spotted Kristine. He couldn't help but to smile. She cupped her hands over her mouth. Tears glimmered in her eyes. Her skin, red from blush and sun, glowed and shined. Her hair had darkened with sweat. Daniel opened his arms, and they took hold of one another.

She smelled of sunscreen and felt soft and warm. So warm that the cold melted off his bones and sank to his feet.

"I'm sorry," he said, letting her go.

"You're cut up?" She ran her fingertips over his bandaged arms. Her eyes scanned his face.

"I'll be OK," Daniel said. "Can we go? I just want to get out of here if that's cool with you."

So many people wanted to shake his hand. They were so elated for whatever reason. Daniel felt like a fool, but was thankful for their kindness. The rangers gave him more bandages and ointment but reiterated that he should go to the hospital. Kristine assured them she'd make him go if he took a turn for the worse.

Eventually, Daniel and Kristine started down the trail. Kristine talked excitedly about everything that had happened after he fell. She had run to the gift shop near the Swinging Bridge, and so many people came together to help her get him out.

"Things happened so fast, but when I looked at my watch, it had been hours." Kristine wiped away tears. "We shined flashlights in the hole and couldn't find you. I thought you were dead."

Daniel took her hands. "I'm sorry."

She looked down at his hands and turned them over. "Your hands. They're not torn up at all."

"Wish it were the same for my face."

She touched his cheek. "It's not that bad. Looks kind of cool, actually." They resumed a casual pace down the trail. "I think God had his hand on this, somehow. Know what I mean?"

Daniel rubbed his chest and chuckled.

Kristine pulled a strand of red hair behind her ear and smiled nervously. "Don't laugh. I mean it."

"I have to tell you something." Daniel froze. The chill returned. He gazed into her warm eyes. "While I was in that hole, I..."

Though she was beaming, her eyes were wary. "What?"

Daniel swallowed. "This is going to sound insane, but I fell into Hell."

Kristine's forehead wrinkled. She squinted down the trail. "You mean that literally?"

"I know how it sounds, but it's true."

"You mean that literally." Kristine started walking, but her movements became rigid and slow. She placed her hand on a tree as she stepped down a stairway of stones. Daniel could almost see the gears spinning out of control inside her head. "You died and went to Hell?"

"I was alive the whole time. But yeah, I was in Hell."

The trail ended, and they crossed a narrow road that curved upward toward the summit. In the parking lot, sunlight reflected off glass and shiny quarter-panels.

"You sure it wasn't a dream?"

"I was there," Daniel said, "for sure."

"Tell me everything."

Daniel and Kristine slapped dirt off him the best they could before hopping into Kristine's car. The leather interior was clean and soft. It smelled new and sweet with air freshener. He took his wallet out from the glove box and pocketed it before buckling up for the ride down Grandfather Mountain. They drove to a nearby diner, which, surprisingly, wasn't too busy.

He went to the bathroom and looked in the mirror. Hundreds of scratches ran from either side of his face, from his ears to his nose, all along his jaw, and around his mouth. After washing up, he joined Kristine at a booth, where they ordered coffee.

Daniel told her everything. She listened intently, staring into her mug.

"You believe it really happened?"

Daniel spun his mug in a slow circle. "It's crazy, I know."

"Call it crazy if you want, but you've got to be feeling pretty good right now. Like you've got a second chance at life." She raised her mug to her lips. "What do you plan to do with it?"

Daniel reached for the diamond ring in his pocket. Gazing into her eyes, he considered proposing. He wanted it more than anything, but fear pooled at the bottom of his heart. Something about the moment wasn't right. A strange sadness bloomed within. He returned his hand to the table and leaned forward.

"I'm going to reach out to my parents," he said. "I've wanted to do that for so long, but keep talking myself out of it."

Kristine ran a finger over her ear. "You told me they kicked you out and disowned you."

"I came home drunk and pushed my father to the floor." Daniel wiped the itchiness from his eyes. "I was practically begging them to kick me out, but I don't think they disowned me." He sent a hand through his hair. "I think that's a lie that I told myself, so I wouldn't ever go back. To never try."

"Then you should." Kristine took Daniel's hand and squeezed. "Don't put it off either."

Don't put it off. He dug into his pocket.

Kristine scowled at her cellphone. "We've got to get going or I'm going to be late for work."

Daniel let go of the ring and picked up the check instead.

They drove back to Boone. Red, orange, and gold blended along the horizon. Overhead, the sky darkened. Kristine pulled into Daniel's apartment complex and parked beside his car. He couldn't propose here. The thought of proposing at all made him feel ashamed for reasons he couldn't explain.

"What's wrong?" Kristine took his hand and squeezed.

Daniel shook his head. "Nothing. You need to get to work."

"I've got some time. What is it?"

Daniel couldn't bring himself to look at her. He fixed his eyes on the gearshift. Her smooth legs shifted slightly as she turned to him. The love he had for her felt selfish. Maybe he only wanted her for a time. To use her until he grew tired of her. The thought of tossing her aside for another someday hurt him. Maybe he wouldn't do that this week or next year even. But deep down, he feared he'd abandon her—even their children, if they had any. *Maybe love is a weakness.*

"Daniel?"

"Sorry." He closed his eyes and sniffed. "I'm still processing everything."

"That's understandable." Kristine ran her fingertips over his scar to the back of his neck, massaging it lightly. "You've been through a lot today."

"I want to be good." Daniel lowered his head. "To you and everybody else."

"Look at me." Kristine's face seemed to glow in the dim light of the setting sun. Her eyes were full of acceptance. Her smile beamed with kindness. It was everything he needed. "You are better than you think."

He sucked in a breath. Tears breached. "I love you, Kristine." The words came out of nowhere. It hadn't even crossed his mind to say it. He felt vulnerable in the silence that followed.

"I love you too." She kissed his cheek. The love he felt in that moment was overwhelming. He hugged her.

She laughed. "You really need a bath."

Daniel let her go and stepped out. "See you tomorrow then."

He watched her drive off and then walked upstairs to his apartment. Inside, the lingering warmth and smell of his living room sent shivers up his spine. Pale yellow light gleamed from his lamps. Somehow, it comforted his eyes. The soft carpet thudded lightly as he slowly made his way to the kitchen. And Kristine loved him. *Heaven, I'm in Heaven...*

He placed his wallet and the ring on the counter. Across the room, he saw the telephone sitting by the couch. *Don't put it off.* After a deep breath, he walked to the phone and picked it up. Dialing his parents' old number sent shock waves through his body. When it rang on the other end, his heart thumped in his chest. Deep breaths did little to settle his nerves.

"Hello?" It sounded like his mother.

"Yeah... hi." Daniel paced the floor. "Is this the Strong residence?"

With a quivering gasp, his mother said, "Daniel?" He imagined her sitting down at the kitchen table with her hand over her mouth. His father would likely be sitting across from her, looking up from his paperback novel with a stern expression.

"It's me, Mom." Emotions were welling up fast. He paused at the countertop and exhaled. "How are you doing?"

"Oh, Daniel—" She sobbed. "We've missed you so much."

"I've missed you too." Daniel swallowed. He heard his father whispering. *That's Daniel?* His mother would be nodding. "Sorry Mom. I've been meaning to do this for a long time." He wiped his eyes.

"It's OK," she said, gushing. "It's just so nice to hear your voice. Your father's here. He wants to talk to you. I love you so much."

"I love you too." Daniel was worried his father would tell him not to call again and hang up.

"Daniel?"

"Hi Dad." Daniel pressed his palm against his head and ran it through his hair several times. "I'm sorry I haven't called until now. Shouldn't have left the way I did. Years ago."

An uncomfortable silence followed until his father said, "Your mother and I have prayed for this since the night you left. Are you doin' all right?"

It relieved him to hear solemn joy in his father's voice, but deep within, Daniel felt pained. The forgiveness and love coming from the other end of the phone overwhelmed him. Tears streaked down his face. "I am. Looking forward to catching up with you two."

"Good," his father said shakily. "That's really good. We are too."

Daniel heard the smile on his father's face. It eased the tension swarming within. He began pacing again. "A lot's happened since I left. I was in the service, but I'm a student at Appalachian State now. The GI Bill helps a lot, but I work part-time delivering for Dominos."

"You're smart. You'll get there. I know you will."

There was another moment of awkwardness. "I mean it Dad. I'm sorry for everything."

"We are too," his father said. "I was hard on you. I shouldn't have told you to go."

"Is it OK if I come home and visit," he asked, "tomorrow, maybe?"

"Tomorrow?"

"I'm off and school's out, so—there's no better time, really."

"Sure. You're welcome here anytime." His father's voice broke.

"There's a girl I'd like you to meet, too." Daniel paused at the edge of his living room and gazed at the engagement ring. "We've been dating for a few months, and I really like her."

"We'd love to meet her," his father said. "Is she comin' too?"

"I don't know. Haven't asked her yet. I'll call and let you know before I leave in the morning."

"OK, we'll be up." His father chuckled nervously. "Love you, son."

"Love you too."

Daniel set the phone on the counter and exhaled. He felt light, as if he might float away. He turned his attention to what had to be done. The trip home would take him about eight hours, but he loved road trips, especially ones that included Kristine. He'd text her now if he hadn't lost his smartphone. The joy running through him made it difficult for him to think. There were tons of things he had to do, yet he didn't know what he should be doing.

Finally, he realized he needed a shower. When he started for it, he felt something else in his pocket. He pulled it out. It was the keystone, but it had changed. The spiral was gone. The smooth surface was translucent, with a light-blue sheen that glowed like the moon.

He was about to squeeze it until something in the hallway caught his eye. Was there a shadow watching him, or was it only darkness? The edges of the light oscillated due to the wobble in the ceiling fan.

"Beau?"

In the silence, the ceiling fan chain tapped the side of the light fixture. He set the stone beside his wallet and went for a hot shower. It took him a moment to unwrap the bandages. They were bloodied, but just before he stepped into the steaming water, he saw his arms were no longer scarred. He went to the mirror. The scratches on his face. All of them were gone. How did he heal so fast? Was it some sort of hangover left by the cold winds of Hell or what? Daniel didn't know, and rather than worry about it for another second, he jumped into the shower.

Afterward, he threw on shorts and a t-shirt and headed for the couch. The phone was ringing on the counter. He recognized the number but couldn't place it.

"Hello."

"Sergeant Strong." It was Sergeant Bobby Faircloth, the friend who had called about Captain Jones. "You doing all right?"

"Yeah." Daniel walked over to the couch and plopped down. "Sorry, I hung up last time."

"It's all good," Bobby said. "Just wanted you to know that Captain Jones's funeral is on Monday at fifteen-hundred hours. That's three in the afternoon in case you—"

"I think I remember military time, thank you." Daniel chuckled.

"If you can make it, it's at Southridge Funeral Services in Fayetteville. Just come to the barracks, though, and ride with me. OK?"

Bobby's voice was deep and sorrowful. Daniel had spoken little with Bobby since leaving the military, but he could tell something was wrong. "Are you doing all right?"

"It's been a crazy few months," Bobby said. "Hard to lose Captain Jones. Treated us like brothers. You know."

"Yeah, I know." Daniel thought about what he had learned in Hell about his former commander. This was a chance to see if it was true. "I have to ask. Did Captain Jones kill his brother and himself over his wife?"

"You caught it on the news, huh?" Bobby said solemnly. "It's actually worse than what they're saying. He did it all in front of his kid, too."

Daniel balled his fist and squeezed his eyes shut. "I'll be there. I'm visiting my parents tomorrow down in Georgia. Still, I promise I'll be there."

"Good," Bobby said. "I told you thousands of times to get that done, and if you can't make it Monday, I understand."

"I'll see you Monday."

"All right," Bobby said. "We'll catch up, then. Later."

Kristine would have to close tonight, so he'd have to call her in the morning. He wasn't sure if she could make the trip or not. She had planned to get in more work hours over the break.

With so many thoughts and emotions running through his head, he thought he may never sleep. He tried some TV, ate a bowl of cereal, and even thought about getting a cheap cellphone, but decided to put it off for tomorrow. Nothing could settle his thoughts, and the hour was getting late. He lumbered to his bed, crawled under the covers, and stared at the ceiling. Millions of shadows shuffled about in the darkness. Faint blue and green lights swayed in his vision. Dark slanted eyes glared at him. He twisted to his side, pretending it was his imagination.

Then came the whispering voices—barely discernable. One spoke over all the others. *I saved you from death and this is what you do? Oh Daniel. There will be no rest. I got plans for you, friend.* A high-pitched tone rang in his ears, and he closed his eyes.

BEAU

Rain poured in droves, and Beau sat on the hillside looking down upon the town of Grayton. He rocked back and forth, seething, and fearing for whatever happened to Daniel. Whatever it was, it would've happened by now. He shook his head, gritting his teeth, and sobbed.

"Why are you crying, mister?" someone asked from behind.

Beau turned. A tall man in a cowboy hat stood a few feet away. Wearing denim jeans that stretched over his brown leather boots and a button-up flannel shirt, the man seemed resourceful and out of place from the city down the hill.

"Why do you want to know?" Beau looked up into the stoic face of the stranger.

"Fair question," the cowboy replied. He stepped up and sat next to Beau, regarding the dismal city. "You've been sittin' here for a while. I've been watchin' ya."

"No reason to be miserable anywhere else." Beau massaged his sore forearms.

"They say misery loves company," the cowboy said. "You sure you want that kind of company?"

"Is there another kind here in Limbo?" Beau picked up a rock and threw it down the hill. It bounced once, then splashed into a steaming pothole.

"You had better company the last time you were here," the cowboy said with a hint of laughter.

Beau locked eyes with the stranger. "What's your name?"

"The name's Chance. And you're Beau."

"You know who I am," Beau gasped. He didn't trust this man. Only a demon would know who he was. "What do you want?"

"I'm only here to deliver a message." Chance turned his head and smiled at Beau. "Your fella, Daniel, he made it home. Didn't make no deal with Satan, either. Thought you'd like to know."

Beau felt relieved to hear this, but didn't believe it. "How would you know?"

"I got reliable sources, mister." Chance reached into his pocket. "Now why don't you try being miserable at the bus stop down in Grayton for a while? The bus is on the way, so you might want to hurry. There's a particular little girl who wants to see you on the other side."

Tears filled Beau's eyes. "Angela?"

"She's a sweetheart, I tell ya." Chance took Beau's hand and placed nine coins in it. "Looks nothing like you. A blessing, I believe."

Beau chuckled. "Thank you."

Chance stood up and started toward the desert. "You shouldn't thank the messenger."

Knowing what this man was, Beau became filled with anger. He came to his feet. "Hey!"

Chance turned. His thumbs rested on his belt. "Yessir?"

"Why didn't you help sooner?"

"Well now," Chance pushed his hat up higher on his head. "What makes you think I didn't?" He walked off and shouted, "Don't miss the bus!"

CHARLES

In the third chamber of Violence, laying in the searing sands of the dreadful desert, Marcus stared at a harvester's pocket watch, unable to move. Coming up beside him, Charles grimaced at the lake of tears. A faint stench *did* linger in the silvery haze wafting from the waters. How he had stomached it before was a wonder, but it didn't matter. He came here for one last thing.

He reached down and pried his prized watch from Marcus's hand, who groaned like an injured feral cat in the presence of humans. "Oh, shut it, you," Charles said.

He clasped the chain to a buttonhole in his vest and tucked the watch into the appropriate pocket. His new shoes were tarnished, but the distressed look seemed stylish in a way. He righted his bowler hat, pulled on the lapels of his coat, and tightened his too tight necktie.

"Are you all set now?" Beelzebub asked. His voice buzzed like a thousand flies.

"Just one more thing." Heartless Charles reached into the inside pocket of his coat, retrieved the flask, and set it in the outstretched hand of Marcus. "That'll do." He turned to his commander. "What's next, sir?"

"We're heading topside," Beelzebub said, "for unfinished business."

"What business is that, sir?"

"Daniel Strong."

Charles grinned. "Let's go, then."

Thanks for Reading

If you want to be one of the first to know about new releases and updates, sign up for our mailing list by visiting **www.descendantpublishing.com**. Scroll to the bottom of the page and fill out the form with your name and email.

Please leave a review for *Infernal Fall*. Reviews go a long way in helping the authors you love get noticed by other readers. So if you enjoyed *Infernal Fall* please leave leave a review on Amazon and recommend it to friends and family. YOU are our greatest asset for spreading the word about EPIC stories!

Acknowledgements

I was stop-lossed. Not sure if it's in the dictionary, but what it means to the soldier who's wishing to leave the military is that your contract has been involuntarily extended. I wanted out because my plate was full. Full-time job. Full-time school. Military obligations. I had no time for myself. One person who helped me through this is now my wife, Sarah Mitchell. As I lived in Iraq working with Iraqi Security Forces, she turned on the news every day and worried. My whole family worried. My hell was different from hers. Her hell was different from theirs. What pulled us through was hope. I think hope is the greatest strength we have. Sometimes it's all we have, and it can lead us back into faith.

I hope you enjoyed this story. I have so many people to thank for its materialization. Jamie Chavez helped me stay true to my word and helped me clear up much of the mess. Multiple writing groups, especially Word Weavers, the Serious Writer Club, and Novel Blueprint helped me navigate the waters of writing a story. Taking part in the Novel Writing Intensive with Steven James and Robert Dugoni brought my writing to a new level. Descendant Publishing has been more than a publisher to me. They have been more than professional and have listened to me, a first-time author, with ears that hear. Dawn Carter, their editor, helped to polish this story up some more. Renee Kennedy and Laura Smith were fantastic beta readers and went the extra mile to help us clean this work up. I also thank YOU for reading this story and hope you will read my future works. I have a free short story available to you now on my website (https://www.bryantimothymitchell.com). Expect more over time.

This story wasn't easy to write. A journey into Hell requires a mind to be there. We've all been there, and nobody likes it. It's oxymoronic that we always go back. Some of us feel we have no choice. There's a sense of being trapped, and all I can say is that the Holy Spirit is with you. So hold on to that, and remember—always—you are loved. God bless you and keep you—forever.

Your friend,
Bryan Timothy Mitchell

About the Author

The hardest thing I've ever done is share a piece of my soul with others. It makes me feel vulnerable. Like a thief who just got spotted by the police with his pants down. Can't run away now. Gotta face whatever judgement awaits. That's how I feel when I share my stories. I cringe like a baby tasting a lemon and look at the reader all weird, hoping they want more.

While I cringe, eye twitching, neck straining, there's one thing that holds me together, and that is the truth. Like me. Love me. Hate me. It's not my decision. The important thing is the olive branch that I've extended. I'm trying to connect with you and honored you're making the effort to hear me out. This is what storytelling is. It's who we are. It's how we connect and grow together.

If you happen to look up at me while reading and see a ghastly face trembling like Hulk Hogan waking up from a bearhug, just know, I'm happy you gave me the opportunity, pal, and I encourage you to pass along the olive branch to others in your life because we all need to make ourselves vulnerable to be real. We've all written terrible prose. We've all fallen short of Shakespeare. Forgive yourself and others for those wordy sentences and write the good write.

Sorry, I can't end with that. Let's simmer it down a little. I invite you to visit my website and to subscribe to my newsletter. You'll be the first to know when I have new works coming out. If you take me up on this invitation be sure to say hello.

Look for the sequel to *Infernal Fall*, *Almost Paradise* By Bryan Timothy Mitchell to be released in 2023.

Connect with me:

https://www.bryantimothymitchell.com

https://twitter.com/btmitchell78

https://www.facebook.com/bryantimothymitchell

MORE FROM THE PUBLISHER

CONTINUE YOUR EPIC JOURNEY WITH MORE GREAT READS...

Descendants of Light Series
Book 1: The Watcher Key
By: Troy Hooker

Descendants of Light Series
Book 2: The Watcher Tower
By: Troy Hooker

Descendants of Light Series
Book 3: The Watcher Revealed
By: Troy Hooker

DESCENDANT
PUBLISHING

Look for more EPIC stories at:
www.descendantpublishing.com

Made in the USA
Columbia, SC
22 April 2024

28f4bbaa-14d0-4e67-9d68-e2e1ecb19ef2R01